TRADITORÈ

Book Eight

Salvaggio's Light

An Epic Contemporary Romance Serial

By C. L. Cattano

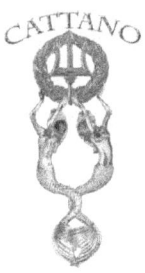

VAGARY PUBLISHING

Traditorè
Book Eight
Salvaggio's Light
A Vagary Publishing Book
Copyright © 2018 by C. L. Cattano
Cover Art, Title Page Art and Typesetting Copyright © 2018 by Chynsia Hinesley

Published by:

VAGARY PUBLISHING

www.vagarypublishing.com
inquiry@vagarypublishing.com

Rogena Mitchell-Jones, Independent Literary Editor
RMJ Manuscript Services LLC *www.rogenamitchell.com*

ISBN: 978-1-947852-07-5
First Edition

WARNING

It is suggested readers of this story be adults over the age of eighteen.

This dramatic romance series has many scenes describing sex as well as intense emotional scenes and acts of violence.

This is a serial story with themes that flow from one book into another with lots of twists and turns. Reading this series from the beginning is highly suggested, or the reader may not be able to follow all of the story-lines.

Go to the Salvaggio's Light Facebook page to join other readers who are talking about the series.
www.facebook.com/SalvaggiosLight/

Join the C L Cattano mailing list and check out my website at www.clcattano.com

Acknowledgments

THANK YOU TO those who have continued the journey so far. Only two more books to go! Those frustrating cliffhangers have tested you and the one in this book will do the same. I can't help it – I love cliffhangers! Your dedication to the story humbles me and I appreciate you all.

Dedication

For Marie — who only likes drama in books.

Salvaggio's Light

An Epic Contemporary Romance Serial

*Coming Soon

"Into the eternal darkness, into fire and into ice."
— Dante Alighieri, *The Divine Comedy*

1

The next day...

RAFE SALVAGGIO SAT behind her desk looking through all the paperwork stacked in front of her and all the emails on her computer. Some of it needed to be looked over for her signature, some only needed a reply, and she needed to forward others on to her lawyer Katheryn or to the CPA office at Hawthorn Financial. It seemed like since she inherited her father's business, she had just as much paperwork to take care of as she did when she owned her business.

She had decided to start overseeing a lot of things again when she was put on leave from the school, even though the people who were taking care of them did a decent job. She figured they could always be hired again if she went back to work. Until then, it gave her something to work on and made her feel like she wasn't just home wasting time.

Every morning, after Eden headed to work, and Bronte went to day school or with Lydia, Rafe took time to check on things and work for herself—literally. She reviewed all her financial and investment matters, including ones she had inherited from her father, made sure things were still on track from the sale of their businesses, and other small matters that she needed to take care of for the day. There wasn't always a lot, but some days, it kept her busy for a few hours or until it was time to go to her doctor's appointment on session days.

She had put a lot of it off for the last week because of her pizza oven project, so she decided to get it under control this morning instead of waiting until Monday. She finally sent off her last email and stood up to stretch, happy she had finished before Eden brought Bronte home from having breakfast at the Kiki with Letty and shopping.

Finished for the day, Rafe headed to the kitchen. She poured some orange juice, and then was trying to decide if she wanted anything to eat when the doorbell rang. *It begins again*, thought Rafe with a sigh. She then went to answer the door, hoping she was wrong.

"Good morning," said Julia with a smile. She held up a sack of food in one hand and a drink tray in the other. "I brought bagels and coffee."

"Is this your new job, delivering bagels and coffee?" asked Rafe flippantly.

"Very funny," said Julia with a smirk. "Can I come in?"

Rafe let the door open then turned and walked away as Julia followed her to the kitchen.

Julia put the bagels out and a cup of coffee in front of Rafe, then sat down at the counter. "How are you this morning," she asked then sipped her coffee.

"Fine," said Rafe as she took the lid off her coffee and looked inside. She took a small taste and made a face at the unpleasant flavor. She put the lid back on and drank her orange juice instead.

Julia could already tell she wasn't going to have an easy time talking to Rafe this morning. "So, how did things go last night after we all left? Did you just stay in your room?"

Rafe just glared at her as she broke off a piece of bagel and ate it.

"Come on," Julia cajoled. "You have to talk to someone."

"I do talk to someone," said Rafe with a shrug. "She's a very good therapist too."

"Rafe, you need to talk to Eden," she said exasperated, "and to your friends. We want to help you."

"What exactly do you want me to talk to you about?"

"Well, first, what the hell were you doing last night with Abby's date?" she asked. "Why would you act so Machiavellian in front of Eden? Are you sending her a message you want out?" she asked hiding her hopefulness at the possibility that Rafe was trying to push Eden away.

Rafe sighed because she knew she would regret letting the silver-haired pain in her ass into the house this morning. "I didn't do anything wrong. She was a nice woman who I was being polite to in my home. That's all. No messages."

"You were flirting with her." Julia scoffed.

"No," Rafe said firmly, "I wasn't. If I had decided to start flirting with women again, I wouldn't let her leave with someone else." She thought about last night and her conversation with Eden about Darcella and knew Julia had been talking to her about it. "If you do anything, or say anything, to make Eden think I'm cheating on her or doing even the smallest thing wrong, *you will* regret it," she said venomously. "You need to keep out of my personal life."

"Me?" Julia laughed haughtily. "You're the one blowing off Eden to speak French to a pretty girl with blue streaks in her hair. You were giving her those smoky looks and practically purring to her as you talked!"

"What is it with everyone telling me how I'm looking at or talking to people?" Rafe complained. "I know you heard and understood just about every word I said, and you know I said nothing wrong." She scowled at Julia. "And I wasn't purring. I was just speaking French well," she said annoyed.

"Okay, you're right," Julia conceded, "you didn't say anything wrong—that I heard. But the girl was all over you. Both Eden and Abby saw it, and neither was happy about it."

"She was being nice. She missed home and was just happy to talk about it with someone. I know how she feels," said Rafe with a shrug as she thought about how much she missed Italy and tried to remember how long it had been since she had been there. "It was the only thing we had in common. She wasn't doing anything wrong either, and you know it. I don't know why you would let anyone think there was anything more going on," she said in frustration.

Julia shook her head at what was, in her opinion, Rafe's overreaction. Maybe Julia did let them make more of it than there was. It just seemed Rafe was up to her old bad behavior. "Fine," said Julia. "I'm sorry. I was wrong," she conceded wishing she wasn't wrong at all.

"Good," said Rafe as she leaned on the counter. "Anything else? I have things to do."

"Yes, as a matter of fact, there is," said Julia switching back into the ever-frustrating friend mode. Helping Eden meant not letting Rafe get away with the rest of what went down yesterday. "You completely disregarded Eden," she said accusingly. "You blew her off after she gave you a gift. Then you shut us all out when you got upset about what Letty said about your father. I don't think we should have to make crazy promises to you so you'll talk to us, especially Eden. You can't do that to her, put her in a position where she's damned if she does and damned if she doesn't." Julia knew all about making promises to Rafe and the consequences for breaking them.

Rafe just glared at her for a moment and wondered why Julia was being so hard on her right now. Rafe couldn't understand why she, and everyone else, was putting her under a microscope and getting on to her about Eden all the time. She had enough to deal with right now without them making it harder.

"First, I didn't disregard Eden. In case you missed it, the whole point of yesterday was for Eden. Second, all of you need to stop talking about my father. I don't understand why you're all suddenly bringing him up all the time. I don't care how you felt about him. He's my father, and I don't like it when you talk badly about him," she said firmly. She looked down at the half-eaten bagel then up at Julia. "You know what else? What I say to Eden, and what we talk about, and how we talk about things is none of your business."

Julia could not believe Rafe was being so obtuse. "You did disregard her. She was trying to give you a gift, and you barely acknowledged her. She was hurt, Rafe, and confused by how you treated her. She's been hurt and confused about a lot of things you do. What are you trying to accomplish? You give her a gift and compliment her, then the next minute, you're beating her down or disregarding her."

"You know what? I don't want to talk to you about this," said Rafe holding in her anger. "Eden hasn't told me she's having a problem. I think you're the one having a problem," she said with a scowl. "Maybe you should go back to work for your father. You obviously have too much time on your hands!"

"Of course, she hasn't told you!" she said in frustration. "She's been walking on eggshells again. She's so worried about upsetting you and making you angry that she feels like she can't talk to you."

"She seems to be able to talk to me just fine!" said Rafe hotly. "She talks all the time. She almost never stops talking! I guess, what you're really saying, is Eden and I aren't talking about what you think we should be talking about! Well, too bad!" she said and wadded up the napkin and remaining bagel, then threw it in the trash angrily. She then dumped the untouched coffee in the sink and threw the cup away.

She didn't know what Julia expected from her after less than two months of therapy sessions. She was doing the best she could to work through everything. "I think we're done here," she said holding in her anger and frustration. "Just so you know... I've been doing the best I can right now! We–Eden and I, are doing the best we can right now! We don't need a third wheel in our relationship making things worse and causing more problems than we already have raining down on us!" Rafe took a calming breath. "I think you need to leave now before she gets home with Bronte," she said and walked out of the kitchen toward her room.

"Rafe!" Julia called as she followed her. "I'm trying to help you, not make more problems." She got to the bedroom as the door slammed closed. "Rafe, come on!" She knocked on the door. "She may talk, but you don't talk back and answer her. You haven't touched her or kissed her since you got back. She's upset because you haven't told her that you love her. She feels like you don't want her here," she tried to explain. Julia heard the front door open and Eden talking to Bronte. "Shit," Julia said under her breath and went to meet Eden.

Eden walked into the house and left the door open for Abby, Erica, and Jude, who were coming over to swim. As she put Bronte down in her play area in the living room, she looked up and saw Julia and the concerned look on her face. "What's going on?" she asked worriedly as she looked past her. "Where's Rafe?"

Before Julia could answer her, the others came in the front door. At the same time, Rafe came out of her room in her workout clothes, and Eden fought to calm herself.

"Great, the rest of the inquisition is here," Rafe said sourly. She frowned at everyone gathered in the house as they watched her as if they expected something from her. She took another breath and let it out slowly, and then walked up to Eden, took her in her arms, and kissed her deeply. *"Ti voglio,"*[1] she whispered, and then kissed her again. "I want you here," she said huskily. "I love you," she said and ran her hands over her and kissed her neck and shoulder. Eden started to wrap her arms around her. *"Ti amo,* Eden," she said then kissed her once more quickly on her lips. She then let go of her brusquely leaving her stunned and confused. Rafe turned and faced Julia and the others. "There. Now are you all happy you got to dictate what happens in our relationship?" she asked resentfully.

Turning back to Eden, she gave her a false smile. "I'm sorry you feel like you can't talk to me and are walking on eggshells. Just tell your lictors everything I'm doing wrong or what you need from me, and have them put it on a list, and maybe they can email it to me, or better yet, come over and beat me over the head with it in person. Then I'll put them on my schedule to take whatever punishment they think I deserve if I don't fulfill your demands or somehow commit another crime against you."

She walked over and picked up Bronte. "We're going out for a while." Rafe started to walk to the patio doors then stopped and turned around. "Oh, and my father is off limits, so don't talk about him." She held Eden's eyes for a moment, wondering if she would keep her promise, then walked out of the house.

---

[1] I want you

She unlocked the brake on the jogging stroller and began wheeling it out the back gate with Bronte on her hip.

With wide eyes, Eden stood stunned and reeling from Rafe's kiss as she watched her walk out of the house with Bronte. She turned to Julia as anger flashed through her body. They had discussed giving Rafe space and not setting her off, and obviously, Julia pushed Rafe's buttons again. "What the heck did you say to her?" she snapped.

"Yeah, what the fuck?" asked Abby. "Why's she so mad, and what the hell are lictors?" She immediately pulled out her phone to look it up.

Julia felt a bit of guilt at seeing Eden's worried and angry face. "I'm sorry. I was just trying to talk to her about what happened yesterday."

Eden sat down slowly on the couch and ran her hand through her golden hair. "Julia, she was doing so much better this morning—and *now*..." Eden threw her hands up in frustration. "Her birthday is in two weeks. I thought we could all have a good day together and convince her to get out of the house and talk about what she would like to do for her birthday. Now she's upset with everyone again," she complained.

"What exactly did you say to her?" asked Jude as they all sat down around Eden.

"Why does she think we're going to punish her?" asked Erica.

"I just talked to her about the things she did yesterday with the flirting, disregarding Eden, and not talking to us about things," said Julia exasperated. "I just asked her why she was doing those things and what she was trying to accomplish."

"You know, Darcella told me last night she thought we should see other people," said Abby disgruntled. "What did Rafe say to her?"

"Abby…" Eden sighed, putting a comforting hand on her shoulder. "She told me she just asked the girl not to play games with your heart. She didn't want her to hurt you."

Abby was shocked at first then rolled her eyes and continued messing with her phone.

"So, she talked to you about it?" asked Julia. "I thought she wasn't talking about things to you."

"Most of the time, she doesn't say much," Eden affirmed, "but last night, after all of you left, we actually talked a little, and it was good."

"Okay, okay," Abby interrupted as she held up her phone, "I got it! Lictors are like bodyguards to Roman magistrates who, at the magistrate's command, could make arrests and carry out capital punishment," she read and pulled a face.

"Harsh," said Erica with a grimace.

Eden couldn't hide her worry. "She's been doing so much better the last couple of weeks. I thought you weren't going to challenge her, and you were going to go easy on her and just talk, not make her feel like she is being punished."

"It wasn't what I intended," Julia assured her. "I just wanted her to start talking to us about things so we can help her."

"At least she kissed you and told you she loves you finally," volunteered Abby.

"Oh, god!" Eden put her head in her hands. Based on Rafe's reaction, she didn't know if it was really good at all.

2

AFTER ESCAPING EVERYONE, Rafe Salvaggio secured Bronte in the jogging stroller and then ran them to the park and around the foot trail until she burned off most of her anger. She wheeled the stroller to the fountain and got water for her and Bronte. Moving to a bench, she took Bronte out of the stroller so they could use the restroom and have a little run around the playground.

They made their way to the slides first then the swings where Rafe pushed Bronte high, and she laughed as she swung through the air. Soon, Bronte wanted out to explore the playset with the slide again, and Rafe followed her around along with the other mothers who were there following their own children.

Bronte jumped from one of the lower platforms to the ground into the dirt then brushed hands together to get the dirt off and went back to do it again.

"You've got a little daredevil there," one of the mothers said with a laugh. "How old is she?"

"She just turned two last month," said Rafe proudly.

"She's so petite," said the mother. "Mine's the one in the green," she said as she pointed to a little girl on the playset. "She'll be four in a few months, and she's still a bit timid with things. I think she's going to be tall and lanky like her father." She laughed again. "They grow up so fast."

"They do," said Rafe with a nod as she watched Bronte play. She looked up, and in the distance, she saw a familiar person approaching. She was just glad she was coming without her posse following. "Bronte," she called, "your mommy's coming. Do you want to run and meet her or play?" She watched as Bronte signed the word *play* and went under the slide with the other children. "Okay, you can play," Rafe acknowledged her signing.

"Well, color me impressed and embarrassed," said the mother. "I'm impressed a two-year-old is using sign language and embarrassed because I thought she was your daughter. I'm sorry," she said as she blushed.

It was Rafe's turn to laugh. "She's my daughter," Rafe told her with a smile as Eden came up to them. "This is her birth mother, Eden. Eden, this is," she paused, "I'm sorry, what's your name?"

"I'm Pamela," she said as she shook Eden's hand and Eden returned the greeting. "I didn't get your name," she said to Rafe.

"Rafe," she answered as they shook hands. "Bronte is under the slide," she told Eden.

Eden looked under the slide and saw Bronte with the other kids playing. She smiled at Rafe. "Looks like she's having fun."

"Well, it was nice meeting you both. It looks like I'm needed on the swings." Pamela laughed and took off after her little girl.

"Bye," said Rafe with a small laugh.

"Everyone's at the house swimming," said Eden as she watched Bronte play. "Do you want to head back?"

"In a bit," said Rafe with a small smile. "Let's just let her play for a while longer," she said then went after Bronte who had decided to climb up the rock wall. Rafe helped her get to the top of the wall then lifted her off and flew her around while she giggled. Then she let her back onto the ground where she decided she had to do it all over again.

Eden watched as the two played, and she laughed at their antics until Rafe flew Bronte into her arms. "Well, hello, flying girl," she said to Bronte and kissed her dirt covered cheek.

Bronte struggled to get down from Eden's arms, and when she let her loose, the little girl ran for the rock wall, and Rafe lifted her up and put her on her shoulders.

"I think it's time to get home, B Girl." She turned to Eden. "Can you grab the stroller?"

"Sure," said Eden. She got the stroller and pushed it as she walked next to Rafe and Bronte. She looked over at Rafe as she held on to Bronte's legs, and the little girl wrapped her arms around her head. "Rafe," she said softly.

Rafe looked over at Eden. "Yeah," she said as she jiggled Bronte.

"The next time you kiss me like you did and tell me you love me," she said matter-of-factly, "you better do it because you want to and mean it, not because you were told to do it or you were forced."

Rafe laughed and bumped her lightly. "Sounds like a good plan," she said with a wink as Eden stumbled a bit and laughed.

Eden couldn't stop grinning at Rafe's playfulness. She hoped, when they got home, the girls wouldn't say anything upsetting to her again. After walking for a while, Rafe took Bronte off her shoulders, and they stopped and secured her in the stroller. Eden pushed the stroller, and they walked in silence for a while.

When they got close to the house, Eden slowed down. "What would you like for your birthday?" she asked casually.

Rafe slowed to match Eden's pace and thought about what she wanted. Mostly, she wanted to be left alone by all the people interfering in her life, but she knew it wasn't what Eden wanted to hear. "I don't know," she said. "I really don't need anything."

"Would you want to go out to celebrate?" Eden asked. "Abby said you went out with everyone last year."

"I'll think about it," she answered as she pushed open the gate to the backyard and was about to hold it open so Eden could get through. Then she saw Jude, Erica, and Flynn in the pool and Julia, Abby and Stacey in the lounge chairs. "I didn't know all of them would be here," she grumbled because now Flynn and Stacey were there too. "I'm not really in the mood to deal with all of them." She held Eden back from going through the gate and pulled it closed quietly.

"What are you doing?" Eden asked confused.

"I," she hesitated. "Let's not go home right now."

"Rafe," she said with a sigh, "they know I went after you, and they're expecting us back. Besides, where would we go? Bronte will want lunch soon."

"Maybe we can take a run to the Kiki and sneak in the back door. We can just eat in the kitchen or something," Rafe suggested hopefully.

"We can't barge in on Ephraim during Sunday lunch," said Eden sensibly. "What if we just go in, and I'll tell them you have a headache."

Rafe frowned. "I hate being trapped in my own house," she groaned. "At least it won't be a lie. Just thinking about them all ganging up on me is giving me a headache."

"I don't think they're going to gang up on you," said Eden. "They're just worried about you."

Doubt etched on Rafe's face. "Let's just get this over with," she said and opened the gate again.

They went through the gate, pushing Bronte in her stroller and the girls looked over as they made it to the patio. Rafe prepared herself for the onslaught she dreaded might come and held the stroller while Eden got Bronte out. She followed Eden inside as the girls watched them but said nothing. They made it to the kitchen and got some water then sat at the kitchen counter.

Eden watched Rafe as she drained her glass and knew she had to do something to help her stay in a good place. She didn't want her to have another bad night. "I have an idea," she said softly as she helped Bronte with her cup.

Rafe gave her a small smile. "Yeah? What is it?"

"Why don't you take Bronte and get cleaned up, because you're both sweat and dirt covered," she said and wrinkled her nose.

"Your mommy thinks we're gross and stinky." Rafe laughed and tickled Bronte.

Eden laughed with her and nodded as Bronte giggled. "Disgusting," she teased. "When you're all clean, go upstairs to play and maybe watch a movie," she suggested. "In the meantime, I'll make you some lunch and take it up. Then I'll go out and tell the girls you two need some quiet time. I'll stay with them until they leave. When they're gone, I'll come up to let you know."

Rafe swept Bronte up in her arms and kissed her cheek. "You have a smart mommy," she said then smiled at Eden. "Thank you. It's a great idea. We'll see you in a little while," she said and carried Bronte to her room.

Eden watched her walk away and then started getting lunch together for them. As she worked, Julia came inside and sat at the counter.

"So," said Julia tentatively, "how is she?"

"I think she's better," Eden said as she cut up an apple. "She went for a run, and I found her playing in the park with Bronte. I told you she'd probably go there."

"Did she say anything?"

"She just doesn't want to be ganged up on anymore," said Eden. "You know you're not going to get anywhere if you make her mad. I don't understand why you do it," she said frustrated.

"Believe me, I didn't mean to upset her," said Julia defensively.

"Maybe everyone should back off her for a while," said Eden as she put some peanut butter on the plate next to the apples. She hoped Julia would get the not so subtle hint. "Maybe you two just can't talk right now without making each other mad or saying the wrong things. I know you've been her best friend most of her life, but every time you talk to her, something happens. It makes things harder, Julia."

"She has to talk sometime," said Julia emphatically, not liking the idea of being shut out. "She has to start talking and working through things. I'm trying to help you too, Eden."

"I know," said Eden softly as she added some veggies and crackers to the lunch plates. "It's just, she seems so much better since she's been taking her new medication. Maybe those other meds were the real cause of all the things she said and did. If they were, then we shouldn't treat her like she is still on them and still doing those things," she said, hoping Julia would see her reasoning. "She's actually been laughing and playful again. It's got to mean something."

Julia sighed and thought about the situation. "Yeah, and she did kiss you and touch you, finally."

"I don't want her doing it if it's forced, though, if it's not real," said Eden aggravated. "She just did it because she was mad at you. I don't want her to have to fake her way through things just to keep us off her back. If she starts faking things, we'll never know if she's really getting better."

Julia could see how upset Eden was getting. "You're right, you're right," she surrendered. "We need to think of a better way to get her to open up."

"I'm going to take this upstairs for Rafe and Bronte. They need some quiet time," she explained as she put the lunch plates and drinks on a tray. "I'll meet you outside in a bit." She picked up the tray of food and headed upstairs.

Julia got up and went back outside with the girls. She knew Rafe just didn't want to come out, and Eden was helping her. To Julia, it seemed Eden was enabling Rafe's behavior more than she was helping her change it. She wondered again if she should call Greer and Kate to help or for advice. She sat down on the lounger and then picked up her drink and waited for Eden while the others swam.

Abby swam to the edge of the pool and looked up at Julia. "So, what's going on with Boo Radley?"

"Rafe has sequestered herself in the house again," she said annoyed and rolled her eyes at Abby's literary reference.

"It seems like she never wants to spend time with us anymore," said Abby concerned. "She's alone even when we're all here."

"I know," said Julia. "I just don't know how to get through to her. When Eden gets out here, we're going to have to figure out what to try next to help her."

3

FINALLY ALONE AFTER talking to the girls, Eden Kingsley began to understand a little of how Rafe was feeling as far as being ganged up on by them. They all had opinions about what to do about helping Rafe. Julia kept reminding her she needed to grow up and not depend on Rafe so much, but it seemed like they all depended on her a lot too. They wanted Rafe to hang out or go places or talk to them or help them just as much as Eden wanted Rafe to talk to her and hold her and get back to their lives, and be happy. She didn't know how many of their suggestions and ideas would help, but they had a lot of them.

As soon as the girls and Flynn left, Eden went up to check on Rafe and Bronte and found them asleep on the sofa while a Blu-ray disc repeated its music on the main menu page. She looked lovingly at the matching pair with their dark hair and swarthy skin holding each other while they slept, and she smiled. She loved them so much.

Regret surged through Eden over everything that had happened, for the time Rafe had lost with both of them, and for what they were going through now. It was good to see Rafe able to sleep again. The insomnia she suffered compounded a lot of her problems, and now she was actually able to take a nap instead of trying to think up another project to do.

She took a breath and held back the tears her emotions threatened to release. It seemed like crying was becoming an unwanted friend. It helped to release some anxiety, but she didn't want to do it. She turned the TV volume down then turned off everything. After quietly gathering the dishes, she took them downstairs. She was happy to see they ate everything, but she wasn't sure who ate the most. Bronte had been eating a lot lately while Rafe, though she was eating more than before, still only seemed to snack. When she finished putting the dishes in the dishwasher, she took a glass of water to the living room and sat down on the couch to try to relax for a while.

As Eden drank her water and relaxed, she looked up at the painting over the fireplace. It was the one Rafe had done of Eden when they first met. She was standing in a garden holding an apple. No one ever believed Rafe hadn't talked her into posing nude for the painting. Rafe thought it was all very funny back then. Eden smiled as she remembered the name people began to call her and the one she had such a problem with after she left Rafe.

She understood now what it meant.

Salvaggio's Paradise.

Eden thought about it a lot, and right now it seemed like she was very far away from paradise, and she wasn't sure if it would ever come back. Laying back on the couch, Eden thought about all the things Julia had been telling her about Rafe over the past couple of weeks. She really didn't know what to make of it all.

So many things Julia said seemed unbelievable. As Eden contemplated the things Rafe had told her about her past she realized, after hearing all Julia had to say, they seemed sparse and glossed over. Then she pondered the secrets she had promised to keep now, about Rafe's first kiss and her father.

She found herself thinking a lot about what Rafe had told her. She still had no guess as to why, or how, or what those events had to do with Rafe's friend who died in Italy or her mothers' death. She sighed in frustration about the whole situation. Eden knew it would take time to recover after everything, but she was beginning to wonder if they really could recover from all of it.

She felt the air move and looked up as Rafe sat down in the chair across from her. "Did you have a good nap?"

"Yeah, thanks for saving me," Rafe said with a small smile. "Bronte is in her bed. She probably won't sleep much longer, though."

"It's okay," she said and sat her water glass on the floor beside the couch. "It's been a hard day, so we should relax while we can."

"I'm sorry," said Rafe softly.

Eden looked over at her with a wrinkled brow. "Why? What for?"

"For today. For using you when I was mad, for leaving you alone with the girls to take their backlash, for putting you between them and me." She leaned forward to look into her eyes. "I really am sorry."

Eden chuckled. "It's okay. I get it, really. They can be a lot to handle when they're mad and frustrated."

Rafe leaned back, happy she understood. "Yes, they can."

"Can I ask you a question?" Eden asked softly.

"Sure," she said, "you can ask me whatever you want. I don't want you thinking you have to walk on eggshells around me like Julia says you do."

Eden sat up and faced Rafe. "She told you what I said?" She watched Rafe nod. "I guess I do. Sometimes I just don't know what to do, and it seems like lately, everything I do is wrong. I don't mean to do things wrong," she said getting nervous. "I just think, sometimes, you need some affection, and I know I do. I know you think I do the things I do for myself, but it's not just for me. I think you need me sometimes even though you say you don't."

Rafe watched her as she rambled on and could see she was nervous. It made her sad. Eden used to tell her everything, and now she could barely ask her a question. She wondered when Eden stopped feeling safe with her. Was it before Jake, before they decided to start a family, or even before then? "So, what's your question?"

"Well," she started, "Julia told me some things I'm a little confused about." She wrung her hands nervously. "Have you really never forgiven me for anything I've asked forgiveness for?" She looked into Rafe's surprised face then back down at her hands.

Fucking, Julia, thought Rafe angrily. "What did she say?" she asked calmly.

"She said you don't forgive the way I understand it, and you've never given forgiveness to anyone, and you won't or can't give it," she answered softly. "So does it mean you've never forgiven me? Does it mean I always have to live knowing no matter what I do, I'll never be forgiven by you?"

Rafe knew she was referring to the type of forgiveness she learned in Sunday school class when she was young, a type of forgiveness that made no sense in her mind. She sighed and ran her hands through her hair. "No," she said softly, "it isn't what it means. It just means you don't need forgiveness from me and neither does anyone else."

"I do though," she said as she looked up at her. "It's going to be very hard for me to live knowing you won't forgive me."

"Listen," said Rafe then sighed heavily, "I don't want to debate philosophy with you right now. I don't want you to worry about my views on it. If it's something you need, then take it. You have it. You don't even have to ask for it because it is yours however you define it."

"Okay," said Eden not sure exactly what Rafe was doing. "She told me a lot of other things I didn't know about you too." The look on Rafe's face said she was torn between confusion and anger. "I wasn't going to tell you she told me the things she did," she continued, "but the more I think about them, the more I wonder if I really know you. And then I find myself getting angry. I get angry because you have secrets you keep, but you've been so angry and have problems with the ones I've had. I don't think it's fair."

Rafe fought to control herself. "I see," she said softly. "Julia can tell you anything she wants to tell you. She can also answer all your questions and explain everything about me, because she apparently knows everything and is in control of all the information, and when and how people receive it."

"Don't blame her, Rafe," said Eden seeing Rafe's defensiveness. "She's telling me things because she's worried, and she said I needed to know some things to be able to understand you better."

"Well," said Rafe as she stood up, "I guess you really don't need to talk to me then." She walked out of the living room and grabbed her keys. "I won't be home for dinner tonight," she said and walked out the door.

"Rafe!" Eden called. "Don't be mad at me! I do need to talk with you! Come back!" she called as she followed her out. "Rafe!" she called as she watched her get into her car. "Dang it!" she said to herself as Rafe pulled out and drove away.

She went back inside and tried to figure out who she should call. She knew Rafe was mad at all the girls, including Letty, so she had no idea where Rafe would go. She heard Bronte calling from her room, so she went to check on her. She would just have to wait for Rafe to calm down and come home. Anxiety buzzed through her at the thought that Rafe might not come home again.

4

ON THE DAY before her birthday, Rafe Salvaggio was enjoying some alone time. Everyone dropping by to 'check-in' over the last couple of weeks had been getting on her nerves. Julia was especially pushing her luck by telling Eden things and inserting herself where she didn't belong. Everyone had some advice or opinion about how she was handling matters with Eden. Rafe was also tired of being told she had to get out and have fun or go to dinner or any other innumerable things she just didn't want to do. She knew, once tomorrow came around, there was the possibility other people would be at her house which she didn't want to deal with. They may even come over and try to convince her to go out somewhere again or deliver more unwanted advice.

It all led to the realization she needed to make a change. At her therapy session, she told Dr. Conrad she wanted to stop going. She just had too much pressure from home, and she felt she could not balance doing the therapy and trying to manage all the shit her so-called friends were raining down on her about Eden. Maybe if she stayed away from all of her friends and their pressure, things would be better.

Plus, she finally decided she didn't want to go back to work at the Conservatory. Since her time away, she couldn't see herself there anymore. They were taking too much time deciding what they were going to do, and the therapy was just for them in order to cover their asses anyway.

The doctor didn't like the idea of her quitting, of course, but she couldn't force anyone to go to sessions. Since Rafe was turning in her resignation, the doctor agreed to write up a notice of patient's voluntary discharge and her review for the school with a notice that all further sessions were the responsibility of the patient. Rafe had typed up her resignation letter the night before and would send it along with the letter from the doctor on Monday after her last session.

Rafe decided to manage things herself by keeping the prescription for a while, maybe check in with the doctor occasionally, and make sure to stay away from stressors. The meds helped with her mind so she could get sleep, and though they didn't stop them, they did make her dreams less intense most times. She hated taking the meds because they made her feel disoriented sometimes, and she hated the off-kilter feeling more than the dreams. The only reason she kept taking them was that she promised Kate.

The more Rafe thought about it, the more she realized she never promised Kate she would take this particular pill. With this realization, she decided to stop taking them as of today. The nightmares were not as bad anymore, though she knew they would never completely go away. She was sure she could handle them. She would keep the pills and take them again if she thought she needed them.

Rafe's phone rang, interrupting her thoughts. She checked the caller ID. It was Julia, the last person she wanted to talk to—so she declined the call. Seconds later, the phone rang again.

"Fuck," Rafe cursed quietly then answered the phone. "Hello," she said unhappily.

"Rafe, I need to talk with you. Where are you?" asked Julia.

"What is it?"

"I'd like to talk to you in person," she said firmly.

"I'm not available right now," she answered. "What do you want?"

"Where are you? I know you're not home because I'm at your house, and I called Eden, and she says she doesn't know where you are, either."

"What do you want, Julia?"

"I need to talk to you in person."

"Well, it will have to be some other time, maybe next week, or the week after."

"No, I need to talk to you today. Tell me where you are, and I'll meet you."

Rafe sighed and shook her head. She just wanted a few fucking hours for herself today. It didn't seem like a lot to ask. It seemed like she had no time alone since they ganged up on her about Eden a couple of weeks ago. She finally decided not to go back to the house today so no one could show up and try to tag along. "I'll be home later tonight," she said hoping it would satisfy her.

"I need to talk to you today. It's important, and I don't want to do it over the phone."

Rafe considered just hanging up on her but knew she would never hear the end of it. Just like she hadn't heard the end of it about walking out on her conversation with Eden. *Fucking Julia,* she thought. "Fine, I'm in Long Beach," she lied.

"Long Beach?" she asked angrily. "What the hell are you doing there?"

"None of your business," Rafe answered. Her calm voice in no way represented her true emotions. "I'm busy right now. I'll call you when I'm back," she said and hung up the phone.

She knew Julia would be livid on the other end, but she decided she couldn't care less. She got out of her car and grabbed the duffel bag from her trunk then walked into the massage boutique.

"Hey, Rafe," said Jude with a smile. "You made it right on time."

"Thanks for setting this up for me," she said warmly. "I think this has been a lot of help."

"I think you're right," she said and motioned to the woman next to her. "Susy will be your experience associate again today, just like you asked."

"Hi, Susy," said Rafe as she shook her hand. She turned to Jude fretfully. "This is still just between you and me right now, right? I just need this so I can relax. I just need some alone time, you know?"

"I get it," said Jude with an easy smile, "don't worry. Just follow Susy, and she'll get you started." She could see Rafe really needed her time here. "Rafe, don't forget to take it easy when you stand up this time. I don't want you getting another dizzy spell and getting hurt."

"Thanks," said Rafe. "I will. It's just the meds. They make me light headed sometimes," she said as she followed Susy. Jude was the only person who seemed to understand she needed to be able to relax. Her time at Jude's massage company seemed to help take the tension from her body better than any drug.

She followed Susy to the locker room, got a robe from the shelf, and then took her clothes off and put on the robe. Susy was there when she came out and led her to the soaking room.

"Do you remember how long to stay in each one?" asked Susy, averting her eyes as Rafe opened her robe.

"I do," said Rafe as she took off her robe and climbed into the first of three different temperature soaking tubs, the last was hot and had lots of powerful jets.

"Okay, I'll set this timer so you don't lose track of time," she said with a smile. "It'll give off a chime when it's time to switch."

"Got it," said Rafe as she leaned back in the water. She closed her eyes and just tried to focus on her breathing.

Jude had a great set up with soaking baths, jetted water therapy, and heated lumbar loungers, massage therapists and a lot of different massage options and treatments.

Rafe was unsure if it would really help the first time she came, but it had helped her more than she could have imagined. She decided to do whatever Jude recommended. Jude and Susy came through with a program for her, and it not only helped, but Rafe actually enjoyed it.

Jude had come over a few weeks ago. Rafe knew it was to babysit and was annoyed at first. As they hung out, Jude was happy just to keep quiet company with her as Rafe did projects or they shared a few beers. At some point, Jude mentioned Rafe looked like she had some tense muscles based on the way she walked around and sat.

Rafe let Jude check her muscles for tenderness and found her muscles were all knotted up. Jude suggested Rafe get a massage. Rafe had seen this as an opportunity to have alone time and, at the same time, get some help relaxing. Jude, in turn, thought Rafe needed the sessions, so she agreed not to tell anyone Rafe was going to her massage company. This way no one would decide to encroach on her relaxation time.

After Rafe went through the last bath, Susy came back into the room. "Are you ready for your massage?" she asked softly and scanned a file as Rafe put on her robe. "Or would you like to go to the sauna or to the lumbar chairs."

"I think I'll go ahead and do the massage. Can you give me some extra time today? It looks like I may have a hard night." She did not look forward to dealing with Julia when she got home.

Susy smiled. "Sure. Jude said to take as much time as you needed."

"Great," said Rafe. "Can you make sure not to put on the music with the high pitched flutes again? It drives me crazy," she said with a chuckle.

"Sure, follow me." She led Rafe into a small room with a massage table. She turned down the music, switching to a new

CD that she hoped Rafe would approve of, and then checked her supplies. "I'll knock in a few minutes," she said and left Rafe alone in the room.

Rafe took off her robe and got on the heated table then waited for Susy to knock. When Susy began the massage, Rafe was thankful for either Susy just not being a talker or Jude telling her not to talk except when necessary.

As her muscles warmed from the kneading, Rafe closed her eyes and tried to think about what she wanted to do with herself now since she had quit therapy. What was important? She could only think of two things, Eden and Bronte. Everyone else could go to hell. She and Eden needed time to figure out if they really could have a life together or if they had nothing left to save. She wished they would all just stay out of her life right now. Everything was going fine until they started pushing in. Julia was telling Eden stories and things about her, and who knew how it was coming off. It seemed like it was making Eden think badly of her, just as she knew it would. It was exactly why she never wanted to tell her about all of the stuff in her past. It was the past, and it should have stayed there. Now it was adding to the problems they already had. Rafe wondered if Julia was doing it on purpose just to piss her off.

"Just relax," said Susy. "Listen to the music and try not to think," she said softly.

Rafe took a deep breath and tried to push everything from her mind. The one thing not leaving her mind was the image of Eden.

5

JULIA HAWTHORN WAITED impatiently for Rafe to get home. She sat watching Eden play with Bronte in the living room. Bronte was taking Eden pretend food she had made in her little kitchen, and Eden pretended to eat it. If not for their antics, she would have had a frown on her face. Bronte had brought her over a few treats, and she placed them on the table after she pretended to eat them.

"Are you sure you don't know what she's doing in Long Beach?" Julia asked Eden again.

"No," said Eden as she shook her head and helped Bronte pretend to cook. She wondered how many times Julia was going to ask the same question. "She left before we were up this morning," she repeated just as many times. "She'll be home soon. She likes to hang out with Bronte before bed. Sometimes they do yoga together. It's really cute," she said with a small smile as the vision of the two in their poses filled her mind. Lately, they even let her join in, and she loved their time together. She could see whatever was upsetting Julia must be big because she still looked angry. "Are you going to tell me why you're so upset with her?"

"Don't worry, you'll probably find out soon enough," said Julia peevishly. "I just need to ask her about some things first. I don't want to worry you any more than I have to if it's nothing." She perked up as she heard a car engine outside cut off and then a car door close.

"I think she's here," said Eden as Bronte handed her more toy food.

Julia went to the front door to look. "It's her," she announced and went out the door to confront Rafe. She met Rafe as she walked up the driveway toward her. "Glad you finally made it home. I need to talk with you." She looked past Rafe and saw she had her father's car. "Why are you driving the Spyder again? I thought you weren't taking off in it and driving crazy anymore."

Rafe stopped and just glared at her for a moment. "What do you want?" she asked evenly, ignoring her question. It was none of her business if and when she drove her papa's car.

"I got a call from the office this morning," she said and crossed her arms as she stared at Rafe.

"Great. I'm glad they want you to come back," said Rafe, knowing it wasn't what she was talking about but not giving her the satisfaction of letting her know.

"You know what I'm talking about!" she said her voice rising with irritation. "What are you doing? Are you getting ready to move all your accounts from the company?"

Rafe crossed her arms to mimic Julia. "Since you're on leave from the firm right now, I'm not discussing my financial plans with you."

"Damn it, Rafe!" Julia exclaimed heatedly and tried to stare her down. "Are you planning on leaving Eden?" she burst out suddenly. "Is it the reason why you're suddenly disappearing for hours again? Were you in Long Beach running half-naked on the beach again? Are you purposely trying to fuck things up with Eden?"

Rafe said nothing, and Julia got angrier. "I knew I should have convinced Eden and Letty to have you placed!" Julia yelled. "I should have called Greer! As a matter of fact, I think I will call her and tell her everything that's going on. Maybe she can talk some sense into you!" she yelled in frustration.

Rafe turned and began to walk back to the car. Julia knew she had handled things badly, so she went after her. "Come on, Rafe, don't leave. I'm sorry," she said as she followed her. "It's just Eden has been trying so hard, and when you met her, you changed so dramatically. I know you love her. Why are you turning back into the person you were before you met her? Secretive and going on crazy adventures alone," she demanded, more out of jealousy than concern. She wanted to be the one on those adventures again. "I know it's what you're doing with all the disappearing. It's just like before when you would disappear anywhere from days to months, and then, suddenly, you were back after some wild adventure. I thought you were over pulling those stunts!"

Rafe opened the car door then turned to look at the person who was supposed to be one of her best friends. Julia had no fucking clue what was going on, and Rafe just wanted her to stop interfering and go away. She was making things worse with all her guessing and projecting. Normally, Julia would just watch from the sidelines and make a suggestion every once in a while. Now she was inserting herself and telling Eden things she knew she didn't want Eden to know. Rafe had no idea why she was so interested in getting involved all of a sudden.

"Why are you doing this, Julia? You have no idea what's going on, and you're the one fucking things up for me. Why? I thought you were my friend. I thought you wanted things to work out with Eden and me. Do you realize you're driving us further apart with all the things you're doing? Do you? Now since you've talked her into having *high-fucking-tea* and had all your *special fucking talks* with her, she hates me!"

"She doesn't hate you," Julia insisted with exasperation. She knew Rafe was comparing her with her mother and her gossiping tea parties, and she did not like it. "She's worried."

"Fine, she's worried, and you've not helped," said Rafe evenly.

"Just talk to me," demanded Julia. "You have to talk to us and stop pushing us away."

"No, I don't," said Rafe flatly. "You all need to back off and stop pressuring me. Stop interfering in my life and my relationship with Eden!"

"We're trying to help you save your relationship!" Julia declared angrily. "Since you met her and fell in love with her, you've changed. For the better! You couldn't even commit to Greer because of her, for fuck's sake! She's the reason you changed for the better, and you need to make sure you don't go back to the person you were before you met her," said Julia trying to reason with Rafe. Julia was positive, if Rafe regressed into her adventure-seeking state again, there would be absolutely no place for her or Eden in Rafe's life.

"Is that really your problem?" Rafe laughed bitterly. "You think I'm going to regress into who I used to be? I think I should be insulted, but I'm not. The person who should be insulted is Eden. You really think I'm with her to better myself or something? I think you've been hanging out with Abby too much!" Rafe decided she couldn't talk to Julia anymore. Julia had no idea what she was talking about, and Rafe was in no mood to educate her. She thought her massage would relax her enough she could deal with things, but this was too much. She looked behind Julia and saw Eden come out holding Bronte. She was torn between the desire to go inside with Eden and just getting in the car and leaving.

Eden had heard Julia yelling at Rafe. Concerned, she came out to see what was going on. She saw Rafe just looking at Julia angrily, then when Rafe turned her attention toward her, Eden could see how hurt she was and knew Julia had pushed Rafe too far. "Julia, why don't you give her some space? Maybe you can talk to her when you calm down. She needs to come inside and have dinner with Bronte right now," she said firmly.

"Right," said Rafe in relief. "You should go," she said and closed her car door. "I need to go inside now." She walked up to Eden and took Bronte then walked into the house.

"Eden, you have no idea what she's doing." Julia stopped herself in frustration. She couldn't tell Eden what was happening without risking breach of confidentiality. Her father would not be happy if Rafe sued and they were fined, not to mention having her license revoked. The only option was talking to Rafe directly. She needed to know why Rafe called the office and requested three years' worth of financials, an updated net worth report, and a list of all her accounts with balances. The girls had to get it to Katheryn by the end of business today. *Is she moving her money or is she planning to leave again? Last time she tried to leave town, she only had a day to plan. Now she has had months.*

Eden faced Julia nervously. The only reason she could think of for Julia being so hesitant to tell her what was going on, when she clearly wanted to tell, was it had something to do with Hawthorn Financial and Rafe's accounts. "Does it have to do with something at work?" she asked tentatively.

"You know I can't divulge anything to do with work," said Julia, her body tense. *Even if Eden guessed, she could not confirm anything.*

"Well," she said hesitantly, "maybe it's nothing." Julia's demeanor made Eden certain Rafe was doing something with her money, and it concerned Julia. *Maybe Rafe was planning to leave again.* Julia shifted her feet, and Eden didn't want what she was thinking to be true. "She was talking about buying back into her old company," she revealed. "Maybe she just needs to know if she can afford it."

"Right," Julia scoffed, knowing *Rafe could buy her old company back four times over or more with the amounts in her accounts now and the aggressive investing Rafe had been doing. Who knew what Rafe had from the sale of her father's business and his other financial accounts, not to mention if she sold the properties she had inherited.* She didn't want to upset Eden, and she couldn't discuss Rafe's finances with her, but she at least wanted to help if she could. "I'll go for now, but I have to talk with her again, and soon," she said as she stormed off to her car and took off.

Eden watched her go, the feelings of anger and frustration she left behind stirring up the anxiety inside. When she went back into the house, she found Rafe in the kitchen with Bronte looking through the refrigerator.

"How would you like to go out to eat?" she asked Rafe hiding her anxiety. "Maybe we can go to the bistro or try something new so we can get out of here."

Rafe turned around and looked gratefully at Eden. She loved her for those words, but she knew she wasn't really going to be good company. She walked over and handed Bronte back to her. "I think your mommy can find something really good to eat." She rubbed her neck and glanced at Eden. "I'm sorry. I just need to go lay down for a while."

"Okay," said Eden softly and watched with worry as Rafe walked back to her room.

Eden made dinner and knocked on Rafe's door to let her know it was ready, but there was no answer. She opened the door and saw Rafe was already in bed. She had been working on her computer when she fell asleep. She went over and closed the laptop then put it on the nightstand. "Rafe," she said softly, "dinner is ready. Do you want to come out and eat with Bronte?"

Rafe opened her eyes to Eden looking down at her with concern. "Sure," she said and sat up. She put her hand to her head and sat still for a moment.

"Are you okay?" asked Eden. "Dizzy spell?"

"Yeah," Rafe groaned, "I'm okay." She felt the wave of dizziness pass and moved to get out of bed slowly. "I keep forgetting," she said then followed Eden out of the bedroom.

Bronte came running down the hall signing she had to potty, so Eden took her to the bathroom while Rafe went into the dining room.

The table was set, and the food was already on the table, so there was nothing for Rafe to do but sit down. As she sat, Rafe looked over everything on the table Eden had made. There was a roast chicken, small potatoes, salad, and broccoli—for some unholy reason, Bronte loved to eat broccoli. She looked at the plates all in their places, everyday plates for her and Eden and a purple plastic one for Bronte.

It was a family table.

Rafe leaned on the table with her elbows and put her face in her hands. She knew she had sat at a table like this almost every night since she came home, but for some reason tonight, the scene suddenly struck her. She felt tears seep out of her eyes as she realized what was in front of her. This was all she ever really wanted since she and Eden had begun talking about having a baby all those years ago. A family she could come home to, spend time with, love, and not be alone.

She didn't know if she would ever figure out the true reasons Eden had done the things she did or if Eden even really knew herself. She knew one thing—they had to build trust again somehow. She could see Eden was trying and knew she wasn't being easy on her, but it had been so hard to focus on getting through everything in therapy to get back to work. Coming home and seeing her, and thinking about the things Eden had done, they both had done, was hard, so she did her best to avoid her and everything else. She just wanted all the turmoil inside her to end, but she didn't know how to stop it yet.

"Hey, babe," Eden said with concern as she came in with Bronte. "Are you okay?"

"I'm fine," said Rafe as she wiped away any traitor tears and sat up. "Everything looks good," she said and smiled as Eden got Bronte into her chair.

Rafe spent more time looking at her family than eating.

6

TODAY WAS SPECIAL. Eden Kingsley decided she would fix a nice birthday breakfast for Rafe that they could share. By arranging for Letty to pick Bronte up early this morning, Eden hoped to have some positive time together before Letty brought Bronte back home and everyone showed up for the birthday party. It seemed like they hadn't been alone for the last two weeks. Rafe would shut down every time one of their friends came over, or she would disappear for hours at a time. It was almost a stalemate between Rafe and their friends. Rafe was winning so far, but Eden knew it wasn't fair because there were more of them.

It looked to Eden like everything they tried just made Rafe dig in more. Julia coming over and upsetting her again last night hadn't helped. If Julia was right and Rafe was planning to leave, then they all had obviously pushed her too far because before they started coming over, she seemed to be doing better.

Last night Rafe was very quiet even while they played with Bronte. They watched a movie together upstairs, and Bronte fell asleep. After putting Bronte to bed, Rafe went out and put the top up on her father's car for the night, then sat outside beside the pool. It looked to Eden like she had a lot going on in her head, so she just left her alone except to tell her goodnight.

Eden knocked on Rafe's door. "Rafe," she called, "Bronte is going with Letty and wants a kiss and to show you her outfit. Can we come in?" As she opened the door, Rafe was there and took Bronte. She could tell as she looked in the room Rafe had been working on her computer in bed.

"*Sei molto carina*, B Girl,"[2] said Rafe and kissed her. "I didn't know she was going this soon or I would have come out earlier."

"It's okay," said Eden reassuringly. "She had a nice breakfast. Then we had to have a bath and played in the water for a while. We just played dress up with her Halloween costumes until Letty got here. I thought you were still asleep."

"Oh," said Rafe softly, "well, at least I got to see you in your new clothes," Rafe said to Bronte with a smile then kissed

---

[2] You're very pretty, B Girl,

her and growled playfully. "Let's go see Zia Letty," she said and carried Bronte into the living room where Letty was waiting.

"Hi *Cugina*, happy birthday," Letty said happily. "There's my B!" she said as she held her hands out to Bronte and gave Rafe a serious look. "We've missed you at the KiKi. Ephraim's been wanting you to try the new lunch pizzas you inspired."

"I'm sure they're great," said Rafe as she released Bronte into her arms. "I've not been very good company."

"Everyone says you're avoiding them," she revealed as she hugged Bronte.

"Avoiding them?" Rafe scoffed. "I can't seem to get rid of them lately."

"But," said Eden as she put a hand cautiously on Rafe, "we're going to have a quiet morning today. No company. No distractions."

"Oh, well," Letty winked at Eden, "we girls will get out of here and see you later," she said and took Bronte to the front door. They kissed Bronte goodbye again and then Letty left with her.

"I'm surprised she didn't mention the car," said Rafe as she arched her brow.

Eden laughed. "Oh, she mentioned it."

"She did?"

"Yeah," Eden confirmed with a shrug. "I told her you were taking me out in it," she said and grinned.

"Really?" Rafe asked slyly and watched Eden nod. "Well, maybe I will," she said with a smile, "maybe."

Eden saw Rafe's smile and immediately changed her plans for the morning. She went to the closet and grabbed a jacket and a scarf. "I'm ready," she said as she beamed and headed out to the car.

"Eden," Rafe called in annoyance, "I said maybe. What about my breakfast?" she called, but Eden was already out the door. Rafe stood there for a minute then laughed softly. "Okay," she said and grabbed her keys then followed her out. She locked the front door then ran to catch up to her. When they got to the car, she unlocked and opened the passenger door. "M'lady," she said with a flourish and Eden slid inside. She ran around to the driver's side and got in. She pulled her father's cap out of the glove box, put it on, and then started the engine. She looked over at Eden. "Want to make the neighbors worry?" she asked with a grin as she revved the engine. Then she backed out of the driveway quickly, and the tires screamed as she peeled out down the street while Eden laughed, glad Rafe was happy.

7

DRIVING TOWARD THE highway, Rafe Salvaggio made the decision to take them down the 405. She weaved through traffic then got off the 405, making her way to the coast highway to drive along the ocean toward Newport Beach. She wanted to be somewhere far away from everyone they knew.

As she drove, Rafe looked over at Eden who was looking out her window enjoying the view. The sun shining on her face and hair was dazzling, and anyone would think Eden was a native Californian with her golden locks and glowing skin. It had been years since she had gone anywhere with Eden in this car. She frowned a bit remembering the last time she wanted to take her somewhere in it and what Jake had done. She could still see his smirking face.

She noticed, in her irritation, she had picked up her speed, so she let off the gas to slow down. She caught Eden looking at her and smiled. Eden leaned her head back and enjoyed the ride, and Rafe was glad they could just drive and not have to talk. They drove for an hour or so and made it to Newport Beach. Rafe took them to Balboa Peninsula and parked. She looked over at Eden. "We're early enough maybe we can walk around for a while then get in somewhere for lunch without much of a wait."

Eden looked over at Rafe in her father's cap. "You look very sexy in this," she said. Eden took it off Rafe's head and put it on herself, giving Rafe a smile. "How does it look on me?"

Rafe laughed and pushed the hat back on Eden's head so she could see her eyes. "Very charming," she said as Eden took the cap off and put it and her scarf in the glove box.

"I may wear it on the drive home if you put the top down." She heard Rafe chuckle as she got out of the car.

They met at the front of the car and began their walk to the main street of shops and restaurants. Eden took hold of

Rafe's arm a bit possessively, and when Rafe didn't resist, she felt a swell of happiness inside her.

The morning was spent going through shops, looking at art, and enjoying watching all of the people who were out appreciating the day like they were doing. They bought some fresh fruit for a light morning snack and watched some of the boats take people on whale watching cruises and other outings for sightseeing and fun. Walking along the pier, they stopped to enjoy the sight of the ocean and watch as people reeled in fish or just stopped to talk.

After they walked a while longer, they headed back to the shops and found an Italian restaurant to try. As Rafe predicted, they didn't have to wait long for a table. Rafe ordered the Chef's Special Butternut Squash Ravioli, Eden had the Pollo Florentina, and they shared a good bottle of wine.

As they ate quietly and enjoyed the excellent food, Eden gazed at Rafe until she looked back. "So, I was just thinking about the bad dream you had," she said cautiously. "You said some things, and I was wondering if you remember."

Rafe frowned at the memory. "I remember everything," she said and shrugged. "But it was just a dream. It wasn't real." She didn't tell Eden she had other dreams since then, just not ones bad enough to take her out of her room. She knew she was supposed to tell someone, but since she wasn't going to therapy anymore after Monday, she wouldn't have to follow any doctor's orders.

"Oh, I know," said Eden reassuringly. "I was just wondering if you could tell me who Maria is," she said and then sipped her wine.

"Maria," said Rafe with a confused frown.

"Yes, you told me I should go to the grotto with Maria, and she would explain everything," she revealed. "So, I thought she might be a real person. Is she?"

Rafe considered her thoughtfully and sighed. The thing she didn't know was how much Eden heard of what she had said out loud. "Yes, she's real. I told you about her."

"You did?"

"Yes, she's the zingara. Gypsy girl."

"Oh," Eden said slowly as understanding formed in her mind. Maria was the girl Rafe had her first kiss with. "So, you're dreaming about your first kiss and me, together. Interesting," she said and took a bite of her food.

"Hmph," grunted Rafe. "Are you going to try and psychoanalyze my dreams now?"

"Well, it is hard to analyze your dream by just one thing, but she was your first, and I intend to be your last. So, yes, I think it's interesting," she said and locked eyes with Rafe.

"Interesting," said Rafe as she arched her eyebrow then took a sip of her wine.

Eden saw Rafe wasn't going to elaborate, so she continued. She hoped, since Rafe was in a good mood, she would want to talk about the dream today. "What's the grotto we were supposed to be going into? Why did we have to go there? What was she supposed to explain to me?"

Rafe sat her fork down carefully and leaned back in her chair. "If you don't mind," she said softly, "I'd rather not talk about it right now, if ever. It meant nothing. It was just," she hesitated, "just a dream. One I'd rather forget." She hoped Eden would drop the subject. Rafe really didn't want to talk about her broken mind right now and have Eden looking back at her with pity in her eyes.

Looking across the table, Eden could see Rafe was on the edge of being upset, and it wasn't what she wanted today. "Okay, I'm sorry," she said and nodded. "You're right. It was just a dream. We don't have to talk about it." She took the last sip of her wine while Rafe was just playing with her food. "Are you finished? Maybe we can go walk on the boardwalk again or on the beach."

"I'm finished," said Rafe and motioned for the check. They paid and left the restaurant and began walking toward the beach.

Rafe felt Eden take her arm again, and it felt good to have her there. She knew she needed to tell Eden some of the things going on, but it seemed like every time she tried, Julia or someone would say or do something, and it just made things harder. Since they started coming around all the time a few weeks ago, it seemed like she and Eden had no real alone time together.

They got to the beach and just enjoyed walking on the sand for a while and watching all the activity on the water. After a while, Rafe noticed Eden had slowed down. "Are you okay," she asked worriedly. "Are you in pain?"

"No." Eden laughed softly. "I'm not in pain. I told you I'm okay. I'm just tired. Can we sit down somewhere?"

"Sure," said Rafe. "How about over there." She pointed to a shaded, dry spot with not many people around. She led Eden over, and they sat down in the sand. Eden leaned against her and Rafe decided she should probably talk to her now because she might not get a chance again the way things were going.

"I don't like everyone babysitting me," Rafe said suddenly. "It makes it hard for me to think about the things I'm working on in therapy," she hesitated, knowing she wouldn't be going to therapy anymore. "It makes it hard for me to talk to you."

"I can tell you don't like it," Eden said with a small smile. "Maybe we can talk to them about it together."

Rafe nodded thoughtfully. "I don't like Julia telling you things and making you angry with me, and I don't like the others always pressuring me to talk."

Eden put her hand on Rafe's leg. "They just want to help you, babe."

"They're not helping," she complained and cocked her head in frustration. "Do you remember when you were going to therapy and you had things to tell me but you said you needed time?"

"Yes, I remember," she nodded wondering if she should mention she was still going to therapy.

"Well, I need time too," she said softly. "It's hard sometimes, to focus on what I need to do to make sure I can get through therapy to go back to work, then come home to a bunch of separate issues to figure out. I was doing my best to just focus on the job first, and then I thought I could work on us, but I just can't do it when they're always there pushing me when I'm not ready."

Eden felt a little confused. "I thought some of those things were mixed together, and you were getting help with both work and personal issues."

"Yeah, some things get mixed, but the underlying issue with getting back to work is the PTSD and stressors." Rafe sighed. "I have to be able to go back to the school and the classroom and not think about the anger I was feeling and everything making me feel those phantom pains. So, we were treating the PTSD as a separate issue hoping it would help some with everything else."

"Oh," Eden said and quirked her lips into a slight frown. "I wish you would have told me sooner. Maybe I could have been a better help."

"I should have," Rafe admitted, "but I think dealing with the meds just made it so I couldn't think to tell you or ask for help."

"Well, I'm glad your new meds are better," Eden said softly, and she berated herself again for not seeing Rafe's side effects sooner.

Rafe sat quietly looking out at the rolling blue ocean for a while then looked over at Eden who was toying with the sand. "I don't understand why they won't leave me alone so I can figure things out," she said irritated. "They think they're telling me things I don't know, but I do. They tell me you're going to leave me again because I won't talk to you," she paused, "and it scares me. You got mad at me for not being fair with secrets, but I can say the same because you're not being fair about giving me the time I need until I'm ready to talk."

Eden took a breath and wished Julia had never told Rafe she was going to leave. She understood very well how Rafe felt—more than Rafe knew—about the need for time to talk about things.

"What are we going to do, babe? It feels like no matter what we do, we're in this place where we can't move forward. At this very moment, the only thing I can think about is how you're letting me touch you again, and nothing else really matters. I miss you. I miss being close to you. I know a lot of things had to do with your medications, and I even messed those up for you." She ran her fingers through the sand. "I don't even really know what things were because of the medication and what things weren't."

"Well, you don't have to worry about it anymore," Rafe said softly.

"What? Why?" asked Eden concerned.

"I quit," she said matter-of-factly

"You quit? What did you quit?"

"Therapy."

"Rafe, you can't quit therapy!" said Eden in frustration.

"Why not?" she asked annoyed. "I was only going so I could get my job at the Conservatory back, and I've decided to hand in my resignation."

Eden was shocked, and she swallowed nervously. "Does," she hesitated, "does this mean I'm going to have to move out of the house?"

"No," Rafe shook her head, "not unless you want to."

"Well, what are you going to do?" she asked troubled. "We both signed the agreement saying we have to be gainfully employed."

"I know. It's why I was getting all my financial information from the Hawthorn Financial Firm," she said and studied Eden for a moment deciding not to tell her the other reason for requesting the information. "Eden, I don't think I should stay. I think I need to get away for a while."

"What?" Eden choked as tears formed in her eyes then ran down her face.

Rafe saw the tears falling from Eden's eyes and was angry with herself. This wasn't the way the news was supposed to come out. She leaned over and wiped a tear away then pulled her face close and gave her a small kiss on her forehead. "I'm sorry," she said. "I didn't mean to make you cry."

Eden looked up at Rafe and loved her for the fact she never told her to stop crying or that she shouldn't cry. She understood it was something she had a hard time controlling. "Rafe, please, I wish you would stay," she said and looked down to wipe away another tear.

"Eden," said Rafe as she pulled her face up so she would look at her. "I want you and Bronte to come with me," she said softly. "I want us all to take some time and just be together without everyone pushing us. Maybe, if we can just be alone for a while, we can figure things out."

Eden's mind reeled with confusion, unsure if she was following what was happening. "I don't understand. Why do we have to go away? Can't we just tell them to stop pushing?"

"I've tried," said Rafe as she shook her head. "They just push harder, and now they're telling you things and telling me things, and when we sit down together, we find out they aren't true at all. I don't understand why they couldn't just give me some time," she said again rubbing her temples. "I know we didn't talk a lot, and I know I said some hurtful things to you, but I'm hurting too. Now, suddenly, Julia is involved, telling you who knows what, and it's just making things worse."

"How can we just leave," she said doubtfully. "What about Letty and my job and the house, everything we have here and our friends?"

"Fuck them." Rafe grinned, happy at the thought of getting away. She wanted Eden to be happy about it too. "I gave all my financial information to Katheryn, and the paperwork is signed so she can help take care of things while I'm away. I have enough money so we can go anywhere we want." Her eyes brightened with excitement, and for a split second, she debated on whether or not she should tell Eden about the money she inherited. She decided not to say anything because it wouldn't matter if Eden refused to go. "We can go to Italy and see Gabri and live there for a while. I know we can find things to do there to keep us busy but also give us the time we need together to figure out everything."

Eden saw the fevered excitement in Rafe's eyes and was not sure what to think or say. She didn't know if Rafe had been pushed and was having another break, or maybe she was right and having time together would help them. "I don't know," she said nervously. "Leaving everything behind is kind of scary." Who was she kidding? It was terrifying.

"We don't have to be gone forever," said Rafe. "We can come back whenever we feel like we're ready."

"What about your nightmares and your PTSD? You can't ignore it and hope it'll go away."

"I know, I know," said Rafe not willing to tell her how, in her dreams, Maria keeps begging her to come home to Italy. She knew they were just dreams, but she thought it could be her subconscious telling her that she needed to go back. She felt she had to listen. "I can keep my medicine, and I can get a doctor in Italy or wherever we go. Maybe we can get help for us too. I'll do whatever you want. We have to be able to figure things out, and I think the best thing to do is to go somewhere where we can just concentrate on us instead of fighting with everyone who keeps pushing us apart. We'll be away from Julia and the others, away from Jake and his group, away from the place where there are so many things to remind us of all the pain we've been in for the past few years."

"You must have been thinking about this a lot. It seems like you have a lot of answers," said Eden nervously. "It's a lot to wrap my head around."

"I know it is," said Rafe heavily. She could see Eden's uncertainty. Rafe knew such a big change would be hard for her because of Eden's anxiety, but she had overcome her fear before with her parents, and with Jake. "I don't want you to tell anyone right away. I want you just to think about it yourself for a while first. I know they'll try to talk you out of it, and I want you to think seriously about it without them chiming in. We can tell them together if you decide."

"Okay, I'll think about it."

Rafe looked out at the ocean for a while and then looked back at Eden. "I really need this, Eden. If you decide you can't go, I think I still need to go. And, if I go to Italy, I'd like to take Bronte to visit Gabri for a while. I've sent him pictures, but I want them to meet."

The old anxiety Jake put in her tried to surface, but Eden pushed it down. "I want them to meet too," she said as she looked down, trying to hide her anxiety. "Maybe I can come along for the visit too, if I decide to stay here."

"Absolutely," said Rafe knowing Eden didn't like to be too far from Bronte. "I'd like you to come."

"Can I ask you a question? It's a little off topic."

Rafe laughed softly. "Sure."

"Where have you been going when you disappear?" she asked warily. "Are you just out driving around in your father's car for a few hours to Long Beach and back?"

"Well," said Rafe a bit sheepishly, "it's kind of a secret so the girls can't find me. If I tell you, will you let me keep it a secret?"

"Do I have to swear on my life?"

Rafe chuckled. "No."

"Okay, we can keep it a secret."

"I go to Jude's massage place," she revealed.

"What?" Eden laughed in disbelief. "You go get a massage for three hours?"

"Yeah." Rafe laughed along with her. "It's a great place. I usually get the works so it can take a while. It does help me relax after dealing with all of them."

"Hmm, maybe I should try the place out," said Eden with a smile. "We can both go get secret massages."

Rafe leaned over close to her ear. "Ask for Susy," she purred then leaned back and winked.

"Susy?" Eden raised an eyebrow. "Well, if you recommend her, I'll definitely ask for her." Eden leaned into Rafe. It felt good being alone with her, especially when she was in a good mood and wanted to talk. Maybe Rafe was right, and they just needed more time alone together. "Can I ask another question?"

"You have a lot of questions," said Rafe softly. "So, let's cut out asking for the question and just ask what you want," she said and gave her a small smile. "Okay?"

"Okay," said Eden softly. "Why don't you want Julia telling me about you? She's just told me some little things about your school days."

"I'll bet she told you more than little things," said Rafe, her face shadowed with annoyance.

"She told me about the dance you two did and other things that happened in school like how you protected her from her arch nemesis Rebecca," she revealed and bit her lip. "Why can't she tell me things?"

Rafe scoffed at the mention of Rebecca. Julia always hated her, but Rafe never knew why. Julia accused her of all kinds of things, but Rebecca was very nice. Rafe could never tell Julia she had dated Rebecca for a while. Rebecca didn't want to witness another of Julia's jealous rages or be on the receiving end of her temper. So they kept things secret from everyone. One of them would discretely knock on a piece of wood as a signal to meet after school. The last time they met was just after an incident with one of the instructors. Rafe had knocked on Rebecca's desk right in front of her, and Rebecca was upset because the signal wasn't discrete. It ended up being for the best that no one knew about them in the end. Now Rebecca was a senator and following in her father's footsteps.

Rafe pulled out of her memory and refocused on Eden. "I don't want her telling you things because it takes away my chance to tell you. It's like stealing a moment with you from me. I don't want her to tell you, or anyone else, things because it's my life and my story. If I choose to tell it, I will, and I should have the choice not to tell it. There are some things I'd just really rather leave in the past and other things should really only matter to me."

Eden shifted herself and looked out at the ocean. "When she told me those things," she hesitated, "I kind of felt like I didn't know you."

"You know me. You just don't know the old me," said Rafe. It was frustrating because anything Julia said would be tinted as the truth according to Julia. Most of the time, Julia had no idea what was happening or why things had happened. She still had no idea what she was talking about most of the time. "You only need to know me now," Rafe continued. "I don't think you'd like who I used to be."

"I'd like to know all about you. Good and bad," she said. "I already like you, more than like you. I love you, and I'm not sure whatever you did while you were young could stop how I feel."

"We'll see," said Rafe then took a breath and started to get up. "Let's go have some fun."

"Okay," said Eden understanding she would get no more from Rafe on the subject. "Help me up." She reached out her hand wondering what Rafe had in mind.

After being pulled up, Eden brushed the sand off herself, and they started walking. Rafe reached out and took Eden's hand, and she felt Rafe's warmth travel through her. She loved the days when Rafe was feeling good like this and wished days like this would never end.

8

RAFE SALVAGGIO COULDN'T help smiling as she led Eden to the Fun Zone. As they walked around, they took in all the rides and shops. She remembered going to Coney Island when she first came to America and how much fun she had trying everything and exploring. The whole experience was nothing like anything she knew in Italy. The first time she had been told they were going to an arcade, she thought they meant a place to shop, not to play. Awed by the sights and sounds, she couldn't get enough. She liked all the different games most of all and spent a lot of time in the summer going to different arcades and learning all the games.

She pulled Eden along in the direction of the arcade. "How about we find some air conditioning," she said and led her past the Zoltar case and into the arcade. She stopped inside then looked around and saw a lot of familiar games.

Eden shook her head and smiled because of the grin on Rafe's face. "So, what are we going to do in here?"

"Play," she grinned and arched her eyebrows. "What games do you like?"

"I don't know," said Eden, "I've never really been in an arcade before."

"What?" Rafe asked surprised. "But you grew up in America, how could you not go to one of these?"

Eden laughed at her surprise. "Remember, I lived outside a small town when I was growing up, and there was no arcade in town. My parents were very strict, and I could only go on the rides at the carnival because all the games were a form of gambling. They probably considered arcades dens of sin. So, if I didn't want to be a sinner, I could never go to any."

"Well, I'm probably the biggest sinner you'll ever know then," said Rafe with a wink, "because I spent a lot of time in arcades when I was younger. Come on, I'll show you how to sin with the big girls." She grinned and took Eden's hand again.

"Oh, in my parent's eyes, I think you've already accomplished your mission," she teased as Rafe led her through the arcade.

"Okay," said Rafe as they stopped in front of the redemption counter, "the first thing you do is pick out what you want."

Eden looked up at all the prizes. Each one had a card with the number of tickets needed to claim the item attached. "Shouldn't I win some tickets first?"

"Amateur," Rafe joked. "No, first pick out what we want then we'll have a goal. Once we have a goal, we'll go check out the games and figure out what we need to be playing in order to win the prize we want."

"Wouldn't it be cheaper to just go buy the toy we want?" she asked innocently.

Rafe gave her a look like she was out of her mind. "Buy the toy? No," she said and shook her head, "you can buy a toy anytime, but then you don't have the satisfaction of winning!" she exclaimed with a grin. "It's not about the money, it's about the challenge."

"Oh, my god," said Eden with a dramatic sigh. "I hope you're not planning to teach your heathen philosophy to Bronte."

"Oh, she'll learn," Rafe assured her with a laugh, "and she'll be a winner!" She winked. "Now pick some goals for us."

Eden contemplated the prizes again and considered carefully. "Okay," she said when she finally made her decision.

"Let's go for the monkey, the diving game for the pool, and the lava lamp."

"The lava lamp, really?" asked Rafe surprised.

"Yeah, I wanted one as a kid, and I couldn't have one. I figure since I'm already in the den of sin, I might as well get something else I was told would lead me into a life of depravity."

Rafe laughed heartily and shrugged. "Okay, let's see what damage we can do!" She went to the counter and got tokens then brought them back to Eden.

Eden took the baggie filled with tokens Rafe gave her. "Wow! This is a lot of tokens."

"Yep, and we got some free ones because it's my birthday," she said and couldn't stop her grin. "We need a lot because you picked prizes worth a lot of tickets. Follow me."

They made a circuit around the arcade looking at all the different games. Finally, Rafe stood in front of one she thought was promising.

"This is where we'll start," she declared. "This is a game of skill and timing, but we can get a lot of tickets if we do well. Okay," she said as she looked over the game, "if you get a coin in the truck bed you get eight tickets. If you get the coin through the slot under the red numbers, you get the number of tickets shown. But if you can hit the little wire, you will dump the truck, and every coin will give you six or more tickets depending on what lights are lit up. You just have to know the secret to winning," she said knowingly and grinned.

"The secret to winning," Eden repeated skeptically as she looked over the 'Big Haul' game. It had four dump trucks filled with tokens and an arm moving back and forth. "Okay, what's the secret?"

Rafe leaned in close so her lips were close to Eden's ear. "Stick with me," she whispered slyly then gave her a wink.

Eden watched as Rafe laid out her tokens then started to insert them to play. On her fifth try, the horns and whistles went off, and the truck dumped the coins. Suddenly, tickets started pouring out of the machine, and Rafe grinned proudly at Eden.

Eden couldn't help her excited laugh. "Oh, my, gosh! I can't believe you got it so fast!"

Rafe laughed at Eden's amazement. "There should be over a thousand tickets if the truck was full. It's a great start."

"It's fantastic!" Eden laughed as the tickets continued to pour out of the machine. She couldn't believe how excited it made her to watch the dump truck empty and the tickets come out of the machine. She couldn't wait for Rafe to do it again.

When the tickets stopped, Rafe went to work again, and after a few coins, the next truck dumped more tokens, and the tickets rolled out again. Rafe had the tickets set up so they piled neatly at her feet as they came out.

Eden couldn't control herself and hugged Rafe in her excitement. "How many this time?" she asked eagerly.

"A little less than last time because there were fewer tokens," said Rafe as she watched Eden smile. "Do you want to try?"

"Yeah!" she said excitedly and stood in front of the machine.

Eden got her tokens ready remembering what she watched Rafe do and began inserting the coins. Rafe watched Eden concentrate as the long red arm swung back and forth then released her coins.

As she played, Eden got her coins closer to the truck and then she got some of the tokens in the truck bed, but she hadn't hit the dump wire. "So close." Eden groaned in frustration and tried again. "Okay, I need to take a step back. I'm getting frustrated," she said and looked over at Rafe who just grinned at her. "How'd you do it? What's the secret?" she asked finding herself wanting to desperately dump the truck and win all those tickets.

"You were doing great," Rafe insisted. "You just need a little more practice." She took Eden's place in front of the machine and dumped the third truck with her second coin.

"No fair!" said Eden playfully as the tickets came pouring out again. "Are you this good at all the games?"

Rafe laughed and shook her head. "There are a lot of new games in here so, probably not," she said as the tickets finally stopped coming. "Let's go play some other ones. The last truck doesn't have much in it right now." She tore off the tickets then picked up her bag of coins and led Eden to the other games.

They played several different games. Rafe won more tickets with each token, and Eden was able to add a few to the stack too. Rafe would tell Eden about the games she knew how to play and then they would try them out. They moved to another game, and Rafe smiled at Eden. It was one Rafe knew well.

"Okay, this game is Break the Bank," explained Rafe. "It's similar to the truck game, and we can win a lot of tickets." She rolled a coin into the game and got twenty tickets. "It's all about timing. Why don't you try this one for a while, and I'll go see what else I can find. When I come back, we'll have a little competition to see who can break the bank first." She smiled and wiggled her eyebrows playfully.

"Okay," said Eden and put her coins on the machine. "You're on!"

"Remember, don't use all your coins, and just take your time," said Rafe as she walked toward some other games.

"Right," said Eden. Then she turned back to the game and began doing her best to win tickets.

9

AFTER TAKING HER time and figuring out the 'Break the Bank' game, Eden Kingsley had won a good number of tickets and was proud of herself. She looked around and wondered where Rafe had gone because it had been about twenty minutes. She heard a commotion coming from the other side of the arcade, so she picked up her tickets to go find Rafe and to see what was happening.

Eden saw a group surrounding the basketball game and, through a gap in the crowd, saw Rafe playing against a teenager. It seemed like Rafe never had an empty hand as she threw the balls up and never missed, even though it seemed like she wasn't looking at the basket. The time was up, and the crowd erupted around Rafe who had the highest score. She laughed as she high-fived the kids. She then tore off the tickets and handed them to a little boy standing close to her.

Rafe turned and saw Eden watching her and smiled. "Great game," she said to the kids and laughed at whatever they were saying. "It's time for me to go." The kids begged her to stay, but she fended them off. The little boy followed Rafe as she made her way to Eden.

"That was cool," said the boy as he looked up at Rafe. "Here's all your tickets," he said and handed Rafe a bulging plastic grocery bag.

"Thanks," said Rafe as she took the bag. She reached inside, took out a bundle of tickets, and handed them to him. "I think these will help you get the prize you're working for. Thanks for letting me take your turn."

"No problem!" The boy grinned at the tickets in his hand then ran off to join his friends.

"What's going on?" asked Eden as the boy and his friends ran to the redemption counter.

"Nothing. Just a little friendly competition," she said with a smile.

"How did you make those baskets?" she asked in amazement. "You weren't even looking at the hoop."

"Peripheral game playing," she said nonchalantly. "Are you ready to break the bank?"

Eden shook her head in wonder and emotions of hope and happiness ran through her seeing Rafe so playful and hearing her laugh with childlike delight. They went back to the game she had been practicing and arranged their tokens on the machine.

Rafe observed Eden didn't have many tokens left, so she stacked her tokens then counted out coins of her own to match. "Okay," she said with a smile as she added more tokens to Eden's pile, "whoever has the most tickets when the coins run out wins. Ready?"

"Wait, are you giving me more coins?" Eden laughed as she picked up her first token and Rafe nodded. "Well, I'll take them!" she said and started putting coins in and playing the game.

Rafe chuckled at her cheating then focused on the game. She put her coins in strategically, and soon, she had unlocked a lock and tickets poured out while Eden groaned and complained beside her. She laughed as Eden bumped her trying to make her miss.

"You are such a cheater!" Rafe complained as she laughed. "No wonder your parents were worried about your downfall into depravity!" She growled playfully as she continued to play and unlock a second lock.

"No!" yelled Eden. "Look at all the tickets you're getting!" she whined with happy banter as Rafe's tickets kept pouring out while hers were coming out in short bursts. "How are you getting them so fast?"

"Talent," she said with an impish grin and adjusted her aim. She looked over at Eden's side of the machine. "Oh, no," she said mockingly, "Eden's running out of tokens! And look, she has a tiny pile of tickets. So sad!" She laughed as she hit a bonus slot and was rewarded with more tickets.

"Yes!" Eden yelled as she unlocked her first lock. Her tickets flowed out of the machine and wound around her feet. "What the heck," she complained and tried to untangle herself and make her tickets stack neatly like Rafe's. She gave up, went back to the game, and suddenly found herself with no more tokens. "Dang it, I'm out," she said dejectedly and watched as Rafe unlocked the final lock. She reached over, stole some of Rafe's tokens, and started plugging them into the machine.

"Thief!" Rafe laughed and snatched the rest of her tokens from the top of the machine. She sent the final coins toward the bonus target and broke the bank in four coins. "And that is how you do it, baby!" She laughed as tickets stacked at her feet.

"Look at all those tickets! This is so crazy," Eden shrieked with disbelief and envy. "I think some of those are mine!" She grinned and reached for the tickets.

"Oh, no," said Rafe and blocked Eden from the stack. She pulled off what was out of the machine and put them in her grocery bag then turned and smirked at Eden as the rest of the tickets continued to pour out. "So, how many tickets do you have?" she asked with an arched brow.

"I'm not even close," said Eden as she held up her stack of tickets and sighed then looked covetously at all the tickets still coming out of Rafe's machine.

"You did great," said Rafe. "You just need a little more practice."

Eden watched Rafe tear the last tickets from the machine. "Have you been hanging out in arcades when you disappear too?"

Rafe laughed. "No. I spent a lot of time in them when I was younger, though. When we moved to New York some friends of my father took us to Coney Island, and I was hooked. I looked for them everywhere from then on. It was a good way to make friends, and I had enough allowance to get really good."

"So, you've not played for years, but you still won all those?" she asked crossed between envy and annoyance.

Rafe beamed. "It's like riding a bike. Especially on the games that I grew up playing. Like I said, I probably wouldn't be very good at the newer games," she guessed. "But we're here to win, so we have to go with what we know." She took Eden's arm and led her to the Skee-Ball™ game. "This one I like. It's similar to bocce ball because you have to be in total control of the ball. It's not a big ticket game, but it's fun." She pulled a few tokens from her pocket and stacked them on the game. She put a coin in the machine then pulled the lever to release the balls.

"It looks more like bowling to me," said Eden as she nicked a coin and put it in for her game.

"Bowling," said Rafe in bewilderment. "I don't think I've been bowling."

"Really?" said Eden in surprise. "Well, I was pretty good at it in gym at school. It was the only time I was allowed to go into the bowling alley." She lifted her eyebrows playfully. "Another den of sin according to my parents. Maybe I'll take you some time."

"Okay," Rafe agreed with a shrug. She tossed her ball down the lane with a slight flick of her wrist. "Yes," she said as the ball dropped into the one hundred cup in the corner of the game. "I still have the touch." She smiled and threw another ball with the same result.

"Maybe I won't take you," said Eden with a small pout, then laughed and shook her head at how good Rafe was at the game. She started her own game and hit the cups in the center with random luck.

Eden threw her last balls and only managed three tickets. She glanced at the clock on her phone as Rafe continued to play and saw it was getting late. People would soon be showing up at the house, and they wouldn't be there. As Rafe tore her pile of tickets away, Eden couldn't help but laugh again at the smile of satisfaction on her face. "Do you think we have enough tickets? We're going to be late for your birthday party."

Rafe grimaced because she would much rather stay away from everyone. "Maybe we can skip it," she said looking at Eden questioningly.

"Rafe," Eden said with a sigh, "we can't skip it. I gave Letty the key, and she'll be there waiting with Bronte."

"Well, then," said Rafe with disappointment that they had to return to the real world, "we better go turn in all these tickets and see if we made our goal." She put her tickets in the grocery bag then motioned for Eden to follow her to the redemption counter.

At the counter, the attendant put the tickets on a scale to count them. Rafe laughed at Eden's expression when the total came up to more than they needed to get all the things she had picked. While the attendant got out their prizes, they looked over the other prizes to see what they could get for their remaining tickets.

"How about these," Rafe suggested as she picked up the display for mood rings. "I used to give these to all my girlfriends when I was younger, but I don't think I ever got one for you," she said and smiled remembering her youth.

"A mood ring," said Eden as she considered the rings and studied the color chart. "This could be useful," she said playfully. "I could just look at the ring and know your mood. Maybe we should get two," she suggested as she tried on the ring Rafe gave her. "Oh, look," she said as the ring began to change colors. "I must be feeling happy because it's turning pink." She looked up from the ring at Rafe, and a warm surge went through her at the way she was looking back at her. She looked away, picked up one of the rings from the display, and slid it on Rafe's finger. "I've never given a girlfriend a ring before," she said softly and watched the color change on Rafe's ring. "It looks like you're an orange color," she said reading the chart. "Troubled," she read then nodded her agreement with the result.

"Yeah, probably about dealing with everyone tonight," she said wryly. "Here," she said and took the display and tore off the color chart. "Keep this so you can remember all the moods," she said with a wink.

Eden took the piece of cardboard with a soft laugh. "Thanks." She looked guiltily over at the attendant and wondered if they would get in trouble for tearing up the display box. "What else can we get?"

They picked out another toy for Bronte and left the last of the tickets to the next kid who came to the counter. The attendant said nothing about the torn display box to Eden's relief. With their bags of prizes in hand, they walked past the Zoltar and out onto the boardwalk.

Rafe set a slow pace on their way back to the car. She wasn't in any hurry to get home, knowing the possibility of everyone there ganging up on her. She knew the mood ring was just a chemical reaction to the amount of heat in her body, but she really did feel troubled about dealing with them. She felt Eden lean into her and take her arm and was glad they were being quiet right now.

The change in Rafe seemed to be immediate. As soon as they walked out of the arcade, Eden could feel it. The playfulness was gone, and Rafe was suddenly quiet and tense. The good day was now teetering on the edge of turning into a bad night. Eden knew the thought of the party tonight had

Rafe on edge. Rafe had reluctantly agreed to it and was torn about whether to have it at the house or have it somewhere she could leave if she thought she needed to. In the end, Rafe's reluctance to deal with even more people meant the party would be held at the house with just friends and family.

10

WITH THE CONVERTIBLE top down, Rafe Salvaggio drove back to Los Angeles and thought the trip went well. She hadn't planned to ask Eden to go with her to Italy, but it did feel good to know Eden had at least agreed to think about going. She could tell Eden would probably say no in the end. She knew it meant things would probably never be resolved and they would separate, but the moment of hope she felt was worth the future pain she knew would come.

She wished they could have skipped going home and had stayed to play more to prolong their last good memory. She looked over at Eden, who was wearing her father's cap and smiled. She looked good. Rafe thought today proved her point that they needed time alone together to figure things out, but she knew they probably would not get what they needed.

She let Eden ask all the questions today, and maybe they would have another time where she could ask some hard questions of her own. Maybe this could be the first day of healing for them so they could live a good life apart.

Since she wouldn't be going to therapy to get back her job now, she could just focus on her relationship with Eden until she left for Italy. Maybe they could work things out so, at the very least, they could be good parents for Bronte like Eden said she kept hoping when she was with Jake. Maybe Eden would finally be able to find the happiness with someone else, maybe even with a man—like Jake said she needed. She knew he was crazy, but he might have been right about Eden.

She pulled into Rick's Auto Storage, parked in front of the office, and cut the engine.

"So, the secret garage is revealed," said Eden as she took off the driving cap.

"Secret?" asked Rafe. "I don't think this place is a secret, it has a sign."

Eden laughed. "Julia and Abby are both obsessed about where you store the car," she revealed. "I admit I was curious too."

Rafe rolled her eyes. "It's Rick. He always takes care of the car. You know him," she said and got out of the car.

"Hey, Ms. Salvaggio," said Rick happily as he came out of the office with his book. He looked over and saw Eden close the passenger door. "Hey, Ms. Kingsley, it's been a long time." He smiled kindly then looked over at Rafe with surprise. He knew they had broken up and things were bad for a while.

"Yes, it has," said Rafe as she took the book from Rick and found her page.

"It's good to see you again," said Eden and walked around to the back of the car.

"Good to see you too," said Rick and took the book back from Rafe. "Here are the keys to your car and its right over there," he said as he pointed. "Any instructions?"

"Just a detail and gas," said Rafe as she got into the trunk and got their prizes. "We drove to the ocean again."

"No problem," said Rick as Rafe handed Eden one of the bags.

Eden took the bag from Rafe and noticed there were several other things in the trunk. "Do we need to take any of these things?" she asked pointing into the trunk.

"Nope," Rafe said and closed the trunk quickly.

"I guess I should have known about Rick," said Eden as she put her bag in the backseat then got into the other car with Rafe. "You're very loyal to people who you let in your life, business and personal."

Rafe just laughed softly as she put on her seatbelt. She pulled out and drove them toward home. "I can't believe they thought where I parked my car was a secret. It's just strange. They really need to focus on something else."

"So," Eden started with a nervous smile, "are you going to tell Julia why you asked for the information on your accounts? I have a feeling it was why she was concerned and wanted to talk to you. She wouldn't tell me her reasons, but she may be worried you're planning to move everything."

"I think I'll let her worry for a while," said Rafe wryly.

"You're so mean," she said with a giggle, and Rafe smiled back at her.

"She deserves it," said Rafe with a wrinkled brow. "She threatened to call Greer and make you and Letty have me placed somewhere."

Eden whipped her head around in shock, her good mood cut off. "She did what?"

"It's what she was yelling at me about last night," she revealed with annoyance.

"I'm so sorry! She shouldn't be saying those kinds of things to you," said Eden wondering what else Julia had said to her along those lines. It made her angry, and she could tell it made Rafe angry too.

"Don't worry. It won't be as easy to do it to me again," she said assuredly. "I took Letty's power of attorney away. If Julia tries anything, she'll have to go through a lot of legal hoops and other things to even begin getting anywhere close to putting me in one of those places again."

Eden looked away so Rafe couldn't see the look of concern on her face. She knew she would have to have a hard conversation with Julia and the others.

She would also have to convince Rafe not to leave home and to continue her therapy. She looked back at Rafe and touched her arm. "I don't think she would really try to do something against your will. I think she's just really worried about you."

"Yeah, and I don't understand her," said Rafe as she held the steering wheel tightly. "Why is she so fucking worried all of a sudden? She's supposed to be taking time off work to find another job or something, but it seems like, for the past three weeks, she's always hanging around. It's really getting on my nerves. She should just go back to work for her father."

They pulled up to the house and saw there were already a lot of cars there, and by the sound of things, Letty and the girls had already started the party. They got their prizes then walked up to the front door and went inside the house to meet their guests.

"Happy birthday, Rafe!" Abby called out as she saw her and Eden walk in the door.

"Thanks," said Rafe with a small smile. She didn't feel very happy at the moment, though.

"Whatcha got there?" Abby asked and pointed to the bags they were carrying.

"We won prizes!" said Eden happily. "Apparently, Rafe is a hustler at arcade games." She laughed at Abby's surprised expression and put the bag on the couch pulling out the contents.

"Oh! A lava lamp!" screeched Abby happily. "Let's plug it in." They pulled the lamp out of its box, sat it on a side table, and after plugging it in, they turned it on.

"Well, this is anticlimactic," said Eden as a light came on, but nothing happened.

"You have to let it warm up," said Abby, "kind of like Rafe." Abby looked up at Rafe feeling snarky.

Rafe shook her head and sighed heavily as the criticisms began. "I'm going to take B Girl her monkey," she said and walked away with the toy.

Eden waited until Rafe was out of the room then turned to Abby. "She's had a good day, Abby. Please, don't ruin it by making her mad."

"Sor-ry," said the freckled faced woman. "I was just joking around." Abby huffed as she got up then went to the sound system and scrolled through her iPod to change the music.

"I need to talk to all of you, but I don't know if it'll be tonight," said Eden. "Until then, just take it easy on her, okay?"

"Sure," said Abby as she perked up in interest. "Is everything okay?" She nodded her head to the beat of the eclectic Ginger Doss music streaming from the speakers.

Eden bit her lip. "I don't know."

"Flynn said he heard the car take off like a bat out of hell this morning," said Abby suspiciously. "Did something happen?"

"No," said Eden reassuringly. "Rafe was just showing off." She smiled at the memory. "Come on. Let's go join the party."

11

AFTER FINISHING DINNER, Rafe Salvaggio endured an unremarkable rendition of Happy Birthday on her thirty-fifth birthday. She blew out the candles on her birthday cake then Letty cut and served it along with gelato to everyone. Rafe made sure she sat next to Eden at the table and tried not to be alone with any one person for fear of any hissing they might be planning on doing in her direction.

Rafe looked over at Bronte and decided she must have had a busy time with Letty because she was falling asleep in her cake. She tried to clean her up a bit, and Eden came to the rescue.

"I think I'll take her inside and get her cleaned up and put to bed," said Eden softly as she touched Rafe's leg. "I'll be back soon." She got up and took Bronte from her booster seat then carried her inside.

Abby immediately took Eden's seat. "Have some more wine," she said and filled Rafe's glass. "So, it looks like you two had a good day," she said trying to sound casual. Rafe just glared at her then took a sip of wine. "I saw you guys have matching rings," she said with a sly smiled. "What are they all about? Are you guys good now?"

Rafe glanced at her mood ring, which was currently black, and she was angry she had forgotten to take it off. "It's just an arcade prize." She took it off her finger. "Here, you can have it," she said and laid it on the table.

"Oh, no," said Abby putting her hands up. "It's bad mojo to take someone's matching mood ring," she declared as if she were still in high school. Rafe just stared at her without saying a word. "Well, are you going to put it back on?" Rafe ignored her and took a sip of wine. "Jesus, Rafe, I was just joking with you," she said and left the table in a huff. "She's all yours," she said to Julia as she passed her and went to talk to Jude by the pool.

Julia watched Rafe and considered how she wanted to deal with her tonight. She didn't want to upset Eden by being confrontational, but Rafe had been polite yet distant the entire night. It seemed she was avoiding speaking at all if she could. Julia wondered if she could get her drunk enough so she would start talking like she did when she needed a place to live. Rafe hardly ever got angry when she was drunk. Unfortunately, it looked like Rafe was on high alert tonight so her plan may not work.

Rafe sat her glass on the table and looked up to see Julia glaring at her. She knew Julia was forming up to go on the attack. She decided to go on the offensive before Julia could start pressing again. "So, have you found a job you want to do yet?"

"No," said Julia hoping this was an opening she could use. "Are you going to tell me why you need all your financial information?"

Rafe ignored her question. "I think I'll call your father and tell him you're just screwing around and wasting your time and his money," said Rafe and picked up her wine glass.

Julia disregarded Rafe's threat because her father knew the real reason she was taking time off. "Are you suddenly being nice to Eden because you're planning to leave?"

"You need to leave me alone and go get laid," said Rafe crossly. "Or are you pressing me, so I'll leave because you think then you'll have a shot at Eden? I'm sure she'll fall willingly into your waiting arms soon."

"Fuck you," said Julia nastily. She knew Rafe was throwing it in her face all the times she dated women after her—specifically the last woman, Andrea.

Rafe smirked. "You aren't worth my time," she said and took a sip of wine. "But it does seem like you're very obsessed with her lately."

"I'm not obsessed with her," said Julia annoyed. "I'm concerned about you both, and you know it."

"Well, it seems to me like you should start being more concerned about yourself," said Rafe calmly, "or are you planning to become one of those arrogant debutants who feel entitled to waste the money their family worked hard making to give you a better chance? I know how much your father hates those types. You must be becoming a big disappointment to him."

"My father knows exactly what I'm doing, Rafe, unlike yours ever did!" fumed Julia. "You're such a fucking asshole! I don't know what my father sees in you!'

"Oh, the jealousy!" Rafe laughed rakishly. "Is your childish jealousy why you're fucking with my life and grooming Eden as your next lover? Your daddy likes me more than you, so you're jealous and want to try to take me down a notch and fuck another one of my girlfriends? Maybe I'll fly to New York and have a special meeting with your father to talk to him about you. We can discuss what a disappointment you've become."

"I'm not jealous of you, and my father isn't disappointed in me!" hissed Julia angrily. "I'm not going after Eden, and you fucking know it!" She clenched her fists and took a breath, angry at Rafe's accusations, although she couldn't deny the past. "I know what you're doing! You're trying to push me and everyone else away! Well, it won't work! You're so fucked up, you can't see anything right anymore!"

"Oh? What am I supposed to see?" asked Rafe calmly. "The fact you're all ganging up on me and making it hard for me to get better? Or maybe it's you really don't want me to get better at all. I don't think you really want Eden and me to see if we can work things out. Do you want Eden to hate me so you tell her things you know I don't want you to tell her? Do you think maybe you'll have a chance with her? Is it the real reason why you're always spending time with her and trying to get closer to her and are suddenly conveniently here all the time to comfort her?"

"What the fuck are you talking about?" asked Julia at a loss because of her accusations—and it wasn't Eden she wanted at all. "You're being ridiculous!"

"I agree. You are ridiculous!" said Rafe with a forced laugh. "So is all the crap you and Abby have been doing, and the things you've been telling Eden about me! I think, after today, you should go back to work and not come to my house anymore. You're all banned from my life! Don't come over, don't call, avoid Eden and me. We don't want you here," she said then got up and walked into the house.

"Too bad!" yelled Julia as she followed Rafe. "Eden needs us and so do you! You can't ban us from your life! Friendship doesn't work that way!"

Eden walked out of Bronte's room and made her way down the hall quickly as she heard Rafe arguing with Julia. "What's going on?" she asked just above a whisper. "Bronte's asleep."

"See, I told you. I can't get rid of them," said Rafe to Eden with a shrug and went to the kitchen.

Eden turned to Julia confused. "What happened?"

"I have no idea," said Julia flustered. "She was berating me about finding a job then the next thing I know she is banning me from her life."

"Dang it, Julia," she said perturbed. "I told you no confrontations today."

"She started it," Julia insisted. "I hadn't said anything to her, and she started in on me."

"Well, then you shouldn't have taken her bait," she said as she shook her head. "You're both driving me mad. Maybe Rafe is right."

"What? Right about what?" asked Julia in frustration wondering if Rafe told Eden about the circumstances pertaining to all the women they had both dated.

"About needing time and space away from people," explained Eden. "Every time you're here, something happens. Maybe you should give her a break for a while. She's been asking for it, a break from everyone, and you keep telling me to look for things to help her. Maybe giving her space is what will help her."

Abby walked in looking for Eden and found her and Julia. "What the hell is going on? Rafe is out there saying the party is over and everyone has to leave and not to come back."

"Apparently, Rafe is banning us all from her life," said Julia, disgruntled but mildly relieved by Eden's answer.

"Maybe she needs some time alone," said Eden in defense of Rafe. "She's already running away every chance she gets and disappearing all the time."

"So true," scoffed Abby. "Typical Scorpio behavior being all secretive and alone. But it's different right now because she's supposed to be talking about things."

"Maybe she just isn't ready to talk," Eden said knowing it was true. "She's hardly had any time alone and look at what she's doing. Maybe it's time to try something else. Maybe we should try to give her what she's asking for instead of what we think is best. Please," Eden begged them, "don't push her until she does what you're worried she'll do. I don't want her to leave," said Eden desperately.

A tear of frustration and worry ran down Eden's face because Rafe really was planning to leave and threatening to quit therapy. She didn't want them putting more pressure on Rafe by revealing more upsetting news right now. It was information she knew would just cause a bigger mess. She would save it for another day.

Abby gave a hostile look to Julia and threw her hands up in defeat. "All I know is I don't want to see her go into a tailspin again like she did when you were going at her. She barely speaks when I'm here anyway so she may as well be alone. And you know Jude doesn't talk when she's here. They say about one word an hour to each other," she said frustrated. "It's like watching a sloth race."

"You can't do all of this alone, Eden," said Julia in exasperation.

"I know," agreed Eden. "Maybe you should just visit her less for now. I can still talk to you about what's happening. If she starts talking or doing anything I think might be a problem, I can call you. I promise I'll watch her carefully. This way you're not banned, but she has the space she needs, and I get help when I need it."

"Fine," said Julia feeling like the disappointment Rafe accused her of being. "I'm not giving up on this, Eden. She needs to get things right in her head. She needs to get back to being herself."

12

CLOSING THE FRONT door, Eden Kingsley leaned against it for a moment in relief that the confrontation about Rafe with Julia and Abby was behind her. She hadn't planned to have the conversation about giving Rafe space tonight, but apparently, Rafe couldn't wait. She pushed herself away from the door and went to find Rafe.

As Eden went out to the patio, she saw Rafe sitting in one of the double loungers. Rafe's head was back and her eyes closed as she held a scotch in her hand with the bottle of scotch and the ice bucket beside her on the table. It was an obvious sign to Eden that Rafe was prepared to drink herself blind again. Instead of confronting her, Eden decided to leave her alone for now and clean up the dishes from the party. As she picked everything up, she found the mood ring matching hers lying on the table. She looked over at Rafe and sighed then put it in her pocket. When she finished cleaning up, she poured herself a glass of wine and went to join Rafe.

"I think you lost this," said Eden as she took Rafe's hand and put the ring back on her finger. "Don't forget, you have to wear it so I'll know what mood you're in." She smiled as she sat down beside her in the double lounger.

"Is everyone gone?"

"Oh, yes," said Eden. "We're definitely alone now."

"Good," said Rafe and took a sip of her drink.

"I wasn't expecting to have that conversation tonight."

"I'm sorry I put you on the spot. I just thought it would be best to treat it like a bandage and deal with it quickly," said Rafe. "We need time to think about things and space to be able to talk when we're ready."

Eden sat silently for a while then looked over at Rafe. "So, I've been thinking."

"Thinking's good," said Rafe quietly.

"I had a lot of fun with you today." Eden looked down at Rafe's hand and her mood ring. "Your mood ring is blue," she paused, "and so is mine. It means we're both feeling romantic. So," she said dragging the word out, "maybe you should let me have my way with you for your birthday."

Rafe looked down at her ring, confirming it had turned blue. She leaned over and stuck her hand in the ice bucket for a bit then took it out. "Sorry, the ring's black now," she said with a grin.

"Rafe!" Eden laughed. "Not fair!"

Rafe shrugged and wiped her wet hand on her jeans. "Hey, I could have put your hand in the ice bucket, but I was being polite," she said teasingly.

"Well, thanks, I guess." Eden smiled and couldn't help noticing how beautiful Rafe was, especially when she was happy. She wanted to see her happy all the time, but she also wanted to make love to her, and it was driving her mad she couldn't be closer to her. She was dreaming about her all the time, and the ache it caused was becoming unbearable.

On days like this, the need for her was hard to hide and hard to keep inside. No one else she had been with had even come close to making her feel the way just being close to Rafe made her feel. She had railed against her feelings the entire time she was away from Rafe but nothing—no one could erase those voracious feelings for her. No one could replicate it because it was more than just a sexual draw. It was a deep and undeniable love wanting to break free and be poured over and into Rafe, and only her.

Eden took a sip of her wine then gazed over at Rafe again. She knew she had caused her pain, and right now, she had no idea what Rafe was thinking. She only knew Rafe wouldn't—or couldn't—tell her she loved her. Rafe only said it when she was forced, so it did not count. Eden also knew Rafe wasn't sure if they still belonged together. She knew Rafe was not sure if she would change her mind tomorrow, but she was sure. She would never change her mind. *If only I could find a way to make Rafe believe me*, she thought.

"Rafe," she said softly.

"Hmm?" moaned Rafe as she sat with her eyes closed.

"Can I give you a birthday present?" she asked sensuously.

"Sure," said Rafe absently.

Eden got up and made her way into the house and then her room. She walked into her closet and pulled out a box. She took the box to her bed and sat down with it. Opening the box, she looked inside, digging under some papers and photos. She pulled out a small ring box and opened it to make sure the ring inside was straight in its slot.

It was a mother's ring with all three of their birthstones. Bronte's was in the middle, and hers and Rafe's were to each side. She had bought the ring for Rafe after she told her she was pregnant and had moved back in with her before Bronte was born. She meant to give it to her a long time ago, but things kept getting in the way and she never did.

When Rafe came back from Mexico, Eden knew she wanted to give it to her after the adoption on her birthday. She hoped Rafe would like it. After snapping the box closed, she gathered the bigger box and put it back in the closet.

Outside, she found Rafe still in the lounger. She walked over and touched her gently then climbed on the lounger and straddled her. Eden put her hands on each side of Rafe's head and leaned down then gave her a quick kiss. She sat up and presented the small box to her. "Happy birthday," she said with a smile.

Rafe looked up at Eden as she smiled down at her and held her hands out in front of her. She took in her golden hair and perfectly kissable lips and those mesmerizing eyes. Eden was such a beautiful woman. Rafe could still see the girl from the renaissance painting she saw the first time they had met.

"Thank you," said Rafe and took the box from her hand.

Opening the box, she found a silver ring with three gemstones set flush with the metal of the ring with a simple but beautiful scrolling design etched along its sides. The ring was beautiful but simple, unassuming, and the design was in a style Rafe would have picked for herself. Rafe looked at it wondering why Eden was giving her another ring today. "It's beautiful," said Rafe softly.

"It's a mothers ring," said Eden when she saw Rafe's confusion. "See," she said pointing to the gemstones, "there's a stone for Bronte and one for each of us, September for Bronte, October for you, and March for me." She took the ring out of the box and, after taking the mood ring off and putting it in the box, slid the mother's ring onto Rafe's right ring finger. "It looks nice on you."

Rafe looked at the ring then back at Eden, unsure of what to make of it. She had never heard of a mother's ring. "So, does this mean I'm your mother now?" she asked mystified.

Eden laughed at the look on Rafe's face "No," she said. "It's supposed to be the gemstones for all our children, and since this has three places, I had them put in our gemstones rather than leave them empty or putting in something neutral. When I picked it out, I thought, if we had another baby, we could take one of ours out."

Feeling a little overwhelmed, Rafe looked back at the ring. She had no idea Eden wanted to have another baby. They were not even together again officially. She wasn't sure if she was ready to commit to Eden again let alone another baby. She wasn't sure exactly what the ring meant. She looked back up at Eden unsure what to say.

"Thank you," she said softly, thinking Eden should be the one wearing the ring since she was Bronte's birth mother.

"One more thing," said Eden as she pushed Rafe's dark hair back from her face. She leaned forward and kissed Rafe on the lips. Since she didn't feel any resistance from Rafe, she kissed her deeply as she held her face. After a while, she pulled away from their kiss and put her head against Rafe's. "I love you so much," she whispered and kissed her again.

Rafe was caught by surprise by Eden's kiss and knew she should have stopped it, but she tasted so good. The second kiss brought tears to the edge of her eyes because she didn't know if she could make it real. "Please, Ede," she whispered as she turned her head away, "I can't." She wiped her eyes so no tears fell then looked up into Eden's sad eyes. "I'm sorry."

"Oh, Rafe." Eden sighed and caressed Rafe's face. "I wish I could make all the doubts and confusion in your mind just melt away," she whispered and gently kissed her forehead.

There's the pity, thought Rafe, *right there in her eyes.* She looked away, not wanting to see it. She looked down at the ring, the mother's ring, and thought about what it might mean. The thought of having more children, coupled with everything she was dealing with, made her head spin. She couldn't take on another issue between them. She slid the ring off slowly then took Eden's hand, and after placing it in her palm, she closed Eden's hand.

"I don't think I can accept this. You should wear it," said Rafe looking up at Eden sadly. "Thank you for wanting to have more children with me, but I can't think about having more children right now, with you, or with anyone," she said softly.

Eden was confused for a moment, then realized what Rafe must be thinking and smiled. "This is just a ring saying you're a mother," she said with a chuckle. "It's not like an engagement ring to have more children. You're not making a promise if you wear it," she said softly. "I just wanted to give you something to celebrate the adoption and let you know I'm so glad you're Bronte's mother." She slid the ring back on Rafe's finger. "You can accept it," she said and kissed her hand.

"Okay," said Rafe nodding and feeling a bit foolish. "Thank you." She looked up at Eden who was looking down at her with those bright eyes. "For someone who's never given a girl a ring before today, it looks like you're making up for lost time," she said with a small smile as she put the box with the mood ring in it on the table beside her.

"Haha," Eden sang as she moved off Rafe and stretched out lying on her side next to her. "The first one was spontaneous, but the second one was planned," she said as she put one arm under her head and laid the other across Rafe's stomach. "This is nice, being alone together," she said softly. Rafe just sighed as Eden toyed with a button on Rafe's shirt. "I've been thinking about what we talked about today, you quitting therapy. I don't think you should let Julia and the girls bully you into quitting."

Rafe turned her head looking at Eden in confusion. "Bully me? They had nothing to do with my decision."

"I think they did," said Eden softly. "I think all the pressure they were putting on you finally got to be too much, and it's the reason you decided to quit. But now, we're making them stay away, so you don't have to quit."

"Since I'm not going back to work at the school, I don't really have a reason to go anymore," Rafe reminded her then shrugged. "I'll just keep taking my meds, and I should be fine."

Eden worried about what Rafe was saying. She knew even if Rafe wasn't going back to work, she still needed to go to the doctor to work through her PTSD and everything else. "Maybe you can go and talk to her about other things. Maybe about us. If you want me to, when you're ready, I'll go with you, and we can talk about things together. We can go to your doctor, or maybe mine, together. I'll go to whichever one makes you most comfortable."

Rafe knew what Eden was doing. Eden didn't want to talk with her alone. She needed someone there to be on her side. "So, you think we need a referee?" she asked flatly trying to hold back her emotions.

"No," said Eden, trying not to take Rafe's bait and get angry. "I just thought it would be good to have someone there to help us," she said nervously. "I know sometimes I need someone to help me see beyond my immediate emotions, and help me look at things from a different perspective. Sometimes, with my anxiety, it's hard for me to overcome all the emotions causing me not to see clearly. It's why sometimes it takes me awhile to work through things."

Rafe ran her hand through her hair then reached over for her scotch. She took a sip then put it back on the table. "I know," she said, knowing Eden was telling her the truth about her anxiety.

Rafe had been there for Eden when she had anxiety attacks and knew they were hard on her. But Rafe also knew she couldn't let the fact Eden had anxiety problems be a reason not to say what was on her mind and not do what she had to do. Eden may be upset, but she had proven she would get through it eventually. She had done fine on her own before, she could do it again.

"So," said Eden, after waiting to see if Rafe would say anything, "maybe you can talk about going to Italy too. I think you should keep going to therapy until we decide to go or not. Maybe it'll help us decide what to do."

Rafe turned her head to look at Eden again. "I've already decided what I'm going to do," she reminded her, pausing to hold back her irritation at Eden's attempt to manipulate her. "Now you have to decide what you're going to do for yourself," she said as she looked back out at the pool. She didn't see the look of shock on Eden's face. "I'll stay until Christmas for Bronte," she stated firmly, "then, in the new year, I'm leaving."

Eden couldn't help the tears beginning to stray from her eyes. She wiped them away and turned her gaze to Rafe who was staring out into the night. She thought she had more time. She thought she could convince Rafe to stay, but it looked like she would have to get help.

"What about Bronte and me?" she asked softly, trying to keep her hands from shaking. "What will we do when you're gone? Where will we go?"

Rafe closed her eyes for a moment, realizing Eden had already made up her mind she wasn't going, even if she hadn't admitted it out loud. "If you don't come with me," she said softly, "you can stay in the house as long as you want under the cohabitation agreement. I'll make sure you have whatever you need for Bronte." She took a breath and put her hand to her head. "I just hope you'll let me talk to her, and you'll let her come and stay with me wherever I go." *I need to work out how to let Eden go*, she thought. Picking up her drink, she took a sip. "If I can wait to see my child for almost eight months, I think you can do the same for a few weeks while she visits me."

Eden felt the cut of Rafe's words, knowing she was still hurting over the time she lost with Bronte.

"What about therapy?" she asked softly. "If I'm going to Italy with you, I'll need you to get the help I know I can't give you. I need to know we're working on our relationship. I need to know if I'm going, that you love me."

"I'll go to therapy," Rafe conceded softly, knowing if she didn't, Eden would continue to press and possibly get Julia and the others involved. Hearing Eden use the word 'if' told her that Eden was just buying time, and ultimately, it was a lie she was going with her to Italy. So she didn't feel too badly for lying about continuing to go to therapy. "I'll do whatever you want during the time before I leave. If you want me to go to therapy with you, I will. If you want me to kiss you, have sex with you, play house with you, I will. But don't call it love," she said and looked into Eden's tear-stained eyes. "If I can't figure out what we are by the time I need to leave, then I'll understand you won't be going with me."

Eden felt her heart beating hard in her chest at the thought of Rafe leaving and all of the things she was saying. She watched as Rafe calmly sipped her drink. Eden was at a loss for what to say or do. She could feel the anxiety building up inside her and knew she had to take some kind of action or it would overwhelm her.

She sat up and climbed over Rafe, straddling her as she looked into her eyes. She took Rafe's drink from her then took a sip of the scotch. The taste wasn't one she was used to. It was harsh to her pallet and burned its way down her throat. She sat the glass on the table and looked Rafe in the eyes again.

"If we only have two months to figure things out, then we should start tonight," she said softly and kissed Rafe deeply. She pulled away and looked into her eyes again. She loved her so much. She wanted her to feel it and know it was true. "It may not be love to you," she said then swallowed back her anxiety, "but it is for me. I love you," she said and kissed her again.

Rafe pushed her back and held her shoulders as she looked intently into her eyes. "If you do this, you may be breaking your own heart," she said huskily.

"I'm willing to take the chance," said Eden and moved Rafe's hands so she could kiss her again. "I love you," she said between her kisses, "I love you so much." She took hold of Rafe's hands and put them around her. "Hold me," she whispered as she kissed Rafe's ear and neck, "please. I need your touch." She felt Rafe run her warm hands over her gently. "I know you love me," she sighed into her ear. "You're everywhere in me. In my heart, my dreams, my soul," she breathed, "and I'm in yours, I know I am." She kissed her deeply and started to unbutton Rafe's shirt.

Rafe grasped her hands. "No," she said softly, "not this. Not tonight," she said pulling her close so she could hold her tight and taking away Eden's ability to show her the affection she knew would lead them to making love. Eden's smell filled Rafe's senses, and she knew, if she allowed it, she could lose herself in Eden. It would only make everything harder.

"But you said anything I wanted," Eden whispered as she broke free and bent to kissed Rafe again, "I want you."

Rafe pushed her back again, sat up, and moved her body so Eden was flipped onto her back and Rafe was over her. "Therapy first," she said then gave her a small kiss on her forehead. She stood up so she could escape the temptation. She had told Eden not to call it love.

Eden looked into Rafe's eyes then leaned back in exasperation. "You're killing me," she groaned then looked up at her again and smiled. "Happy birthday." Eden watched Rafe give her a small smile then turn and walk into the house.

13

PETULANT SINCE BEING banned from Rafe's life, Julia Hawthorn decided she needed to visit her father in New York. The car service from the airport dropped Julia off at her father's building, and the doorman helped get her luggage inside. The lobby attendant helped her to the elevator where the elevator girl pushed the button for the penthouse. She had hung around her condo in Los Angeles for a week before deciding to leave. It was clear Rafe was probably forcing Eden to stay away and not call for help from any of their friends. *Same old Rafe—always needing to be in control of everyone and everything*, thought Julia

At the penthouse, the elevator opened and the maid got the luggage out of the elevator then took it to the bedroom. Julia went to the kitchen to get the snack and drink the maid had ready for her.

She looked around the familiar surroundings and had a momentary flash of nostalgic homesickness as she saw all the framed society awards her mother had gotten over the years. Julia remembered why she had decided to make a move to California. Julia wanted nothing to do with garden clubs, women's auxiliaries, charity balls or all of the other similar things her mother poured herself into over the years. Her mother was obsessed with all things English, proper and high society, while Julia just wanted to chuck it all in a bin and call it a day.

When they moved back to America, Julia's mother hated it almost as much as Julia did. The difference was her mother could fly back and forth and be the center of attention with intercontinental introductions and be the gossip queen of two continents. Julia had to attend a horrible school, with even more horrible girls, and make use of the English stiff upper lip she never really mastered. She also had to learn to keep her head down, and her mouth closed in order to prevent the onslaught of bullying and teasing she would be subjected to in school by horrible American girls. It was not lost on her that she was American too. She was just different, and being different was a cardinal sin at her new school. At home, she had to deal with mother and her posh gossiping hens whilst hiding every cringe at the mention of anything to do with dressing up in itchy attire to be put on display. Everything may have been more bearable if she had her real friends close, but they were all back in England.

Meeting Rafe had changed her small world for the better. Rafe was like a devil, wrapped up in angel robes and wings, set loose in the City of New York. Where Rafe led, Julia followed—closely, or she would have been left behind. Rafe made everything bearable. Everything was an adventure waiting to happen, a challenge to be won, an enemy to be vanquished. She was also someone the other girls could never push around.

Julia wondered throughout the apartment and went to her father's office where she saw the pictures taken of her and Rafe when they were younger still pinned on his wall after all these years. She and Rafe would come in every once in a while and pin up a new photo for him to try and guess what they were up to that day. He never guessed right, and it was exciting to have a half-secret from her father.

After Rafe went home for the evening, Julia would always tell her father where they had been, so it was not a secret for long. Julia's mother had been horrified upon finding Rafe had put pin holes in the oak wood paneling, but her father told the maid to leave them. Julia had no idea why he kept them pinned up after all these years.

She looked at the last photo, one she had to pin up herself because when they made it to the building later in the evening, Rafe hadn't come up with her. It was from the last day she saw Rafe before she left for Italy. Rafe was turned out of school for her dance routine in the counselor's office, so her father was sending her to a college prep school. Because of the strings her father pulled, there was a place waiting for Rafe as soon as she tested into the college. Because of her father's influence, Rafe would end up starting college in Italy not long after she turned seventeen. Rafe starting college a year before her was always a sore point for Julia, but Rafe always got top scores in all her classes, so it wasn't really a surprise.

At the time of their last outing, Rafe hadn't been to school for months, and Julia hadn't heard a word from her. Out of nowhere, Rafe suddenly called to meet after school. They went to the park to watch the performers display their talents and busk for loose change. They had taken their photo with a girl named Hannah. She was an exquisite dancer, slim and tall with dark skin, and her black hair tied up in a ballerina bun. She was part of a dance group from the performing arts school. Rafe didn't say how she knew Hannah, but it was clear the girl knew Rafe well and had been waiting to see her.

Eventually, Julia learned Rafe had been hanging out near the performing arts school. Apparently, she made a lot of friends over the month before her father decided to send her back to Italy. A twinge of jealousy twisted through Julia because she wasn't involved in Rafe's new adventures. It passed quickly as Hannah and her school friends were nice to hang out with and a lot of fun. Rafe had been joining them for their dances in the park, and soon, Julia found herself part of the group for the day.

While the kids from the dance school did an amazing group dance routine, Rafe would dance around and play in the crowd. The dance group loved Rafe. Julia learned they had made quite a lot of money since Rafe began helping them.

Rafe would show off her talent for picking pockets then sweetly demand a donation to the hat for the return of the item she took. She probably wouldn't have gotten away with it if she were not so beautiful and angelic looking, and if the crowd hadn't been full of nice, generous people.

Everyone thought it was amazing how Rafe could dance close and end up with a wallet, a scarf, a watch—whatever. Some in the crowd even dared Rafe to take things from them, which she loved. When asked how she learned to do those things, Rafe only smiled and winked but never answered.

Julia got to dance around with the hat accepting the bribes paid to get the items back that Rafe had taken stealthily. She flourished the hat with pirouettes and other ballet moves she had learned in ballet class. It was fun to use the moves outside her strict class.

After dancing, they all went out for something to eat, and Julia could see Hannah was in love with Rafe. Whenever they talked about Rafe leaving the next day, Hannah would either tear up or get angry in turns. The night was a whirlwind of emotion with all of the performers in the group, and Julia found herself caught up in it.

They sang, danced, cried, and laughed, and then they finally had to part ways. Rafe and Hannah took the subway with Julia and got her home. Rafe said a quick goodbye then Julia watched her leave with Hannah holding hands and leaning close as they walked down the street.

After they parted ways, Julia saw Rafe sporadically in the summers and several times when they were both at college in Europe. After years of not hearing from her, Julia found out Rafe had moved to California. It seemed like Rafe hadn't changed at all and had somehow become even more beautiful. Life had become exciting and scary again like when they were teenagers, and it seemed like they were spending a lot of time together. They had a lot of fun, dated many women, some who in turn they both dated, and became closer than ever.

Then one day, it all stopped. The next thing Julia knew Rafe was introducing her to Eden, and there was a marked change in her. A change for the better, Julia thought, even though Rafe was with a girl who clearly had issues.

Now she barely recognized her friend in the photos. Rafe wasn't the happy and adventurous person she was before she met Eden, and she wasn't the calm and patient person she turned into when Eden came into her life.

Now she was angry, confused, and hurting, and she was going through things Julia didn't understand. Julia was at a loss about what to do to help her.

"Hello," said Ian Hawthorn as he found his daughter in his office. "Did you have a good flight?" he asked. As she turned to greet him, he gave her a hug and a kiss on her cheek.

"Hi, Daddy," said Julia with a smile and kissed her father back. "It was fine. Is Mother here?"

He chuckled and shook his head. "No, she had to fly to Sweden for a ski trip with her friends. She'll be there through Thanksgiving. I suppose I'll have to join her in a week or so." He noticed she had been looking at the photos pinned to the wall. "Going down memory lane?"

"Yes," Julia confirmed with a sigh. "Rafe is kind of why I'm here. . . besides the fact I missed you." Julia gave him a weak smile.

"I've missed you too," said Ian and could see Julia was unhappy. "What's happening with Rafe? Is she okay?"

Julia leaned into her father and burst into tears. "No," she said as her father held her, feeling safe in his arms. "I've been trying to help her, but she's not doing better. I don't know how to help her, and Eden is just as useless as I am. Now Rafe's mad at me, and Eden has asked me to stay away for a while."

"Oh, honey," he said as he tried to console her. "Come on. Let's sit down, and I'll get you a drink." He led her to the couch, and as she sat down, he went to get her a drink. "Here," he said handing her a glass of water as he sat next to her. "What's going on? I thought she was out of the hospital and getting help at home now. I know she's been running the girls ragged in the California office."

"I know. They called me." She sniffed and took a sip of water wishing her father had given her something stronger, but it was his habit always to offer water first. "I was so mad when she wouldn't move the accounts she inherited from her father to us. Now I'm thinking maybe we dodged a bullet."

"Julia," Ian chastised her, "she has relationships with more financial firms than just us. She probably left the money with people her father did business with for a long time. You can't be angry with her for not putting her money with us even if she put it with some other company."

"I know," said Julia unhappily. "I just don't know what she's doing or why she needs all her financial information. I'm afraid she's going to take off for places unknown again, and Eden won't confront her about it. Whenever I do, Rafe goes into a tailspin. It's why Eden wants me to stay away for a while. I've tried everything from being patient to being downright mean, and nothing works."

Ian took a sip of his drink and thought about Rafe and her situation. He knew his daughter had been infatuated with Rafe for a long time, and it hurt her that Rafe didn't feel the same. But he was glad they remained friends and cared for each other.

"I'm not exactly sure what Rafe went through, but I've dealt with men who suffered from PTSD when I got my first job in England. Our company sponsored a free program helping the elderly get their finances in order and helped them when the old annuities they bought were expiring. They had to find a place for the money so they could live off it if necessary or put it in investments so it could go to their families after they died. A lot of the older men I helped, those who came home from one or more of the many wars their country had been involved with, were scarred in ways you and I just couldn't see. A lot of them had very hard lives when they came home because of the mental and physical trauma they had endured. Consequently, their families were also traumatized. It can be very traumatizing to watch someone you love deteriorate into depression, alcoholism, abusive behavior, suicide and other problems coming from PTSD." He took in his daughter's sad face and understood her sorrow. "I know Rafe wasn't in a war, but she's now fighting one in her own mind. I'm sure it's not easy on her. More is going on than you and I can see or even understand."

"So, how can we help her? I just want the old Rafe back, and I know Eden does too," said Julia and wiped away a tear.

"It seems like Rafe's doing what she needs to do," said Ian confidently. "She's going to a therapist, she's taking her medication, and she's getting out of bed every day. It may not seem like a lot to you and me, but I'm sure it is for her."

"She's supposed to be talking to us, but she won't," said Julia trying not to be angry.

"I'm not surprised. Many people find it hard to talk about their trauma. When they do, it brings up images and thoughts they just don't want to have. If you're trying to force her to talk about things when she's not ready, it's no wonder she's angry with you."

"But I haven't asked her to talk about what happened at the school," said Julia trying to make her stance clear. "I've been trying to get her to talk about Eden."

"Eden," said Ian confused. "I thought we were talking about the school. I thought Rafe and Eden were split. The last thing I knew about them was you were looking for Rafe because she needed to do medical paperwork. When I found Rafe, she was with Greer. I know she and Greer aren't together now, but I didn't know Rafe and Eden were actually trying to get back together. I thought Eden was just helping you with Rafe as a friend."

"Rafe and Eden were trying to get back together and living together again, but something happened, and Rafe left her," Julia explained. "In the aftermath of Eden's injuries, I guess everything caught up with Rafe and she had her breakdown and Eden, Greer, and Abby tracked her down in Mexico where they were able to put her in a hospital for the emergency stay I told you about. Since she's been home, she and Eden have continued to live in the same house and were supposed to be working things out."

"I see," said Ian, "and now you're afraid she is going to run again since she's been asking about her money matters."

"Exactly," said Julia and took a sip of her water.

"Well," Ian began pragmatically, "there's nothing you can do, hon. Rafe has the right to go wherever she wants to go, and she can take her money too if she wants." He saw his daughter about to protest. "I know it's hard, but it's just the way it is. We aren't in charge of the decisions for her life or her money. She pays us to manage her money, and we have to do whatever she directs. We can only advise, nothing more."

"But she's not in her right mind," insisted Julia.

"If she really wanted to leave secretly, I'm sure she could get funds from the accounts she holds with other firms," said Ian.

Julia frowned in shock at the realization her father was right. But his words did nothing to quell her concern. "There has to be a way to help her even if it doesn't involve her accounts, and it's just on a personal level."

"Support her. Listen to her. Be patient," he said calmly. "If she gets to a point where she's a danger to herself or others, then you can get medical professionals and courts involved, but otherwise, there's really nothing more you can do. What has her doctor said?"

"Nothing," said Julia frustrated, not liking what her father was telling her. "We call her and tell her things, but she tells us nothing. She did change the medication when we told her about the side effects Rafe was having, but otherwise, there's just silence."

Ian nodded. "She's probably under instruction from Rafe not to speak with anyone. It's Rafe's right to direct her doctor, too."

"But how are we supposed to help if we don't know what's happening?" Julia asked desperately. "She's pushing us all away. She told me she loves Eden, and she worked so hard to get Eden back, and now she is pushing Eden away too. She even accused me of trying to steal Eden from her and of not wanting her to get better. How could she accuse me of something so untrue?"

Ian pursed his lips knowing Julia had pursued and dated women Rafe had been involved with in the past. He hoped Rafe was wrong about his daughter because it seemed those relationships never worked out the way Julia thought they should. The last one, with Andrea, left her devastated.

"Julia, you have to let go of the idea you're dealing with the Rafe in those pictures," he said as he pointed at the wall of photos. "Our Rafe is probably in there somewhere, but whatever happened to her may have taken the little girl we knew and loved away. You need to stop expecting her to be the same because she may never be."

Ian was saddened by the possibility Rafe may be inalterably changed.

"The families I talked to said they sent away a sweet boy, or a happy man, or a loving husband, and the man they got back wasn't who they sent away. PTSD is a serious illness, and it changes a person. If she ever gets back to the person you and I knew, it will be rare, and it may take a very long time. On a good day, we might see the person we remember sometimes, but the person we know may not be there every day because they're still fighting the war or trauma in their mind. I don't know the extent of Rafe's trauma, and it may not be as bad of a case as some of the men had whose families I dealt with, but it was enough to affect her mind and behavior. Give her a chance to work through things. The medication and treatments they have now are much better today than anything those men had when they came home. Maybe, with time, she'll have a better outcome than we can know. But I can tell you it won't happen overnight, and it won't be easy for her, or her family and friends."

Julia put her head in her hands. "I just want my friend back," she said softly.

"Have you talked to her about the fun times you had?" asked Ian as he studied the photos again. "Sometimes talking about good things is the best thing to do."

"I talked to her about the dance competition we were in," Julia said and gave a small laugh. "I challenged her, and she seemed happy dancing around. She declared herself the winner of the challenge then threw me in the pool."

Ian laughed at the thought. "That sounds like the girl we knew. See? Maybe what she needs are reminders her life wasn't always this bad or hard. Remind her she's been happy and give her hope she can be happy again. Help her get out of her mind and look at the world again in a positive way. She may not always be receptive, but don't let it discourage you. She's probably taking life one day at a time so you'll have to remember to have patience."

"Patience with Rafe," she said with a sigh, "is easier said than done."

Ian chuckled understanding his daughter's plight when it came to having patience with Rafe at times. "Well, maybe you should focus on helping Eden then," he suggested.

"Eden?"

He nodded noting the lack of enthusiasm in his daughter. "Yes. You say they're trying to reconcile but are having problems, and Rafe is pushing her away. Dealing with Rafe being ill is probably even more difficult for Eden than you." He hoped suggesting Julia help Eden have a better relationship with Rafe would curtail the prediction Rafe made about Julia pursuing the woman and hurting their friendship again.

"I'm not sure how I can help her any more than I have," said Julia dejected and unsure if she wanted to help Eden anymore since she told her to keep away from Rafe.

"Well, to start, you can just be there for her," said Ian troubled at seeing his daughter so sad. "There's a very high probability Rafe will succeed at pushing her away, and Eden will need emotional support. I can't tell you the number of couples I saw torn apart by PTSD, even when it was treated. The illness not only changes the person who has it, but it changes the people around them too. It can be like a domino effect of emotional chaos." He put his hand on Julia's shoulder. "You have to remember there's more than one friend involved in this illness. Eden is living with it too. If she's strong and supported by her friends, she'll be able to make the right decisions if things get bad."

"Decisions?" Julia frowned at her father with confusion. "What decisions?"

Ian hesitated because of the delicate nature of what he was about to say to his daughter. He didn't want her to be upset or thinking she should rescue Eden. "She may have to make the decision not to be with Rafe," he said regretfully. "She may have to decide to move on to a different relationship if they can't have a healthy one together because of the PTSD."

"But she loves Rafe," said Julia shaking her head in disagreement with what her father said. "She would never leave her. They just got back together before all this happened." She knew, based on what she thought was happening, if anyone did the leaving this time, it would probably be Rafe.

"Yes, and it's what will make leaving again such a very hard thing for her to do," he said then sipped his water. "It's why she'll need a true friend. One who will understand if someday she finally has to make the decision to leave and will support her while she deals with her grief." He saw the unhappy expression on his daughter's face and sighed. "Maybe you're right," he acquiesced, "maybe she is strong enough and will never have to make such a difficult decision. But it means she'll need a staunch friend all the more, to help her through the difficult times ahead of her."

Julia thought about how Rafe was treating Eden. It seemed like she was already the one always trying to help Eden when it came to Rafe. She realized her father was right. Eden probably needed more help than Rafe did at this point. Even with all her talks with Eden, they both failed at helping Rafe. She didn't understand why Rafe was so stubborn and wouldn't let her help or take care of her. Eden probably would be much more receptive to her help. "Thank you," she said with a small smile of appreciation. "I think you may be right, and I've been looking at things all wrong."

"It just shows you care," he said with a smile. "My empathetic little girl, who tries so hard to hide her heart. I love you, my baby girl."

Julia blushed. "Daddy," she said and shook her head because she felt she was too old for baby-talk from him but was guilty of secretly wanting it anyway.

"I hope I've helped and you can help your friends," he said softly.

"You have," she said then took a sip of water. "Can I ask you something?"

"Of course," Ian said with a chuckle.

"Why do you care about Rafe so much?" she asked thoughtfully as she looked at the photos pinned to the wall. "I'm not jealous," she said knowing it wasn't true. "It's just you've always had a soft spot for her, and I was wondering why."

Ian smiled as he thought about Rafe. "I know it sounds strange, but I do think of her as a daughter in a way, and I would do anything for her, just like I would for you," he said candidly. Ian looked over at the photos pinned to the wall. "The first time you brought her home, I was very worried. Your mother was sure she was a street urchin you found in a back alley, despite the school uniform," he revealed with a laugh. "So, I looked up her father and found out the reason she spoke such halting English was they had just moved here from Italy. Of course, once your mother found out she was a *rich* little street urchin, her opinion changed and she tolerated Rafe, except when she was redecorating and putting holes in the woodwork," he said, chuckling softly.

He was referring to the photos pinned on the wall, and the time Rafe talked Julia into letting her paint a mural on her bedroom wall of the pop singer Madonna. Julia had been obsessed with Madonna back then. Ian thought it was actually a very good painting, but his wife insisted on painting over it. He thought it must have been around the time he began to understand his daughter might have been gay. It was always clear about Rafe.

"But I was still concerned," Ian continued, "because she was so wild and unpredictable. When you told me about what her father said to her, I was worried she was being abused." Ian Hawthorn smiled as he remembered the first day he spent exclusively in the company of the young Rafe Salvaggio, and he began to tell Julia the story.

14

IT WAS THE first summer the fourteen-year-old Rafe Salvaggio was in New York. She had been in America for almost six months, and the summer break from school had just begun. Julia and her mother were away in France on vacation. Rafe showed up at the apartment building to see Julia and had waited in the lobby all day. The lobby attendant was getting weary of her and was relieved Mr. Hawthorn was finally home.

When Ian walked into the lobby, Rafe ran right up to him. "I hungry," she informed him with a frown. "Why *eh* you not come home for lunch?"

"I had lunch at work," he said, and it was clear Rafe was confused by his explanation. Later, Ian found out that in Italy, almost everyone goes home for lunch, and her father still had the habit, so Rafe thought people in America did too. "Why are you here today?" he asked, indulging her.

"I want *eh* to see Julia," she said enthusiastically in her heavily accented English. "The man there *eh* him not let me go up," she said pointing accusingly at the lobby attendant who wouldn't let her get on the elevator.

"Julia and her mother have gone to France," he told her, and she looked back at him with an almost heartbreaking expression.

Rafe threw up her hands, "*Tutti mi sta lasciando qui da solo,*"[3] she said and started to walk away.

Ian could only smile kindly because he had no idea what she had said in Italian. It was late, and he worried about her leaving on her own. "Rafe," he called her back, "since you're hungry, and you waited all day, would you like to have dinner with me?"

Rafe smiled, and Ian was surprised when she took his hand in acceptance of his invitation. As they got into the elevator, she gave the lobby attendant a dirty look and a strange hand signal. Ian couldn't stop the grin on his face at her antics.

The elevator opened into the penthouse apartment, and Ian led her to the kitchen. Opening the refrigerator, he began taking out food the maid had prepared so he could heat it up. He noticed Rafe was looking at him almost horrified at what he was preparing, but she recovered and was then very polite.

"You have *eh* wine?" she asked politely.

"Aren't you a little young for wine?" he asked tolerantly.

Rafe just looked with confusion at him as she found the wine rack and took down a bottle of wine. "I not five or *eh* baby," she said as she found the corkscrew. She then proceeded to open the bottle of wine with an enviable skill for such a young person.

Ian was a bit shocked but gave a small laugh. "How old are you?"

"I *eh* very old," she informed him in her accented English. "I am fifteen in October, *eh* this means, *eh* I can drink wine for dinner."

---

[3] Everyone is leaving me here all alone,

"Oh," said Ian understanding it must be a cultural difference. "Julia is already fifteen, and she isn't allowed to drink wine at dinner, or any other time," he informed her, thinking she might try to give wine to Julia at some point.

Rafe frowned at him and then nodded. "She is from England, *eh* she must only *eh* drink tea," she said astutely.

Ian couldn't help but laugh. "Yes, she can have tea. She's an American, but we lived in England a long time, so she has many English habits. Maybe you two can help each other find some good American habits," he suggested, and Rafe just shrugged, so he continued to make their plates quietly.

When the food was ready, they sat at the table and Rafe poured them each a glass of wine. She inspected the food suspiciously and then looked up at Ian sadly. "Is this *eh* all they *fed* you? I *thinks* you were *eh* rich man."

Ian couldn't help laughing at her observation. "This is what they *feed* me," he gently corrected her English, but only one word so she wouldn't be discouraged from speaking. He understood she had to translate in her head before she spoke and was doing incredibly well under the circumstances. Over the past few months, her English had improved, and it was still a mystery to him how she and Julia communicated sometimes. "It's what I asked for," he told her and took a bite of his salmon.

Rafe shrugged and ate the food politely taking a sip of wine with each bite. It was plain to Ian that grilled salmon was not a dish Rafe enjoyed. When Rafe took her last bite, she contemplated Ian for a while.

"Are you *eh* sick?" she asked with concern.

"I'm fine," said Ian, not sure why Rafe was asking her question.

Rafe nodded her head thoughtfully. "Do you need me *eh* make you chamomile tea to help *eh* for your heartache because you family has *eh* abandoned you?"

Ian was a bit shocked at her question. Then he understood she must think it was why he was there alone. "No," said Ian with a small smile and shook his head, "I don't have heartache. They didn't abandon me. Julia and her mother are just on a summer vacation in France," he explained. "I have to stay here for work. They'll be back in a few weeks." He was touched at how worried she was. "You're speaking English very well now," he complimented her.

"Yes," said Rafe with a proud smile. "My mother was *eh* Americano, so I spoke it *eh* best at my school in Italia. Now I speak English *eh* all the time, *eh* have *un* tutor, *eh* makes me better." She took another sip of her wine. "Why you so quiet *eh* if you not sick *eh* have no heartache? I am *eh* good company *eh* know many subjects."

Ian couldn't help but smile at the serious little girl across from him. She was like a miniature adult, so precocious and outgoing trying her best to hold a conversation in a language she barely spoke. He smiled to himself as he realized, despite her small frame, she was a teenager, so she actually was very close to being an adult.

He sipped his wine and told Rafe all about his day at the office of his financial firm. He talked about some employee issues and the financial market and explained how a few of his company's new products worked. He thought she would get bored, but the whole time, she paid close attention and asked a few very good questions.

"This seems simple if *eh* fourteen-year-old *eh* understands," said Rafe thoughtfully. "I think I *eh* come to your office *eh* Monday *eh* I help," she declared. "I help Papa *eh* all the time. I could *eh* be a great help."

Ian was speechless for a moment. "That sounds fine," he agreed, thinking she would forget about it by Monday morning.

After dinner, Ian tried to get Rafe to let him take her home but she informed him she had a 'phone card for the car,' and she pulled out a car service card and a credit card. Ian couldn't believe Rafe's father had given a credit card to a child and she was allowed to call for car service whenever she needed— forgetting just moments ago he had considered her an adult. He noticed the credit card was issued to Salvaggio Real Estate, and it actually had Rafe's name on it. Rafe went to the phone and called the number on the card. Against his better judgment, Ian let her walk out the door when the lobby called to say her car was waiting.

Monday morning, Rafe was waiting in the building lobby where *Hawthorn Financial & Investments* had offices. She was dressed very smartly and held her hand out to Ian as he came into the building.

"I have read all about *eh* financial market *eh* speaked to my papa too. He say *eh* real estate always be *eh* the best investment, but I *eh* still help you," she said as they shook hands.

It was all Ian could do to stop himself from laughing because he understood that she was serious. "Your father sounds like a very smart man," he said graciously.

"Yes," said Rafe with a smile as she agreed about how smart her papa was.

Ian took her upstairs to his office and introduced her to his secretary at the time. "Lois, this is Rafe Salvaggio. She'll be helping me today." The secretary smiled at Rafe. "Please prepare a copy of all the meeting information for Ms. Salvaggio so she can get up to speed before the meeting." He wanted to be as serious as Rafe was about helping.

"Of course, Mr. Hawthorn," said Lois and got to work.

Ian and Rafe went into his office, Ian showed her how to read the ticker, and they talked about trades and the stock market. Rafe pulled out a scrap of paper from her jacket pocket. "I *eh* write down *eh* important industries for best *eh* investment," she informed him and gave him her slip of paper.

Ian was taken aback but scanned the list then looked back up at her. "So why do you feel, after one weekend of looking at the financial market, that these would be good industries to invest in?"

Rafe shrugged and looked openly at him. "I just *eh* think about all I know *eh* from my papa, *eh* what kids at school *eh* speak about," she said matter-of-factly. "I look *eh* political climate, they *eh* teach us in school, *eh* I choose what I think will be *eh* good twenty-year return. My papa, he say *eh* think about my future."

"Well," said Ian with a chuckle, "I have to say I'm impressed." And he was because she had put more thought into her list than a lot of people put into their investment strategies. It also seemed Rafe's father cared a lot about his daughter's education and financial future since it seemed he talked to her extensively about the subjects. Ian reviewed Rafe's list again and knew a few of the industries she listed were doing terrible lately. But no one knows the future, so he gave her the morning financial paper. "Now use this and find a mix of twenty companies you think best represent the industries you chose, and we'll run some projections when you complete the assignment."

"I understand." Rafe took the paper to the small worktable and began looking at the lists of companies. A short time later, Lois came in with the meeting packet for Rafe. Ian told her to read it, and as soon as she was finished, they would go to the meeting.

A short time later, they went to the large conference room for the meeting, and Ian introduced her. All the men in the room either ignored Rafe or made a fuss and shook her hand. It was almost an even split. Rafe sat politely beside Ian and listened to the presentations.

The first presentation was about impending mergers and market trends, and the second was about the euro and its impending effects on markets. At the time, the euro had already had its name, and the European Council had set a date for the currency launch. Soon, they would be selecting the countries to participate in the third stage of the program. The team at Hawthorn Financial was working on the financial and investment implications for clients with international holdings, and where investments should potentially be made or sold once the euro was actually launched as more than an accounting currency in countries where clients had holdings. The presentation team made recommendations and given more directives, then they took a break because Ian had to take some calls.

Lois delivered a soft drink and a snack to Rafe and coffee to the others in the meeting as they either made calls or talked until they could get back to the meeting. When the meeting continued, the discussion led to talking about how everyone was afraid governments were going to collapse, and the international market was going to crash because of the euro. Ian could see Rafe was still listening carefully. When the meeting finally ended, they went back to Ian's office.

"So, what did you think?" Ian asked Rafe as he sat down behind his desk and she sat in a chair across from him.

Rafe looked back at him gravely. "I think *eh* you will be firing *eh* three people *eh* soon," she said flatly. She put a page of the report on his desk without explaining herself further, and before Ian could ask about her statement, she continued, "This page *eh* I think is no right," she said and pointed to a column of numbers. "My father *eh* says future value should be *eh* calculated with *eh* compounding interest. This done with *eh* simple interest," she said. Then she showed him the mistake in the presentation and did the math on a financial calculator. "See, it *eh* change *eh* risk/reward ratio," she stated as she looked at him intently.

Ian was stunned she even had a financial calculator let alone knew how to use it. "Did you borrow your father's calculator?" he asked curiously.

"No," said Rafe absently as she recalculated to check her work, "it *eh* mine now. He give it to me *eh* when we moved to Milano *eh* so I could help him."

"I see," said Ian. Then he looked over the numbers in the report himself finding she was correct. It was a significant mistake and could have lost their clients a lot of money. He stared at her in amazement for a moment. "Are you sure you're only fourteen?" he asked impressed. "I think I'll need to talk to the team responsible for putting this together and find out why they made such a big mistake."

"Yes," Rafe agreed. "I needs to *eh* call my papa," she said firmly. "Can I use *eh* phone?"

"Of course," said Ian wondering if there was a problem she needed to speak with her father about. He listened as she spoke quickly to her father in Italian, without the hesitation she had when speaking English.

After listening on the phone, Rafe spoke a few minutes more and then hung up.

"Is everything all right?" Ian asked her with concern because he understood some of the words like lira and euro in her conversation. The presentation report had indicated the lira would potentially exchange somewhere in the range of two to three thousand liras to one euro, but it was just a projection because the exchange would not take place for another two years.

"Everything *eh* good now," she said with a smile.

Ian had a moment of apprehension and decided he needed to talk to Rafe about insider trading, what it meant and the possible consequences because he wasn't sure what she told her father. "So you understand, if we know something the general public does not know, it's considered insider information, and we can't use the information to make trades for ourselves or our clients. This means we can't tell things to your father everyone else doesn't know."

"I understand," said Rafe with a smile. "Don't worry *eh* my father *eh* good man."

"Okay," said Ian relieved. He found out much later she probably meant her father was good at taking a small amount of information and making a lot of money. Apparently, Ettore had begun following the development of the euro and leveraged both currency and real estate in several countries taking advantage of the chaos and social anxieties of people who didn't understand the exchange.

Ian hadn't forgotten about Rafe's declaration he would be firing three people. He was doubtful about her interpretation of whatever piece of information she heard, making her think he would be firing three people, so he decided to ask a few more questions. "Why do you think I'll be firing three people," he asked calmly as he put away the papers on his desk. "Who are you talking about?"

Rafe looked out the glass wall of Ian's office. "You see *eh* the man there," she nodded to a man in the office across the hall. "It will be him *eh* the two he was talking to *eh* in meeting."

Ian was shocked because the man she pointed out was Mark MacMillan who had been a friend for years. Ian brought Mark in when he first opened the firm while Ian was still in England and was considering making him a principal. He thought about the men MacMillan had been talking to in the conference room and shook his head in disbelief. He had taken care of those guys for years. He had even given them leads and accounts to build their commissions. "Are you sure?" he asked trying not to get upset or angry.

"Si, *eh* I mean, yes," said Rafe forgetting her English for a moment and slipping more into her accent as she spoke faster. "They *eh* talking about *rubare*," said Rafe, "uhm, to steal," she said as she found the English word. "They talk about *eh* taking client list *eh* starting for themselves company *eh* with money. *Eh*, I know about this. My papa *eh* has this happen," she informed him. "He *eh* find out *eh* fire all of them, *eh* so will you," she shrugged like it was common.

Before the end of the day, Ian had called an outside company for a secret internal investigation to take place immediately, and Rafe was on her way to picking out the twenty companies for her investment plan.

Over the next few weeks of summer, Ian did end up firing all three men and had turned them into FINRA and the federal prosecutor, who eventually penalized them all with fines. They prosecuted two of the three and sent them to federal prison for misappropriation of client funds, breach of contract with the company, and other federal violations. None of the three would work in securities again.

Rafe turned in her assignment and worked at the office over the summer months when she could to give what she considered help. Ian was so appreciative of her catching the men who could have ruined his company, and his reputation, he got the board to approve a reward in the form of a UTMA custodial account. Initially funded by the company, Ian added his personal money to it on her birthday each year until she turned eighteen, and then he turned the account over to her.

They used the account to test the companies Rafe chose for her assignment, and Ian had been impressed because she did very well in her decisions to buy, sell, and grow the account. The account was one of the things he and Rafe's father, Ettore Salvaggio, disagreed about many times, especially when it was time to pay taxes.

Ettore thought he should be able to use the money in the account, and Ian should not be the custodian. Ian was sure if he gave the custodianship to Ettore, Rafe would have no money left in the account eventually. Despite their disagreement, Ettore did help Rafe by putting some real estate into the account, but Ian was never sure if it was for Rafe's or Ettore's benefit.

Rafe was indifferent, of course, telling Ian if her papa needed the money, it was fine because she would get all of his money someday. But Ian thought it was best Rafe had something of her own because Ettore was so volatile, and he just didn't trust Ettore Salvaggio after dealing with him a few times.

15

IAN HAWTHORN FINISHED telling Julia the story of his first experience with Rafe. He took a sip of his water to wet his throat then looked over at Julia. "I owe the fact I still have a company to a fourteen-year-old girl," he said with a chuckle, "and I learned a valuable lesson."

Julia frowned at her father confused. "Lesson?"

"Yes." Ian nodded. "I learned help can come from the most unexpected places. I also learned, if I ever meet another kid who owns a financial calculator, and knows how to use it, I should hire them." He laughed but was serious. "Rafe is still helping me, in her way, by sending me strategies she comes up with and information about companies she researches. Sometimes, I wonder if she thinks she owes me something because, after giving her the account when she turned eighteen, I haven't gifted her any more money, but she still feels like she should help me. I just wanted to make sure she had a nice balance in her account to work with by the time she was eighteen, one she had worked to build and let her know I appreciated her help."

"I always wondered why Mother would complain about Rafe's birthday every year," said Julia wishing she knew about what Rafe had done before now. Julia had never really been interested in her father's business until she was trying to figure out what to major in for college. Now she understood her father's relationship with Rafe better. Knowing didn't take away the jealousy she had always felt, but it helped.

Ian sat silently in thoughtful contemplation. He wondered if Julia would ever truly understand the significance of what Rafe had done. He knew his wife still didn't comprehend the amount of gratitude they owed Rafe. With one observation and a few words in broken English, she had assured the future of Hawthorn Financial and Investments. He didn't know if Rafe even understood what she had done. Without Rafe, there would most likely not be a company, and his wife and daughter wouldn't have the life they had become accustomed.

He broke from his thoughts and regarded his daughter. "Have you ever examined those photos closely," Ian asked as he looked across the room at the group of photos.

Julia followed her father's gaze. "They're just snapshots from a Polaroid, or ones we printed from the computer. So, not really," she said dismissively and shrugged. "We were just goofing around in them."

Ian smiled and chuckled softly. "In every one of the photos, Rafe looks like she's in some sort of motion. I don't think she ever slowed down. Some part of her is blurred in each photo," he said motioning toward the photos. "I just noticed it one day."

Julia got up and looked closer at the photos. "You're right," said Julia. "I guess it's just how she is in my head anyway, a constant force in motion. It seemed like she never could make it into the shot before the timer went off." She chuckled at the memory. She went over to the bar and made herself a stronger drink then sat back down. "When I was trying to figure out why she was asking about her accounts, I told her I was worried about her regressing into the person she was before she met Eden." She looked up at her father. "She did change when she met Eden, didn't she?"

"I think so." Ian nodded in thought. "It seemed like it was around the time they met."

"Me too, for the better," she said dryly. "She says Eden wasn't responsible for her change, and she wasn't with her to better herself."

"Well, maybe she just decided to change," said Ian not sure where his daughter was going with her thoughts.

"But, if she didn't change for the better because of Eden, and she just changed for no real reason, it means she may change back for no real reason," pondered Julia. "If she does turn into the old Rafe, Eden doesn't stand a chance, and Abby will have been right all these years to worry."

16

AN INCESSANT KNOCKING interrupted Julia Hawthorn's peaceful slumber. Slowly she opened her Mediterranean blue eyes and checked the clock. It was blurry at first then the white digital numbers came into to focus. Three fifteen. The knocking came again, and she whipped the soft linen sheet off her body and sat up on the edge of the bed.

"Who the bloody hell," she mumbled, cranky, as she pushed her silver locks from her face.

She looked at the phone and saw no missed call from the front desk, so she had no idea who could have gotten in the apartment. She got up and shuffled to her bedroom door wondering if her mother and father had come home early from their Switzerland trip somehow or if someone was sick. She could think of no one else who would be knocking on the bedroom door to her childhood bedroom at this time of night. It was just a guest room now, but she stayed in it sometimes when she came to New York. Since her mother was out of the country, she had decided to stay and work with her father in the New York office for a while.

Julia told herself, and her father, she stayed because she wanted to spend time with him. But she knew there were other reasons. Going back to California meant dealing with the fact she had been pushed away by Rafe once again. On top of the fact that Eden had encouraged her to stay away from Rafe for a while too. She felt shunned and hurt, so she decided to just let them handle things without her and see how they fared. She was sure they would soon regret kicking her out of their lives. In the meantime, she thought staying in New York for a while would do her good. It would give her time to think about the things she had discussed with her father and regroup her emotions. She wanted to be in a good place when she went back to help Eden as her father had suggested. She had to temper her unrequited feelings for Rafe and look at Eden as something other than an object in the way of her desire.

Julia turned the handle on the bedroom door and opened it tentatively and then peeked out. She was sure her eyes were playing tricks on her. "Eden?"

The golden-haired woman was standing outside her door shifting nervously and sniffling. "Julia," she said, and her breathing hitched. "Can I come in?"

"Of course, of course," she answered quickly. Part of her mind was questioning why Eden had no coat and was wearing only baby doll pajamas on such a cold night. But it seemed the rest of her mind was concerned about other things. "What are you doing here? How did you get in the apartment? What's happened?" She let Eden in the room. Her mind and body were both in shock at Eden's presence. She could see Eden was upset and her inner voice told her something had to have happened with Rafe for her to be here.

Eden looked up at Julia with red-rimmed eyes. "I left her," she said softly. "I didn't know where else to go."

Julia led Eden to the bed and sat her down then took her place beside the sensitive blonde. "You left Rafe?" she asked in disbelief. She remembered her father's words. He had said 'Someday, Eden may have to make this choice,' but she didn't think it would be this soon. It had been barely over two weeks. She watched as Eden nodded affirmation. "Oh, I'm so sorry," she said and took Eden into her arms.

"I had too," Eden sobbed into Julia's shoulder. "She just kept pushing, and I couldn't take it anymore."

"It's okay. I understand," whispered Julia. It was hard to miss the heady scent of Eden's hair and the way her soft, warm body fit perfectly into her arms. "I'll take care of you," she promised.

Making her promise to Eden made Julia's heart fill with affection for her. She wanted to take care of her and protect her from getting hurt again, especially by Rafe. In a strange but freeing amorphous moment, she let go of the feelings she had for Rafe and re-focused them all on Eden.

Eden needed her help and her affection, unlike Rafe who had always pushed her away. She and Eden now had the same thing in common, and it meant they understood each other the way no one else could. Julia allowed herself just a little self-congratulations at being right about them falling apart without her there to help. More than a little—a lot, in fact. But she pushed the urge to say 'I told you so' aside in order to help ease Eden's pain.

"I hope you don't mind I came to you." Eden sniffed as she pulled away and looked up at Julia sorrowfully.

Julia looked into Eden's eyes. "No, I don't mind," she said softly. "I know how Rafe can be. She's been pushing me almost from the first time I met her. I think I understand how you must be feeling."

Eden tilted her head as if looking at Julia for the first time. "You do understand, don't you?" She looked away shyly. "I've just been feeling so alone. I need," she whispered then stopped herself.

"What?" Julia asked gently. "What do you need?"

"It's just. . . I can't live like this anymore. I need to be with someone who will hold me and kiss me. I don't think I can live without affection and without knowing I'm loved anymore." Eden looked up at Julia again, heart-melting tears glistening in her soft brown eyes. "The more she pushes me, the more I feel like I'm slowly dying. You understand," she whispered. "I just can't."

"I do," Julia whispered, knowing she had needed and felt the same things when it came to Rafe. "I do understand." She pulled Eden close, wrapping her arms around her. "You deserve better, much better." She lowered her face slowly and pressed her lips to Eden's. The kiss was soft. It was sweet. She felt Eden run her hands down her back as the kiss deepened. *This is happening*, she thought as she ran her hands over Eden. She broke away from their kiss and put her head against Eden's. Their hair intertwined—her silver and Eden's gold, like precious metals in a delicate piece of jewelry. "Are you sure, I mean, this is really unexpected."

"I'm sure." Eden breathed into her mouth and Julia was amazed at the sweetness. "I thought you would help me." Worry crossed her face as she continued. "Unless," she hesitated, "unless I'm wrong, and you don't want to do this. I'll understand." The disappointment in her voice was unmistakable.

"No, no," she stammered softly. "I mean yes, I want to."

"Show me," whispered Eden and gently pulled Julia close.

Eden's small pull was all it took, and Julia put all her doubts aside. She pushed Eden back on the bed and felt Eden surrender to her as they kissed. Drunk with lust, Julia pulled at Eden's silky clothes until, like magic, she was naked against the soft sheets. Just as quickly, Julia stripped off her pajamas and found herself looking down on Eden's body.

The sight meeting Julia's eyes was one she never thought she would see. She had never imagined it, and now she didn't have to imagine anything. Eden's golden hair splayed out around her head. Her full breasts heaved with every breath, and her nipples were at attention waiting to be touched and kissed. Julia ran her hand over Eden's taut stomach and reveled in the sensation of her soft skin. Lower, between Eden's legs, she was shaved and smooth so Julia could see the soft pink between them throve and plead for attention. The perfection made Julia's head spin, and she couldn't wait for one more second to have her.

Pouring kisses over Eden, she made her way from her lips down her body trailing her silver hair behind. Eden's moans of pleasure were in her ears and her mouth watered at Eden's scent and the promises it was making. Julia couldn't wait to taste her and show her just how well she would take care of her.

Just as she was going to make her final descent, the one leading her to bliss, there was a crashing sound jolting them both out of their sexual haze. They scrambled back against the headboard while at the same time trying to cover themselves with the sheet. Julia looked up as the door exploded opened and slammed against the wall.

Her jaw dropped.

It was Rafe.

Julia wiped her hand over her eyes, not quite believing what she was seeing. It looked like Rafe had a set of angel wings as black as her hair. Julia blinked several times. It was true—the wings were there. Somehow Rafe was creating her own light, and it surrounded her, so the expression on her face was evident. It was one of anger and vengeance. Julia trembled and swallowed back the taste of fear developing in her mouth.

"Rafe!" cried Eden in shock.

"Rafe," Julia said shakily, "just, just stay calm. It's not what you think."

Rafe stared back at her with those hard blue-gray eyes, and Julia could feel the waves of anger directed at her. Beside her, she felt Eden trembling, and she remembered the promise she had made to take care of her. Suddenly, she knew she had to stand up to Rafe even though the prospect terrified her.

"Rafe," Julia dragged her name out. "You did this to yourself! You drove her into my bed! Face it, you can't take care of her. You don't even want to take care of her anymore or you would! You knew perfectly well what you were doing and what it would lead to!"

The black wings behind Rafe stretched and Rafe's face contorted into a snarl as she let out a scream of fury. Eden stood up on the bed, her naked body trembling. "Rafe, I'm sorry." She wept.

"Don't tell her you're sorry," Julia complained. She watched in disbelief as Rafe's arms stretched out, reaching from where she was at the door all the way to where Eden was standing on the bed. Rafe seized Eden, and in an instant, she had her clutched close to her body.

"Help!" Eden sobbed. "Julia, help me," she begged and reached out for her. "I can't live trapped without love!"

Julia jumped up to try to rescue Eden and felt Rafe's hand grab her throat and squeeze. "Rafe," she choked. "She can't stay with you! You'll destroy her!"

Rafe answered with a growl and threw Julia against the bedroom wall.

Julia slid down onto the bed disoriented. When she looked up again, Rafe was gone, and she had taken Eden with her "No!" she cried out angrily. "Come back with her! She's mine now!" She scrambled to get off the bed and to the door in order to follow them but felt herself falling.

Abruptly awake, Julia sat straight up in bed. "Bloody hell," she hissed.

It was clear to Julia her father was right. She could see now the need to focus on Eden. There was no doubt Rafe would keep pushing Eden away and was now only holding onto her out of selfishness and passiveness.

Julia decided it was time to return to California and help Eden, and in turn, help herself. Whether or not her help would end up making Eden stay with Rafe or help Eden get away was yet to be determined. It was clear, though, in Rafe's current state, Eden would be much better off with her than with Rafe. Julia vowed to be there when Eden finally smartened up and got out of her situation with Rafe. She knew Eden needed her, and she would never push Eden away.

Her dreams about making love with Rafe again were over. From now on, Julia knew her dreams would be filled with Eden.

17

THE LAST MONTH had been building up to this day, and Eden Kingsley was nervous. Rafe had finally agreed it was time to start going to therapy sessions with her. Rafe insisted when they went to the therapist together, they would go see Dr. Cathcart. Her reasoning was Eden had a longer history with him, and it would help her anxiety levels. Eden wasn't sure if it was the real reason, but she couldn't think of another reason Rafe would insist. Eden was anxious about how the sessions would go and excited they would be taking the first steps to getting their life back together.

Things had just seemed too good to be true for a while, and Eden didn't want it to end. But Eden could tell things were getting strained again lately, and she wasn't sure why. The girls had kept their distance, and Eden made sure they didn't do anything to make Rafe feel pressured or ganged up on. Julia went to New York for a while, but she'd been back for almost two weeks. When she got back, Julia had called and offered her help. Eden was able to talk with Julia on the phone and sometimes meet for lunch because Julia had gone back to work. Fortunately, Julia was still too angry to make visits to the house, so Rafe was still free of her pressure.

Rafe had been more engaged and attentive at home, but Eden was still not sure what Rafe did during the day. She was happy at least that Rafe was home when she got there every evening. It was very comforting, and Eden couldn't wait to get home just to be close to Rafe. It seemed like they laughed a lot and did more things together. But Rafe still stopped everything if it even hinted it might go further than a few kisses and caresses. Sometimes, Rafe stopped engaging in things so abruptly that Eden was left wondering what she was doing wrong while Rafe retreated outside or to her bedroom. The times Eden had tried to address Rafe's reasons for her behavior there was always a seemingly plausible excuse, but it still left Eden feeling uneasy.

Eden was trying to stay positive because, as promised, Rafe had been going to her doctor. However, no matter how often Eden asked, Rafe wouldn't say anything about her therapy. Rafe also refused to discuss what they might talk about when they went to therapy together. Rafe had reminded her several times not to tell her secrets, and Eden kept the things Rafe told her about her father and Maria and Rafe's first kiss to herself.

After dropping Bronte off with Lydia, who had arranged a playdate with some friends, Eden was on her way to their Saturday appointment. She had talked to Dr. Cathcart a lot in the last few weeks about Rafe and what she might want or need to talk about in their session. Eden hoped things would go well today and Dr. Cathcart could convince Rafe not to go to Italy. If everything went well, it would mean their relationship was going in the right direction. Hope for their future helped calm her now.

After parking, Eden rushed into the building and found her way to the doctor's waiting room where she saw Rafe pacing from one end to the other. Eden watched Rafe as she walked and the way her body moved. She took a breath to clear her head of the dizzying rush she had at the sight. She loved seeing Rafe dressed up, but seeing her in clothes similar to those she wore to the work sights she used to visit filled her mind with memories. It was always an appealing contrast to see such a beautiful woman coming home covered in dirt. The way she walked and her body moved in her construction boots was like art in motion. Put the two together, with Rafe's playfulness, especially when she turned up the sex appeal, and Eden couldn't control her own body's reaction.

As Rafe turned, Eden took in her dark hair, and tawny skin and her beautiful face and smile then felt her heart thud in her chest. There was no doubt Rafe was the only person who ever made her heart beat so hard and put her mind and body in such a high state of anticipation and desire.

"Hi," she said as she walked to Rafe and hugged her. "Were you working on another project today?" Rafe's scent made Eden's body tingle and her mind cloud until she had another small wave of dizziness.

"Hi," said Rafe quietly. "Just cleaning up the workshop." She broke away from Eden as the door to the doctor's office opened.

"Eden," the doctor said with a smile, "you both can come in now." He motioned them into the office.

Rafe followed Eden into the office and took in her surroundings. She walked over to the window and looked out at the city then made her way around the room decorated in a sparse modern style. She turned toward Eden and the doctor, and she found they were both looking at her. Eden was sitting on the couch, and the doctor was standing between the couch and two chairs. Rafe walked over to one of the chairs and sat down.

Eden glanced at the doctor then at Rafe. "You're in Doctor Cathcart's chair," she said softly and put her fingertips on Rafe's knee. "You can sit next to me," she said encouragingly.

Rafe looked up at the doctor silently and didn't move from the chair.

"It's fine," said Cathcart. "Sometimes a change in perspective is helpful." He understood Rafe wanted to maintain some control over the meeting, so he took the second chair while Eden took the scene in with confusion. "So, it's good to finally formally meet you, Rafe. I think the last time we crossed paths was when Eden came to me for help with the anxiety over her parents. You used to bring her and stay until we were finished." He held out is hand, and Rafe took it briefly to be polite. "I understand we're going to talk about where you two are in your relationship. Eden has told me you've had a very hard year. Where do you think we should start?"

Rafe gave a frown of disbelief. She didn't understand how Eden could think their problems only came about recently. In her mind, she'd had an onerous three years. She looked hard at Eden and wondered if she should just get up and leave now.

"Do you want me to tell you about things I've been working on in my therapy?" Eden asked nervously, breaking Rafe's silence. "I've been trying to work out some of the issues you've pointed out," she volunteered, feeling the tension building over the last few days appear again.

"Which issues?" Rafe asked calmly.

"The big one mostly. The trust issue," she said. "I'm sure I trust you now, but I think you may be right that I didn't trust you before." She paused and watched Rafe. "I think it's one of the reasons you keep me at arm's distance. Maybe," she hesitated and waited to see if Rafe or Cathcart were going to say anything. When they stayed silent, she continued. "I admit a few times I was angry with you, and I was wrong to be," she said nervously wondering why they were silent. "My anger came from me not trusting in you. But it also came from the fear you didn't want me here and that you didn't love me anymore. Do you love me?" She kept her eyes on Rafe and waited nervously.

After giving some time to see if Rafe would say anything, Cathcart interrupted the silence. "Can you answer Eden's question, Rafe?"

"Is it why you don't want to have sex with me—because you don't love me anymore?" Eden asked nervously as Rafe looked over at the window.

The surreal nature of the conversation, and how it was unfolding, were making Rafe's head hurt. "The reason I don't want to have sex is I don't think we're both on the same page yet," said Rafe softly then turned to Eden. "I don't want one of us to think there is more to us than there is right now."

"What are we right now?" asked Eden and swallowed hard.

"Roommates."

"Oh," said Eden feeling stabbed in the heart. "Don't you want me even a little?"

"Of course I want you." Rafe sighed and rubbed her temples. "Why is it when you're not sure about having sex or getting closer, I have to wait, but when I'm not sure, I get punished?"

"I'm not punishing you," said Eden in confusion about why Rafe would think she was punishing her.

"Then why do you want me to have sex with you when I'm not sure whether or not we can be together again? Do you want me to treat you like a one night stand or someone I pick up in a bar?"

"I just want to be close to you," Eden said softly fighting to control her emotions.

"I waited for you for almost a year," said Rafe as she sat back in her chair. "Then, when you said you'd spend time with me, I waited again because you weren't ready to have sex with me. But now you don't think I should get the same courtesy!" she said with frustration.

"I don't understand," Eden said in dismay. "You said you would do whatever I wanted, including sex." She looked shakily at Cathcart then back at Rafe. "I told you, I know how I feel about you, and I trust you. I love you," she declared as she looked into Rafe's grey-blue eyes.

Rafe ignored her declaration. "I told you I would have sex with you, but you couldn't call it love," said Rafe and shook her head, "but you keep doing it."

"I just," Eden started then stopped to gather herself. "If I love you, then you're not treating me like a one night stand or someone you pick up."

Rafe sighed, shook her head, and leaned forward in her chair. "You're the only one calling it love right now," she said flatly. "So, if I have sex with you, and only you're calling it love, then I'd be treating you like someone I don't have to try and care about, and you, you would be fooling yourself and be vulnerable if we don't work things out."

"So, you don't love me?" she asked shakily.

"I don't know. I keep telling you, I'm trying to figure things out," said Rafe and leaned back again rubbing her temples. The problem was she did love her. She couldn't stop even though she wanted to. She needed to stop, to save herself from sinking into the cold waters of hell. She couldn't tell them that, though. She didn't know if she could deal with the fallout if she revealed her thoughts to them. If she could just let go, she wouldn't have to be here, trapped in this room with Eden, and live with the possibility she would leave again.

"This is good," Cathcart interjected, and Eden snapped her head to look at him angrily, clearly not in agreement anything was good. "We now know where both of you are in the relationship. Eden, you're sure of your feelings, and Rafe, you still need time." He addressed Eden, "Can you continue to give Rafe the time she needs and not pressure her about sex?"

Eden just stared at him for a long moment then turned her eyes to Rafe. She felt like they had just taken a huge step backward from where she thought they were. "I didn't mean to pressure you," she choked out then cleared her throat. "I," she stammered, "I guess I just think sometimes you're sending me signals and I react. I'm sorry. I won't pressure you about sex."

"Now," said Cathcart redirecting them, "let's get back to what Eden was saying about working on trust." He regarded Rafe for a moment. "Eden is saying she trusts you. Can you tell her how you feel about the trust in your relationship?"

Rafe considered his words then looked into Eden's soft brown eyes and frowned. "You want to talk about trust," she ran her hand through her hair and took a deep breath. "I've been trying, but I have no idea if it's possible." She got up, went to the window, and put her head against the cool glass.

"Can you tell Eden how you're trying?" asked Cathcart as Eden's eyes went wide with surprise at Rafe's words because she thought they trusted each other now.

Rafe turned and looked menacingly at Cathcart then went back to her chair across from Eden. "I'm trying to talk with you," she said evenly, "to tell you things," she said thinking about the secrets she had told her. "I'm trying to let you get close again. I'm trying to be how you used to see me." She paused and looked down at her hands then back up at Eden. "I'm trying, but I don't trust you, I can't trust you," she said in frustration. "I don't think you really trust me either or even really want to go to the trouble of trying. I think you're lying to yourself about it and a lot of other things."

Eden was in shock as her eyes filled with tears and her hands shook. She was not expecting anything like this. She thought Rafe believed her when she said she loved her and trusted her. She thought she was doing the right thing in telling Rafe she loved her. "But I," was all Eden could eek out.

Cathcart nodded, acknowledging Rafe's words. "Can you tell Eden what makes you feel like you can't trust her?"

Rafe took a breath to calm herself and worked to find moisture for her dry mouth and lips. She forced herself to look up at Eden. "You tell me you need me to touch you and hold you, but every time I do, something happens. You're either taken away because something happens, or some lie, or you just walk away on your own," said Rafe getting angry at Eden's tears. She never found herself getting angry before at Eden's tears. But now, after listening to Eden cry and beg during her dreams for so long, Rafe found her anger seeping from her subconscious into her reality. "So why should I trust you? Why should I believe anything you say?" She got up and crossed the room to put physical distance between them then turned back to face her. "I don't know if you even believe yourself! You act like all we have to do is make love, and all our problems will magically disappear, but really, right now, it will just cause more problems, more confusion," she railed and spun to pace around the office.

Cathcart watched Rafe as she paced and waited until it looked like she had calmed before he spoke. "Tell her why you think she's lying to herself now," he encouraged calmly.

Eden felt her chest tightening at what was happening as she watched Rafe pace the floor. "I'm not lying," she insisted with a shaking voice. "I'm not leaving you. I do trust you, and I do love you, Rafe. I do," she said firmly.

"How do you know?" asked Rafe with a small laugh and wiped away the bead of sweat flowing from her temple. "You love who you think I am, or who I was. We were apart for over a year. You have no idea who I've become, so how can you trust me? You don't even know what I was doing while you were off with Jake playing house," she said bitterly.

Eden closed her eyes at the jab but knew she was right. Her time and energy were focused on Jake and their relationship, not on Rafe. She did think about Rafe sometimes, but she didn't have any meaningful contact with her, and she had even been relieved when Rafe hadn't confronted her about leaving. "What were you doing?" she asked softly and glanced at Cathcart fearfully. She hoped he could see Rafe might be getting too upset to go on.

"Waiting," Rafe said shortly and sat back down heavily.

"What do you mean?" she asked hesitantly and bit her lip nervously.

"It means I was just waiting to see if you would come back to me again." Rafe shrugged and sat on the edge of the chair in front of Eden. "I waited to see if you really didn't love me anymore. I just couldn't believe it was true," she said with a short manic laugh. "Then you got engaged, and I finally took off my ring," she held up her hand with her bare ring finger, "because I could finally see it was obvious you didn't love me anymore."

"But you still loved her, didn't you?" asked Cathcart. Eden told him the things Greer had said about Rafe and how hard it was for Rafe to move on.

"Yes," said Rafe softly. "Even though I knew you didn't love me anymore, it was hard for me to stop loving you," she admitted and rubbed her head willing the headache trying to form to go away. "I did my best to let you go, but I could never really do it."

She got up and went back to the window wishing the room were bigger so she could get further away. She could feel the heat from the hurt and anger boiling up inside her, and she was trying hard to keep it locked away.

"Everyone, including Greer, could see no matter how hard I tried to push it away I was still in love with you." Rafe laughed so she wouldn't scream. "And now you say you love me, and you really never stopped loving me," she said throwing up her arms in frustration. "But how can it be true?" she asked and turned to look at Eden. "How could someone who loves me, like you claim to love me, take so long to come home? How could you leave like you did?"

She waited for an answer, but it didn't come. She clenched her fists to help hold in her pain. "I finally get out there to start looking for someone new and to try to find love again and then suddenly, there you are. You convince me to take you back, to let you move back in," she stopped and fought for control of herself, "and I wanted you to come home so bad," she said softly and wiped away a traitor tear, "but then, I find out all this other stuff has been going on, and it just makes me wonder if you're lying to yourself as well as to me. And now, I find out you think all our problems started this year but, from where I'm standing, they started long before you left me for Jake. I think you really left me three years ago, and I don't think you're really back!"

18

RAFE SALVAGGIO WALKED over to the mini fridge in Cathcart's office and flung it open. Taking out a bottle of water, she opened it and took a drink. She needed to cool down. She could feel her anger building, and she was determined to stay calm and in control. The anger she felt wasn't one brought on by medication like before. This was a justified, righteous and cleansing anger. Anger that needed to be wielded carefully or it would destroy her and send her back into the darkness she had been struggling against.

Cathcart observed Eden as she watched Rafe and saw her face pale. "Eden," he said calmly, "you and I talked about the events from three years ago, and you were able to work through things, but it seems like Rafe has never gotten the chance to resolve anything from that time."

Eden watched Rafe who was trying to calm herself and could feel the anxiety growing inside her. Her chest was tightening, and her hearing was muffled by the rush of blood racing through her body as her heart beat faster.

She gripped the arm of the couch to steady herself. "She," Eden paused and swallowed, "she has tried to talk about things. Maybe I wasn't listening," she said softly.

She was so busy trying to convince Rafe to take her back she never really thought about what Rafe was saying as anything but an argument against her. She didn't realize Rafe might have been trying to resolve how she was feeling about everything from back then.

Cathcart cleared his throat to get their attention. "Rafe," he started calmly, "you know Eden has been working through her anxieties and has come a long way in accepting truths about her feelings for you. I know she talked to you about the anger at herself she had to work through. She found she was lying to herself when she denied she still loved you after your infidelity. But I think the affair may have affected you too." He paused and saw Eden look at him in misery. He looked back at Rafe who held her water bottle in a death grip. "Having an affair can be as hurtful to the person having it because it is usually caused by something. But it doesn't—" he started to explain.

"Oh, fuck you!" seethed Rafe. "You have no fucking idea what you're talking about! I'm talking about things way before my fuck up! I'm talking about her fucking up!"

"My—" Eden said softly and stopped when she understood Rafe was talking about what she did online.

"Yes, *your*!" growled Rafe. "Your fuck up!"

Rafe paced the floor and held the water bottle tight trying to maintain her control. "I question whether we should have been trying to start a family together in the first place," she said when she calmed herself. "Don't get me wrong, I love Bronte, and wouldn't change things about having her. But maybe you were right, and we should have been figuring out if we were good or not when you were pressuring me to go see a therapist. Maybe I should have taken everything more seriously instead of thinking it was just your anxiety, and you'd work through it. If I had, maybe we wouldn't be in the position we're in right now."

Her eyes raked over Eden who wouldn't. . . or couldn't look back at her. Rafe then turned to look out the window. "Like Julia keeps pounding into me, I wasn't there for you enough, and so I really had no idea what you were feeling and what you were going through. Maybe I shouldn't have just trusted we were good and things would be fine. Julia says it may have just been the hormone treatments and everything else, but maybe, really, it was much more." She turned back and was silent until Eden looked up her again. "Maybe the truth is we don't belong together. If it is the truth, then I don't want to do anything to hurt you... or myself."

Eden swallowed back her anxiety and horror at how fast things were going in a direction she never expected them to go. "It's not the truth, Rafe," she said softly. "We do belong together. I love you."

"Stop saying that!" Rafe screamed at her. "Make her stop!" she demanded of Cathcart. "It's not helpful, and it's not true!"

"Take a breath, Rafe," said Cathcart calmly then redirected to Eden. "Eden, Rafe needs you to help her understand what you were going through and your reasons. You've already told her how you feel, and she knows you feel like you love her. Now, can you help her understand what was happening with you during the time you were going through the things she is talking about?"

Rafe was standing with her arms crossed and looking out the window. Eden couldn't see her face, but she knew from her stance she was frowning. Eden cleared her throat and took a breath. "I think I was just scared. I told you this already, Rafe, when we talked by the pool. It was hard for me because my idea of family included a man, and I had only been in relationships with men before I met you. It was hard for all those years to compete with the five years I was with you."

Rafe shook her head slowly and put her hand to her head. "Bullshit," she said through her teeth. "Those are words Jake put in your mouth!"

"Jake?" said Eden not understanding.

"Yes, Jake!" she said as she turned her angry gaze on her. "Those are his words, his reasoning, not yours! He told me how he put them there! Those words are just an easy excuse not to tell me the truth! What you did has nothing, nothing to do with being gay or how long you were with me! Tell me the truth!" she fumed.

"I'm trying to tell you the truth," said Eden through her tears realizing how thoroughly Jake had infiltrated their lives and was still affecting them. It seemed like he was still coming between them and she didn't know how to stop the destruction of their relationship he and his group had started. She thought about what she was going through and dealing with at the time. She hadn't met Jake yet, so Rafe had to be right about Jake's words not being the truth.

"It seemed like so much was happening then," Eden said shakily trying to remember. "I was feeling overwhelmed. You were gone, and I felt disconnected. I felt like my body was betraying me when I couldn't conceive, and you were so disappointed when the inseminations failed. Then I was afraid maybe I couldn't give you what you wanted, what we wanted. And maybe, it was all my fault, and I needed to talk to someone who had been through what I was going through so I would know what to do."

Rafe turned toward Eden having found a small place of calm for the moment. "Yes, all those things are about the insemination process, I get it. What I just don't understand is when you started to have doubts about us or even why," she said as calmly as she could, "why you wouldn't talk to me?"

Eden looked at Cathcart, and he nodded encouragingly to her. "I think," she said hesitantly, "I think my doubts about us came after I started talking online to people, who I know now were manipulating my feelings. I was convinced I shouldn't bother you with anything, and because you were so upset and disappointed, I should just leave you alone."

Rafe could see Eden was upset, but she was to blame for her own pain. Eden had said nothing new, and it sounded to Rafe like it was very far from anything true. "You think everything is fine now that the adoption has gone through, but really, how do I know you won't have feelings and go away somewhere and make it hard for me again?" She watched as Eden just shook her head. "I'm responsible, and I'm part of Bronte's life on paper, but paper can be changed or taken away with enough money and the right lawyer."

"I would never take her from you," said Eden as tears sprang from her eyes.

Rafe took a breath and let it out slowly because Eden had already proven, if she wanted to leave and take Bronte, she would do it. She ran her hands through her hair and shook her head. "I just don't understand why, if you were having doubts about us, you used the sperm you said you didn't even want."

"When I stopped talking to them," Eden paused and swallowed back her anxiety, "and you were in New York, I realized I shouldn't have doubted you, and we did want the same things. I used the sperm because I realized Gabri was part of you, even though I didn't know him. I used it thinking it would be a perfect surprise for us both if it worked, and if it didn't work, I wouldn't have to tell you my body failed us again," she looked up at Rafe then looked back down at her hands. "Then, it happened," she said softly, "and my world crumbled."

Rafe bristled at her reminder again about her infidelity. "I haven't forgotten I fucked up!" she said scathingly. "But what about you? Where's all the punishment for what you did?"

"I know I did things," she said as she cringed at Rafe's words, "things I shouldn't have done when I was talking to the person online about sex. I'm sorry," she said softly.

"You fuck around, and everyone makes excuses for you!" said Rafe angrily. "You fuck me over with everything you did when you left me, and I should just forget about it all and take you back!" Rafe shut out any sympathy she might have for her. "I may have fucked up, but you were doing something worse to me," she said evenly. "You were going to keep from me the fact you used the sperm my friend gave as a gift, and from all I knew at the time, you were going to keep the baby from me too. I had to find out from a stranger!"

"I meant to tell you myself," said Eden through tears. "I didn't mean for you to find out the way you did, and I wasn't going to keep the baby from you."

"But you did, didn't you? You kept her from me! I felt like I betrayed my friend!" she said angrily. "I betrayed him because he trusted me to take care of the children we might have because of his gift. His gift was out there and not being raised by me, the person he trusts like family! Instead, the baby was being raised by some stranger I didn't know. A stranger you obviously didn't know either! She was out there in danger, and I had no fucking idea!" she yelled, and beads of sweat appeared on her forehead. "I was kept away all those months, and you didn't even care how it hurt me! Did you just want to make sure you broke me completely? How broken do I have to be before you stop crushing me?"

"I didn't want to do those things, Rafe," said Eden and broke down in tears again.

"If it wasn't what you wanted then, when you moved back in while you were pregnant, why did you make me think everything was good again?" she demanded. "Why did you agree to move back in at all if you were just going to leave me? Did you want to see how much more you could hurt me? You told me you wanted to come home! You told me we were a family! You told me you loved me! What was the truth? Were you just using me? When you were in my bed and telling me you loved me, were you lying?

"I wasn't using you," Eden insisted through her tears.

"I think you were!" she fumed. "I think you just hadn't found anyone else yet, and I was the most convenient idiot you could find who would be a temporary placeholder until your feelings changed again!" she growled angrily. "And they did change, because the next thing I know, you're telling me you're having feelings about men. I was fucking stunned," she said with a feverish laugh. "After telling me all those things, and stringing me along, your feelings changed again!"

"I can't help my feelings!" said Eden at the sting of Rafe's words.

"Well, it must be true because barely three months after the baby was born, you were gone—again!" Rafe laughed bitterly. "Are you going to tell me it was the hormones then too? Or am I still to blame because of New York? I just don't know! But of course, it wasn't your fault, because nothing is ever your fault!"

Rafe began to pace the room again and could feel her anger taking over. "Before you suddenly told me you had feelings for men, I thought we were through what happened in New York, I really did. I thought all the questions I had about you using Gabri's gift didn't matter anymore, and we could just move forward again as a family. But according to you, I guess I just hurt you more than I could ever understand, and I deserved to be punished even more because it just keeps coming up! There was nothing I could do but trust you, and you broke me! You didn't talk to me about leaving or say you were even thinking about it. I just came home, and you were gone!"

"You just have to understand, Rafe," Eden started.

"Well, I just don't fucking understand anything!" Rafe fumed interrupting her. "I don't understand why you weren't sure of us, why you had to leave me for Jake, why you lie to me all the time, why you don't care about what I was doing while you were gone or how I was doing or why you think you love me again. Why don't you care who I've become, or how I feel, or what I'm going through?"

"I care, Rafe," sobbed Eden, "I do care!"

19

RAFE TURNED AND paced the room breathing deeply, hoping it would calm her temper. There were so many images flicking through her mind she was having a hard time keeping track of what were memories from long ago and what had happened more currently. The image of her childhood friend Brettito came into her mind and grief surged through her over his death. She thought back to the first time Brettito called her *Eroina,* and how she gave the name to her company for him, then wiped away the tear for him, as it broke free from her eye.

"Then there's my business," said Rafe her voice a low rumble. "I was selling my life's work, and you couldn't give me the courtesy of saying anything about the fact you were leaving me and taking the baby, and maybe, just maybe, I should put a hold on things!" She fumed and paced the room as Cathcart sat silently, and Eden watched her with concern. "By the time I knew what was happening, it was all too late. My life, Eden!" she said as she stopped in front of her with fury and misery in her eyes. "My life was in my company!"

Rafe ran her hands through her hair and pushed her fingers into her temples to press away the pain. "I thought I was doing something great for my family, but really, I was just a fool!" she said bitterly. "I get home from signing contracts, and it's like someone has ripped my heart from my body and crushed it in front of my eyes."

She turned toward Eden again, and her anger took control. "But did you really care? Did you even wonder why I never called you? I was on the fucking floor waiting to be put out of my misery! I had to go stay with Letty because it made me physically sick to walk into my own fucking house! If I had known you fucked him in our bed, I probably would have burned it all down! I should have left then! I should have gone back to Italy and stayed there! I should have listened to Gabri! The only reason I stayed was because of Bronte, and I thought you would come back sooner!"

She sat down in the chair and held her throbbing head in her hands thinking about all she could have avoided if she had just gone to Italy and not stayed in the hell that had taken over her life. But she couldn't go and then have to tell Gabri the baby was being kept from her. She couldn't risk his anger and lose his friendship too. Then she really would have nothing. . . be nothing.

Eden looked helplessly at Cathcart not knowing what to do. Rafe was angry, and there was no way to have an actual conversation the way she was relentlessly ranting and shooting out questions Eden did not even know if she could answer. "I'm sorry," she said softly. "I'm sorry for everything. I don't want you to leave us, Rafe."

Rafe," Cathcart said calmly, "there were a lot of things Eden wasn't in control of happening. You can't put all the blame on her for some of the things happening to either of you. You need to put the blame on the proper person or group. Eden loves you and would never have done some of those things on her own."

Rafe gave Cathcart a stony look. "Yeah, Julia and the others say I can't be angry at her over anything the Stewards and Jake did too, but I think it's bullshit," said Rafe angrily. She turned her anger on Eden. "Everything with them started because you were having doubts or didn't trust me or, whatever, I don't even know. Are those things all my fault too? I have no idea! I can't even fathom what your excuses or answers will be or how you will be able to convince me you're right and I'm wrong. There's nothing I can think of to measure against your claims so I can tell if what you're saying is true or if it's a lie!" Rafe stood and paced the room again. She went to the window and leaned against the cool glass again hoping it would help with the pain in her head.

Cathcart could see Rafe was trying to control herself and waited silently for her. He knew Rafe was spilling out more things than could be handled in one session and he would have to go over the session recording and make a plan to direct both Rafe and Eden so they could either resolve their issues or move on from each other amicably.

He was not sure if the resolution would end up being what Eden said she hoped at this point. He looked up at Rafe, who was holding her chest, and worried she was experiencing more phantom pain.

"Rafe, please tell us if you're having the phantom pains and we can help you. I know what happened at the school and it may be compounding the problems you're having."

Rafe turned her head slowly toward Cathcart with a frown because his voice seemed so far away. She looked down and saw she was holding her hand to her chest and forced it to her side. She thought back to the traumatic day at the Conservatory, and the image of Eden walking away filled her mind.

Looking at Eden, she felt the hurt again from watching her walk away. "I don't understand why you left me alone at the school after everything I went through," she said with the hurt showing in her gray-blue eyes. "I thought you would at least want to tell me you were glad I was okay, but you walked away, you couldn't even be a friend! Then I knew I was right again about you not loving me! I thought you probably wanted me dead and were disappointed I lived because even the possibility of my death didn't seem to concern you," she yelled angrily.

"No, Rafe, it's just not true!" Eden yelled back at her as anger surged through her making her want to lash out. "I never wanted you dead! How can you say that to me? I couldn't come around you! You were with someone, and I was having problems of my own I had to deal with! You were treating me like crap and didn't want to be my friend either!"

"I was protecting myself from you and all your lies!" Rafe fumed at her petty excuses. "Now pile on top of all those things the shit Jake did to me and the things you did to me while the whole fucked up injunction case was happening. Then tell me, how the fuck do I go on with all of this? How do I keep trudging through all of the shit and make it out again so I can have just a little peace? Just a little self-respect? Just a little will to keep getting up in the morning? I don't know. I really don't."

Rafe fought to control herself, but everything kept spilling out. "I wake up, and I think, why? Why do I keep waking up in this nightmare? When can I breathe again without pain? How much longer can I hang on to something clearly killing me inside? How do I stop the seemingly never-ending chaos? I have no answers. I don't think you have them either. I'm not even sure if there are any. Everyone is telling me I should just forget about everything, just brush it away, and everything will be fine. But I'm only human, and I can't forget! They think if I just jump in again that some miracle will make everything fine. I'm not so sure. They tell me I didn't know what was going on with you and they're right."

She glared at Eden with frustration. "But did you even want me to know? You told everyone else in the fucking world what was going on, and I find out three fucking years later! Does that make me the bad guy? Am I so terrible you can't share anything with me? I just, I just don't understand," she breathed heavily and wiped away the sweat from her face. "If I'm so bad, why do they want me to be with you? Why do you want to be with me? Why are we even here right now? You say love, but is it love, really? If we love each other so much, why have we caused each other so much pain?"

"It is love, Rafe, and you're fighting it right now," said Eden as she looked into Rafe's desperate face. "I don't want us to be in pain or cause each other pain. I want us to be happy."

Rafe just stared at Eden not understanding why she was still fighting for anything. "You almost died, Eden! Do you understand? The cop told me you were less than an inch from a bullet in your head! An inch!" she screamed and turned away from her again. "An inch, an inch, an inch," she muttered softly as she paced and the word continued to echo through her head. "All because of more lies and more secrets! All because you don't trust me, and no, you don't love me!"

Eden was feeling sick inside, and her heart felt like it was being squeezed in her chest. "Please, Rafe," she begged, "please don't say that, don't think that."

Involuntarily putting her shaking hand to her head, Rafe couldn't stop the memory of her nightmares from flooding into her mind. She saw the way Eden ignored *Death*, even though he was standing right beside her. She welcomed him with a smile, and the bullet was getting closer. Rafe knew it had to end and didn't know if she could fight anymore against him if Eden was going to keep inviting him to come.

Eden didn't trust her because she didn't love her, just as Death had said, Rafe realized. Eden would never really come back. She would always have to worry about Eden leaving her again, and she couldn't live with the possibility always hanging over her head.

"Maybe this is really just a *cavoli riscaldati*,"[4] said Rafe softly with eyes glazed from her vision of Eden standing happily with Death, "and we're just trying to bring life to a failed relationship, and it won't work," she said as sweat ran down her face. "Maybe we failed, and it's time to move on. Maybe the only thing we have in common now is Bronte."

She looked searchingly at Eden and felt like she was a stranger. "I don't understand when you tell me you can't help your feelings. I don't understand how you can say you love me then a few months later you leave me. If you can't help your feelings, how can you tell me you won't leave me again? How do you know you won't have feelings for someone else? You see what I'm up against?" she asked Cathcart. "It's the unknown, the unknowable! How can you expect me to live in such an imbroglio?" she asked and watched Death just smile as he put his arm around Eden.

---

[4] Re-heated cabbage (Used to mean a relationship which has failed many times.)

"Rafe," said Eden with worry. She could see that something was wrong with Rafe because of the way her eyes had glossed over, and she was looking off into some other world. "Rafe, please, it's not unknowable. I know I'm not leaving you. I know I don't have feelings for anyone else."

"You tell me you need me, and I shouldn't fight against my feelings," said Rafe as she paced angrily, ignoring both Eden and Cathcart as they faded from her vision. The heat was surging through her body while the sound of her jumbled thoughts filled her ears. She could feel an icy cold black wave begin to cover her, and it would have been soothing except for the pain it brought.

"*Ma cerco di controllare i miei sentimenti e capire i miei sentimenti. Non posso avere sentimenti e li seguono ciecamente. Morte esige una scelta e io non posso temporeggiare molto più a lungo,*"[5] said Rafe shakily. She dropped her head down, closed her eyes, and put her hand on her chest in reaction to the pain and the vision she was fighting as the darkness began to fill her mind. She dropped to her knees and shivered.

"Rafe!" Eden yelled. "We can't do this to her!" she said angrily to Cathcart as she ran to her.

Cathcart was at Rafe's side at the same time as Eden, and they helped her from the floor to a chair then Rafe pushed them away.

---

[5] But I try to control my feelings and understand my feelings. I can't have feelings and follow them blindly. Death requires a choice and I can't hold off much longer,

"Rafe," said Cathcart as he held her shoulders and looked into her glazed over eyes. "Rafe, you need to talk to us about what's happening to you. You need to speak English so we can understand you," he said firmly. He knew she was having a mild break, and he needed to get her through it quickly.

Rafe tried to focus. Her eyes found Eden and could see him, the dark man, Death, still standing behind her. "You even tell me in my dreams I need you, I'm part of you," she said shakily trying to focus on Eden and push away her vision. "But what does it mean? Does it mean I have to lose myself to be with you? Does it mean I'm not real anymore?"

Rafe caught sight of Cathcart and wondered why he was looking at her with such an expression. *How can he look at me with pity*, she thought. *He is supposed to be objective.*

"Rafe, take another drink of water," Cathcart suggested. "You've had a small break, and we need to take a step back from everything." He opened Rafe's water bottle for her and helped her take a sip of water while Eden looked on in misery, feeling helpless. "You're okay," he said. "You're in a safe place. Try to relax and focus on my voice." Cathcart spoke softly to Rafe repeatedly telling her to focus and that she was safe. When her eyes began to clear, Cathcart let go of her and stood back. "I think we should cut the session short today," he said softly.

Rafe watched the two of them and the way they looked back at her. She knew what they were thinking. "That's right," she growled softly. "I guess I'm so fucking broken maybe Julia is right, and I should be locked away somewhere again! Well, you can't! I won't be put there again! I saw all the forgotten people there! It was inhumane, and I will not go back! I will not be put somewhere and forgotten!"

Eden shook her head in confusion and then realized Rafe was talking about the mental hospital in Mexico. "Rafe, we would never lock you away! We just wanted you to get better. Everything will be okay. We love you."

"They were in a place without hope!" said Rafe shakily truly terrified they would send her back. "I had to help the forgotten people. I had to force them to care about those people!"

It was clear to Cathcart that Eden had no idea what Rafe was talking about. "Rafe," he said calmly, "Eden and your friends won't forget about you. Take a breath and try to calm yourself. What do you need? Tell us how we can help you right now."

Rafe was at a loss for what he or anyone else could do, or even what she needed. Her body reacted without the help of her confused mind as she stood up from her chair and moved away from them.

"I just don't know anymore!" Rafe said angrily. "There is just too much to figure out! I'm sick. I'm broken. I'm angry," she said and looked back at Eden in pain. "I'm lost in my own mind, and you're trying to tell me everything is fine. It's not fine! It hasn't been fine for a long time from my side of the road. And now, on top of everything, the people who are supposed to be my friends, and even my family, are working against me and trying to send me away!"

She couldn't help the gruff manic laugh coming out of her as she looked feverishly at Eden. "Oh, they all want to help you, and protect you, and defend you, but do they help me?" she asked, pointing to herself and looking to see if they would answer. "Fuck no! They just make my life harder and punish me for whatever the fuck they think I'm doing to you! I try to get help, and they even push me so I can't even think about helping myself! Why are they doing it? Do they think we're wasting our time trying to make things work? Am I missing something? Again, I have no fucking idea!"

Rafe paced the room and could feel the walls closing in around her as waves of blackness threatened to push over her. She felt out of her body and out of control, but her words kept spilling out. It was like something in her mind was waiting for this moment to pull the plug and she couldn't stop the flow. "Sometimes when you tell me you love me, I just want to scream at the top of my lungs and to get away from you because it feels like a lie, and I can't take it! You've proven so many times you don't love me. I must be stupid because I keep coming back for more heartbreak. Maybe, I need to smarten up and just go and try to forget about you. With all your fucking feelings, it shouldn't take you long to forget about me. So maybe it's best for both of us!" she said then stopped and took in their faces filled with pity. She went quickly to the door, yanked it open, and walked out, slamming the door behind her.

Eden and Cathcart ran to the door to follow her.

"Rafe!" Eden cried out as the elevator door closed, and Rafe was taken away. She turned to Cathcart. "What did we do to her? I. . ." she stammered, "I can't believe she means those things. She was so good these last weeks. What happened?"

Cathcart took Eden's arm and led her to a lobby chair. "She had a lot to get out, a lot she's been holding inside for years. Maybe this release is what she needed to help her continue to talk. Now, since the hard part is done, we can answer all her questions. I'll get a transcript of the session and organize all the disjointed things she talked about so we can help her. I'll also call her therapist and let her know what happened. She may have some helpful insights. Give Rafe some space and don't pressure her about sex like you promised. Try to keep things calm at home if you can," he said with empathy. He knew it would be a hard week for them both.

"Okay," said Eden as she nodded, "I need to go. I need to make sure she's okay."

20

AS SHE DROVE, Rafe Salvaggio could feel the hot bile threatening to force its way up her esophagus and the burning sensation caused as she fought to keep it down. The pain was overwhelming every muscle and organ in her body, making it hurt to move or even think about moving. She pushed herself through the pain so she could get away from the source.

Eden.

She knew there would be no answers to her questions because Eden was so thoughtless with her heart. She berated herself for giving her heart away again and thinking Eden cared enough to be thinking about her as much as she thought about Eden.

She had been trying for months to find the answers, and from the look on Eden's face and her silence, Rafe knew those questions would never be answered. She thought she could let things go, and she had tried so hard these last few weeks to find a place where all the pain and lies combined with the torment of what happened that led to Eden almost dying didn't matter, but it seemed impossible. Between her dreams coming back, Eden acting like nothing had happened, and the pressure she felt from the anticipation of having to go to therapy with Eden, she couldn't see anything except hopelessness.

Rafe looked up and had no idea where she was and realized she was lost in more than just her mind right now. She attempted to focus and try to find something familiar, but she didn't recognize anything.

She pulled her car over and turned off the engine then leaned heavily over the steering wheel. After a moment, she decided maybe she would be safer if she just walked or maybe went for a run. She got out of the car and started walking.

She knew she should recognize something because she had lived in this place for years, and it would be impossible for her not to find something she knew soon. She decided she should run in order to get to a familiar place faster. Oblivious to the inappropriateness of the work boots she was wearing, she got out of the car and started down the street.

She ran.

21

PULLING INTO THE driveway at home, Eden Kingsley immediately saw Rafe's car wasn't there and dread flooded her mind. As she opened the car door, Jude and Flynn came out of their house and walked to the driveway.

Jude waved on the way to her Jeep. "Hey, we're going to the bistro for dinner. Do you and Rafe want to come?"

"Yeah, Abby called and said she was desperate for company," said Flynn with a shy smile.

Standing beside her car, Eden tried to reign in her emotions. "Did you see Rafe come home and then leave again?" she asked nervously.

"No," they both said with a shake of their heads.

"Is everything okay?" asked Jude noticing as Eden shifted nervously.

"Is Rafe okay?" asked Flynn.

"I don't know," said Eden and ran her hand over her golden hair. "She left the therapy session upset, and I don't know where she went. I was just going to try to call her again," she said and pulled out her phone.

Jude could see Eden was worried and decided Abby could wait. "I'll call her after you just in case she doesn't want to talk to you right now," she said knowing Rafe sometimes didn't answer Eden's calls now.

"Okay," said Eden. She dialed Rafe and got her voicemail. "Rafe, I'm just making sure you're okay," she said into her phone. "Please, call me or let someone know you're okay. I'm sorry about what happened. I'm home now. I'll see you when you get here. I love you." She hung up and looked worriedly at Jude, and then shook her head as she tried not to get upset.

"She's probably fine," said Jude reassuringly. "She may just want to have some alone time to think or something."

"Right," said Eden softly. "I'm going inside. Lydia should be bringing Bronte home soon." She gathered herself, trying not to cry. "I'm going to call her car storage place and see if she went to get her father's car. If you talk to her, will you let me know?"

"Sure," said Jude and watched Eden walk unsteadily to the house and go inside. She turned to Flynn. "Maybe we should have Abby bring dinner here or something."

"Yeah, but we have to be careful," said Flynn. "Eden told us she doesn't want Rafe to think anyone is ganging up on her and you know how Abby is sometimes."

"Yeah," agreed Jude with a sigh. "Let me try to call Rafe first." She dialed Rafe and got her voice mail, so she hung up. "No sense in leaving a lot of messages. I wish there was a better way to figure out where she's gone."

Flynn shifted uneasily. "Well, there kind of is," he said and blushed slightly.

"There is?" said Jude confused.

"Yeah," he said guiltily, "back when Jake was doing things, I kind of put a tracking app on her and Eden's phones. I was worried after what happened with Bronte in the park that Jake and his group would do something to one of them. I wanted to be able to find them. I never took the app off their phones," he confessed.

Jude was a little bit shocked, but then had a rush of admiration for how much he was looking out for their friends. "Let's use it," said Jude with a shrug. "At the very least, we can reassure Eden she's okay."

"Okay," said Flynn, "I have it set up on my laptop. Let's go in and check it," he said, and they went back into the house.

Flynn went to his room and brought his laptop out to the living room. He turned it on and opened the tracking program. He selected Rafe's phone and waited for the program to find the signal. "It takes a few minutes," he said softly.

Jude looked over Flynn's shoulder, impressed. "This is cool. Why didn't you use this when Rafe took off for Mexico?"

"I tried," said Flynn sheepishly, "but the phone has to be turned on. Rafe had hers turned off so..." he said then shrugged. He didn't want to bore her with tech talk about tracking phones. Rafe wasn't important enough to catch the eye of the NSA, so Flynn was pretty sure there was no Trojan or spy chip on her phone. "Plus, it turned out she didn't have it with her anyway," he reminded her.

"Oh, yeah," Jude nodded, remembering Rafe taking her phone away and turning it off too. If they had left her phone behind, Jude knew it would have been even harder to get Rafe home. "So, you only have Eden and Rafe's phone in there?" she said looking at the tracking list.

"Yeah, it's kind of an invasion of privacy, so I never actually used it again until now," Flynn said nervously. "It was just for emergencies. I don't think Rafe would be happy if she knew. I think Eden might understand, though."

"Well, I think we can keep it to ourselves for now," said Jude. "This is kind of a special situation." There was an alert from the computer, and a graphic appeared over the map on the screen. "Did it find her?"

"Yeah," said Flynn, and he zoomed in on the place the program had pinpointed. "The pin isn't moving, so it looks like she's stopped somewhere." He typed in a couple of commands, and a small window popped up. "Okay, here's the closest address. Give me your phone." He took Jude's phone and entered the address in the maps application. When finished, he handed the phone back to Jude. "There you go."

Jude looked at the map and the address on the phone. "I wonder what she's doing there. It's the complete opposite direction she should be going. I'm not sure if there are even many places around where she could go inside." Jude thought about the area and checked the computer again. "Okay, I'll go see what she's doing. You call Abby and let her know what's happening. When I find Rafe, I'll call and let Eden know. Then I'll try to talk to Rafe about when she'll be going home."

"Okay," said Flynn and closed the computer. "Just don't get me in trouble. I forgot to take this down after everything was over. I'll take the apps off their phones as soon as I can."

"It's okay Flynn," Jude said with a reassuring smile. "I think this one will just be between you and me." Jude walked out of the house, got into her Jeep, and made her way to the other side of town where the app had found Rafe.

22

FINDING THE ADDRESS didn't take Jude Atwood long. Because of Flynn's app, she was able to locate Rafe's car right away. Parking behind it Jude looked around. There was no place open where Rafe could have gone inside. It was all industrial space, and it was the weekend, so most of it was locked up tight.

She stepped out of the Jeep and walked up to Rafe's car. Looking inside, she saw Rafe wasn't there so, on a whim, she pulled the door handle and found the car unlocked. At first, Jude was surprised, and then she was worried. She searched inside the car and found Rafe's phone on the passenger seat. "Shit," she said to herself. She was about to get out and saw the keys were still in the ignition. Fear raced like ice over her. "Son of a bitch," she said then took the keys from the ignition.

She got out of the car with the keys and Rafe's phone. Looking around, she wondered where Rafe was and what had happened to make her leave her keys and phone in the car. She locked Rafe's car and jumped back into her Jeep. "Fuck, fuck, fuck," she said to herself with worry as she tried to decide what to do.

She knew the police would do nothing for twenty-four hours, and if she called Eden, it would only upset her more. She didn't know if Rafe would be angry if she called everyone and then found out nothing was wrong. Looking at her watch, she knew from the time Eden had come home, it had already been about forty-five minutes. Adding the time it took Eden to get home from the therapy session, it totaled a bit over an hour since Rafe left the doctor's office.

Jude knew Rafe ran a lot, and if she was running hard on a good day, she might be able to do a six-minute mile. So she could get maybe ten miles in an hour if she could run hard the whole time. But in which direction, and was she on foot or did she get a ride? She pushed down the fear that someone had taken her against her will. Some creep or someone from the Stewards group. Jude sighed in frustration and considered who she might call for help. It would be dark soon, so there was no time, she decided. She would just have to drive up to ten miles in each direction and hope Rafe was on foot so she would spot her fast. She decided to start in the direction the car was facing and began driving slowly down the street scanning the area for Rafe.

After driving for about six miles, Jude was tempted to turn around and start looking in another direction. She was sweating from nerves because, if Rafe had taken a turn anywhere, she would have missed her. The road she was on was coming to a dead end with railroad tracks crossing it. She drove to the end of the road, and as she turned the car around, she saw movement down the tracks. She stopped and saw someone walking on the tracks. "Rafe," she whispered when recognition hit. "What the hell are you doing?" she asked softly to no one. She parked the car and ran down the tracks until she caught up with her. "Hey, Rafe," she said as she panted from her run. "Rafe, what are you doing," she asked gaspingly.

Rafe, her skin and clothes drenched with sweat, turned and looked with confusion at Jude wondering how she got there and why her voice sounded so far away when she was so close. "*Vado verso l'oceano,*"[6] she said and kept walking.

Jude only understood the word ocean. "Are you going to the ocean? This is the wrong way."

Rafe stopped and frowned, her eyes shifting quickly. "Are you sure?"

"Yeah," said Jude, "I'm sure. Why are you walking? It's way too far to go on foot and in boots. Why'd you leave your car?"

Rafe stared at her not sure how to answer. "I just need to get away," she said with confusion in her voice. "I need to relax for a while."

Jude could see the confusion on Rafe's face, and the edge on her concern for her friend sharpened. "I can help you relax. How about if I take you to see Susy for a massage?" She gently took Rafe's arm to guide her back toward the car. It was clear by the heat of her body and the sweat dripping from her that Rafe had been running. Jude worried that she was dehydrated and might be sick from it.

---

[6] I go to the ocean,

"Yes," said Rafe as she thought about what Jude was saying. "That's our secret," she said allowing Jude to lead her, "but I told Eden, so maybe not." She stopped and pulled her arm from Jude then turned and walked away.

With a worried groan, Jude went after Rafe and tried to act like she was relaxed. "We won't tell Eden about today. Come on," she said and took Rafe's arm again. "Eden's probably at home or something, so we can do what we want." Jude got her to the Jeep and opened the door for her. "If we see her there, we'll drive away and not go inside. Okay?"

Rafe thought about it for a moment. "Okay. I'm tired of walking and thinking," she said as she rubbed her hands over her face and through her damp hair. "It's just too much sometimes."

"I know what you mean," said Jude with a small hesitant smile. "Get in, and I'll take you." She helped Rafe climb into the Jeep and buckled her in, and then quickly ran around to get in herself. Once she was secured in the Jeep, she started it. With a sigh of relief, she put it in drive, heading toward her place of business. "I'm going to call Susy and let her know we're on the way," she said, but Rafe was looking out at the buildings and didn't respond. She dialed Susy and made sure everything was ready for when they got there. Making a quick stop at Rafe's car, Jude retrieved Rafe's duffle bag from the trunk then headed off again.

Jude parked in front of the massage company relieved Rafe had not said or done anything except stare out at the scenery. "Well, we're here, and it looks like everything's good.

Let's hurry and get inside," she said and jumped out of the Jeep then went to get Rafe. She helped her out of the Jeep and then got her bag out of the back. Carefully, she led Rafe inside where Susy was waiting. "Hey, Susy," said Jude as cheerfully as she could. "Look who's here! Our favorite client. Take care of her," she said and let Susy take Rafe and the duffel bag.

"Hi, Rafe," said Susy as she slung the bag over her shoulder and took her arm. Jude had filled Susy in on Rafe's condition, but she still had to hide her shock at the sight of her. "We can start with the baths like we usually do. Then we'll decide what treatments to do after, okay?"

"Sounds good," said Rafe unsteadily. "I just need to relax today."

Jude watched as Susy led Rafe back to the baths then took a shaky breath of relief. She went behind the counter and into her office where she sat down at her desk. Pulling out her phone, she hit the number to call Eden.

23

RELIEVED THE PHONE tracking app worked, Flynn Ogden had called Abby after Jude went to find Rafe. He told Abby what little he knew, leaving out the information about the phone tracking app, and asked her to bring dinner for everyone to Rafe and Eden's house. Abby made it to the house at the same time Lydia brought Bronte home. After Lydia left, they all sat in the kitchen to eat the dinner Abby brought, making sure to save some for Jude and Rafe. At dinner, Eden was trying to contain her worry and take care of Bronte while Flynn and Abby watched her with concern.

"I'm sure Jude will call soon. She told me she thinks she knows where Rafe went," said Flynn, trying not to look guilty about how they found Rafe.

"Why'd she walk out of therapy?" asked Abby with concern. "Did you rake her over the coals again like Julia did?"

"No," Eden said softly then burst into tears because she didn't want to even think about the things Rafe said to her. She didn't think she could handle it if Abby and the others agreed with Rafe and thought their relationship had failed and it was over. She looked up suddenly, her heart leaping in her chest, thinking Rafe was walking in the door. She felt the pain of her heart deflating as Julia walked into the kitchen. She forgot Abby had called her.

"I came as soon as I could," Julia said and sat with everyone. "Have you found her yet? Has she called?"

"No," said Abby as she threw her fork down. "Hopefully, Jude will call soon. She thinks she knows where she is."

"What happened?" asked Julia. "I thought you said things had been really good lately." It looked to Julia like she was right about needing to come back to help Eden. Eden had to see now leaving Rafe was the only solution. But she would wait for Eden to come to the same conclusion on her own.

Eden put Bronte's drink in front of her and steeled herself to talk about what had happened. She didn't want to break the trust of the therapy session, but she felt like she had to tell them something in case Rafe was hurt or decided to leave again.

She sat down and took a painful breath because her anxiety was making her chest contract. "She, she was talking about, things, and got upset. She got so upset that it caused enough stress to bring on her PTSD symptoms." She couldn't hide the misery she was feeling. "She's not doing better," she said and swallowed back her anxiety. "I thought she was because the last couple of weeks had been so good, but I was wrong." She looked down at her hands and clasped them together to stop them from shaking.

"We need to think about placing her again, Eden," said Julia firmly. "She needs more than just a few therapy sessions and a drug to help her sleep."

"I can't," she said looking at Julia fearfully. "She's really upset we placed her before. I think something happened in the hospital in Mexico and it really upset her. She doesn't want to go back to a hospital."

"We would send her to a better one here in the States," said Julia reassuringly. "The place in Mexico may not have been ideal, but we had no choice." She gently put her hand over Eden's. "I'll help you get through this," she assured her. "You have to think clearly about this for Rafe because she can't.

"Can I?" asked Eden in misery. "Can I think clearly for her? I just want our life back, and everything is still crumbling right before my eyes. I don't know what to do for her. I don't know how to get through to her. I won't send her to a hospital unless she agrees to go. I can't!" sobbed Eden pulling her hand away from Julia's. "I don't want her to hate me for placing her against her will on top of everything else I've done to make her so unhappy."

"Maybe Eden should talk to the doctor before she decides anything," said Abby to try to stop the argument and help calm Eden down. "She can't be placed unless a doctor recommends it or Rafe agrees to go anyway."

"Well, maybe we should call Greer and get more advice from her," Julia suggested. "Maybe she and her doctor friend can help us convince Rafe to check herself in somewhere."

Eden shook her head at the thought of getting Greer involved again. She knew Rafe said Greer wasn't a threat, but Eden didn't know if she wanted to test the truth of Rafe's words right now. "I don't know, Julia. I'm afraid to have Greer here again. She may not be as kind as she was before if Rafe starts telling her all the things she was saying in our session," she said as a new round of tears flowed from her. Bronte was calling her, so she wiped her tears then turned to take care of her. "It's okay, baby," she said and took her from her booster chair. "Let's go play now." She carried Bronte to the living room and sat down with her in her play area.

Abby followed her worried. "Eden, you didn't eat. Let me watch her, and you go get some food."

"I'm not hungry," she said softly watching Bronte play.

"Great, now both of you are going to stop eating?" Abby asked in frustration. She had been irate when she found out about the side effects of Rafe's meds. "This isn't good, Eden.

Look at Rafe and how wasted away she still looks. She has got to get some other help somehow. Now, if you stop eating too... What the hell good is starving yourself going to do? What's going to happen to Bronte if you both get sick?"

"I'm not going to stop eating, Abby," Eden said softly. "I'm just not hungry right now. I'm too upset to eat."

Julia and Flynn walked into the room and sat down with them.

"She's actually been eating better since starting her new medication," said Eden as she looked up at everyone from the floor. "I really thought things were starting to turn around for us. After today though—" She put her face in her hands. Bronte walked up to her, patted her head, and hugged her. Eden hugged Bronte back, pulled herself together, and smiled at the baby. "Thank you, Bronte," she said and gave her a kiss. "Can you make Mommy some food in your kitchen?" Bronte smiled and went to her toys to make some food for her mommy.

"Can you tell us what she said," asked Julia. "Maybe we can help you." She wondered if today would be the day Eden would be walking away from Rafe. Seeing her tears made Julia want to comfort Eden as she had in her dreams.

Eden's mobile phone rang. She jumped up and ran to the kitchen for her phone. "Hello," she said hopefully. "Jude, did you find her?"

"I found her," said Jude through the phone. "We should be back there in a few hours. We're just relaxing for a while right now."

"Where are you?" she asked nervously because the last time Rafe was with Jude, they ended up in Mexico.

"We're just across town," said Jude reassuringly. "I promised Rafe I wouldn't say exactly where we are right now. Just know she's safe, and we'll be back soon."

"Well, is she okay?" asked Eden worried about how Rafe left the session.

"She's fine," said Jude. "She just needs some time for herself then she'll be home. We might stop for drinks or something to eat," she said trying to sound casual.

Eden wasn't sure how to respond because, when Rafe left, she did not seem fine at all. "Jude, she had a mild break in session. Please, don't leave her anywhere," she said worriedly.

"Oh, well, she seems fine now," said Jude not wanting to worry Eden with how she had found Rafe. "Like I said, we'll see you in a few hours. I need to go, bye."

Putting the phone down, Eden turned and saw Julia looking at her with concern.

"A mild break?" asked Julia astounded. "Eden, what happened to her? I thought you said she just had some symptoms, not a break. Was it as bad as the one she had when I was here? I thought changing her meds was supposed to stop the things we thought were side effects."

"Dr. Cathcart helped her through it," said Eden shakily. "The medication helps her nightmares, but it won't stop her from feeling stress or stop any effects the stress has on her. She was very upset. She was more than upset, she was furious today."

"I think we had better talk about what happened," said Julia firmly. She was torn now between her concern for Rafe and her newfound affection for Eden. No matter how she thought Rafe was treating Eden, she did want to see Rafe get better. "We're your friends. We're like your family, and we want to help both of you. But we can't if you don't tell us exactly what's going on."

"I don't know if I can tell you!" said Eden angrily. "Everything I do just sets her off more. Getting you all involved again may make her angrier. She told me she didn't want you ganging up on her or to be involved. If I tell you things and you start trying to help, she'll know! Then she'll trust me even less than she already does—if that's even a possibility!"

"You can't let her tie your hands, Eden!" Julia argued. "She's always been very good at controlling people. She convinces you not to talk about something by making threats or making you swear on your life, or making you feel guilty. You can't fall into those traps when you deal with her."

"She hasn't made any threats, Julia. She's made promises! And she's already proven she'll make good on them!" said Eden angrily. "We're lucky we got her back from Mexico! I don't want her to take off again because there's no guarantee we'll get so lucky again! She isn't asking for anything unreasonable. She wants space and to not feel pressured. I think those are reasonable requests. I'm trying to give them to her! Can't you give them to her too? If you can't, you'll drive her away! If you can't, I need you to stay away from her so she'll want to stay!"

"I'm not trying to pressure her. I'm trying to get her the help she needs," said Julia seeing the situation had become too much for Eden. "If you can't make the right decisions, and she won't go voluntary, then we'll have to call Katheryn and get her and Letty to do another emergency placement."

"No," said Eden in frustration. "She won't go, and if you say anything, or threaten her, she'll take off again. If you do anything to make her leave, I'll never forgive you! Never!" she said desperately through her tears.

"What the hell is going on in here?" asked Abby as she interrupted their argument. "Bronte's getting upset. She can hear you yelling at each other. You two need to pull it together," she hissed.

"Maybe the best thing would be if you all left before she gets home," said Eden anxiously knowing her suggestion would make them angry. "If she sees you, she might get mad again, and if you argue with her, who knows what will happen."

Julia shook her head angrily. "You can't be serious," she scoffed. "You tell us she has had a mild break and is sicker, and you think we're just going to walk away? We need to be here to help you convince her to be placed. We need to be here in case she comes home and starts packing her things. We need to be here in case the next break is worse." She needed to be there in case Rafe pushed Eden to her breaking point, and she walked away. She knew she couldn't force Eden to leave.

Eden would have to do it on her own. But she was sure if they got Rafe placed, Eden would see how much better her life was without her. Then Julia could show Eden how much better off she would be if they were together.

24

TO KEEP HERSELF busy, Jude Atwood had been cleaning and doing paperwork while Susy took care of Rafe in one of the treatment rooms. She hoped having the massage, and other treatments would help Rafe feel better tonight like the other times she'd had them. She knew Eden and the others were probably worrying, but she thought it was best to let Rafe have the time to herself that she had asked to have. She also understood very well what it meant having Rafe trust her again, and she wanted to keep the renewed trust between them. Rafe had put herself in her hands before, and Jude felt like she let her down by calling Eden while they were in Mexico. She didn't want to put the trust between them to the test again, especially considering the shape she had found Rafe in out on the railroad tracks.

Thinking about Rafe walking in a daze along the railroad tracks was upsetting. Jude couldn't help thinking about what could have happened to Rafe if she hadn't found her. Rafe could have been a victim of some bad elements hanging around the tracks or hit by a train or who knows what. Jude shook the thoughts from her head and took consolation in the fact she found her before anything bad happened. She would have to get Flynn to help get Rafe's car and hopefully nothing would happen to it overnight.

Susy came out of the back and found Jude folding blankets. "Hey," she said quietly. "She's taking her time getting up and dressed. She had a small dizzy spell in the sauna after I gave her a stress relief salt scrub, but I think she's okay now. What happened to her?"

"She had a very hard day," said Jude softly. "I think she had to talk about some hard things and it triggered her PTSD. I just thought relaxing here would be better for her than anything else. Thanks for staying."

"It's no problem," said Susy with an easy smile. "She was very tense and upset for a while, so I did a few extra treatments to help her relax. If she complains, you can just bill the expense to me."

"Oh, no," said Jude. "I don't think she'll complain, and I did tell you to take care of her, so whatever you did is fine. She always asks for you, so I think she trusts you to make the right call on treatments."

Susy picked up a blanket to help Jude fold. "She's lucky she has you as such a great friend," she said as she folded.

"No," said Jude, "I'm lucky just as much, if not more. She's the one who got me the grant for my art classes and is paying for my art supplies. She's one of the only people in my life who has believed in me and followed through with their promises. I don't know if she even realizes how much her being my friend means to me." Jude gave a small laugh. "She even feeds me at least once a month. When everything fell apart after Chloe left, Rafe was the one who made sure I was okay and brought me beer and food all the time. She even tried to get me to drink chamomile tea." Jude laughed at the memory. "But I couldn't drink it without a lot of sugar, so we switched to beer. She even talked to me about rebuilding and implementing all the ideas I had for the business Chloe never wanted to do."

"Oh, I see," said Susy thoughtfully then chuckled. "Now I know the reason—when we get a new therapist, Chloe comes by and tries to figure out your services menu when you're not here."

"Well, I know she doesn't come over to make peace," said Jude with a smirk and a sigh. "I just hope she doesn't start trying to steal customers again."

"I wouldn't worry," said Susy confidently. "I don't think she can replicate what you've done here. She can buy all the equipment, but you have the vision, and you have people with the right skills and loyalty to your vision."

"Thank you," said Jude as she looked at Susy with a true appreciation for her words. She heard the soft chime telling her someone had walked through the treatment threshold to the lobby. "Let's go see Rafe." They made their way from the laundry area to the waiting room. "How are you feeling?" she asked Rafe.

Rafe smiled half-heartedly at Jude and Susy. "I'm good," she said softly. "You want to get something to eat with me?"

"Sure," said Jude. She was relieved. Although Rafe still looked a bit rough, she did look much more like her old self. "Susy, can you lock up?"

"Absolutely." Susy turned to Rafe with a smile. "Remember, you need to drink lots of water after your treatments. Meaning, go easy on the alcohol if you plan to have a drink with dinner."

"Got it," said Rafe returning Susy's smile with a small one of her own. She nodded to Jude then walked out the door.

"See ya later," said Jude and followed Rafe outside.

"Do you remember where I parked my car?" Rafe asked as she looked around the parking lot.

"You rode with me," said Jude as she motioned to her Jeep. Worry shot through her because Rafe didn't remember abandoning her car. "I'll take you wherever you need to go." After opening the door for Rafe, she ran around the Jeep and climbed in. "So, where do you want to eat?" she asked as she started the car.

"Just take me somewhere," said Rafe softly.

Jude gave a quick nod then drove her to a small bar and grill she sometimes frequented after work. They ordered food and beer along with the water Susy told Rafe she should be drinking. The music was a little loud, but Rafe didn't seem to mind. Jude sat silently and watched Rafe as she watched the people around them talk and mingle. The food finally came, and they ate in silence. Jude noted Rafe didn't eat much, but she drank her water and her beer. Rafe ordered another beer then spent the next hour drinking more beers and talking every once in a while about insignificant things like the people in the bar and the music.

"Maybe we should take off now," suggested Jude. "Eden might be getting worried. It's getting late."

Rafe looked up at her and sighed. "I guess," she said without enthusiasm. "I was hoping I'd be a little drunker than I am so I could just fall asleep when I get home. I don't think I can take talking about things again tonight. Maybe I should order something stronger."

"You don't have to get drunk to keep from talking," Jude assured her. "You can go to your room, and I'll tell everyone you need to go right to bed."

Rafe's mouth twisted as she caught the slip Jude made about everyone waiting at her house. She knew Jude would try, but she doubted she could keep Eden out of her room. She didn't have the luxury of privacy anymore it seemed. The rule about keeping her bedroom door unlocked had turned into an invitation for Eden to come inside whenever she wanted. "Okay," said Rafe with a shrug knowing she had to go home sometime, so it might as well be now.

As they drove toward home, Jude could see Rafe was getting nervous and fidgety. It was plain Rafe was worrying about confronting Eden again. "Are you gonna be okay?" Jude asked as Rafe's distress continued to get worse.

"I think so," said Rafe as a bead of sweat appeared on her head. "Maybe not," she said, her heart beating frantically. "Can you stop the car? I need to get out. I need to get out," she said harshly as Jude hadn't slowed down.

"Okay," said Jude. She pulled over, and Rafe jumped out of the Jeep almost before it had stopped. Then Rafe began to walk down the street. Jude cut the ignition, got out of the Jeep, and followed Rafe. "Where are you going?" she asked as she caught up with her. "It's too far to walk from here."

"I know," she said shakily. "I just had this feeling I should get out. I don't know if I can go back," she said and put her hand to her head and fell dizzily against a building wall. "I don't know what I'm doing anymore. I've been trying not to think about anything, but it's just impossible. Maybe we can go to another bar."

Jude's heart jumped as Rafe wavered again and was relieved when she caught herself. "You can go back," said Jude reassuringly. "Come on," she encouraged as she took her arm to steer her back to the Jeep. "You don't have to know what you're doing today. If you want, maybe we can have a drink at your house out by the pool. You always have the good beer there anyway," she said, coaxing her. "Plus, it's much cheaper to drink at home, and safer."

"She'll just follow us," said Rafe. "I don't know why she wants to be around me." She looked feverishly at Jude as she got in the car. "The girls you break up with who think you hurt them don't seem to ever come back around. Why can't Eden be like them? Just go away, so I don't have to see her pain."

Jude shook her head sadly. "Those girls didn't love me the way Eden loves you," she said thoughtfully. "I think if they had loved me the way Eden loves you, I'd have a hard time letting go too. If they really loved me, I wouldn't have to let go, just like you don't have to let go of Eden. They all let go of me, so there was really nothing I ever had to do. When they let go, I guess it was easier for me to move on too."

Rafe considered Jude's words and knew she was right. She didn't have to let go of Eden. Eden was the one who had to let go. "Okay," she said. "Take me home."

25

WATCHING HER WORLD slowly crumble around her for the past week, Eden Kingsley felt unbalanced and unsure of anything after the last therapy session she and Rafe had with Cathcart. Last week, after Rafe had walked out of the session, Jude had brought Rafe home. They came in the back gate and leaving Rafe outside, Jude came inside to tell them they were going to hang out by the pool and didn't want company. Jude insisted Rafe needed more time and had only agreed to come home if she was left alone. Julia got angry but finally left, and Flynn went to find one of his friends so he could get Rafe's car. Abby stayed for a while but had to leave not long after.

Jude came inside several times for drinks to take out to Rafe, telling Eden each time not to worry. But she worried anyway. Eden could do nothing but go to her room and lay awake until she heard Jude help Rafe into her room. When she went to talk to Jude, she would only say Rafe was fine and to just let her rest. To Eden, it was clear Rafe wasn't fine, and she was so drunk she could barely walk. Eden went to bed unhappy and terrified about what seemed to be happening.

All week, Rafe had been kind but distant. It was unnerving to Eden how Rafe went from being so loving and playful before the therapy sessions started to almost a stranger again. She worried Rafe wouldn't show up today. This morning, Rafe had gravely reminded her not to tell her secrets again, and Eden reassured her she would keep the secrets about her father and Maria. Afterward, Rafe left the house without telling Eden where she was going or even if she would show up to the doctor's appointment.

As she pulled into the parking lot, Eden spotted Rafe's car and a wave of relief cut through her anxiety at knowing at least one fear hadn't happened.

Eden walked nervously into the waiting room where Rafe was sitting in one of the chairs. Another wave of relief ran over her for the fact Rafe looked like she was calm. She hoped Dr. Cathcart would be able to keep things under control today.

She also hoped he had done what he promised in transcribing the last session. Then they could work through everything Rafe was so angry about and not bring on the kind of stress it had caused last week.

She knew it would be hard to work through things because it had taken her a long time to work through her anger with Rafe. But she had worked through it, and she desperately hoped the therapy could help Rafe too so they could be happy together again.

She walked up to Rafe nervously. "Hi," she said softly.

Rafe looked up at Eden and could see she was nervous. She knew Eden was still upset about last week and about how things had been tense at home all week. "Hi," Rafe answered softly and fought the familiar feeling of wanting to walk away. She had done her best all week to do damage control, but the best she could do was to put distance between them. Eden never confronted her about anything, so Rafe was sure Eden was saving up her anger for the therapy session.

The office door opened and Dr. Cathcart came out. "Eden, Rafe, come in," he said softly.

Rafe observed his pleasant yet clinical smile with a frown and followed him into the office, wondering if he would look at her again with pity or if he would be objective like he was supposed to be. She immediately took the same chair she had taken last week and waited for Eden and the doctor to sit down. Neither commented about her choice of chair. The doctor went to his desk and picked up a folder, bringing it back and sitting in the remaining chair.

"What's in the file?" Rafe asked as she nodded toward what he was holding in his hand. So far, every file someone pulled out had been bad news, so she suspected this would be the same.

Cathcart scanned the file then looked up at Rafe. "Last week, I know was hard on both of you," he began, "so I've put together a plan to talk about everything brought up last week in an organized way. The plan is not rigid, so if you feel you need to talk about certain things or if there is something you're not ready to talk about, we can be flexible. Also, some items or issues may fall under more than one category, and it's okay if you think something should be categorized differently or should be added or removed." Cathcart looked over the file. "I think the biggest issue, though they are all important, is the issue of Rafe's feeling of abandonment by you Eden."

Eden looked up in surprise at Dr. Cathcart. "Abandoned?"

"Yes, she seems to have had it for a long time." Cathcart nodded to her then turned to Rafe. "Last session, you spoke the most about Eden leaving you and the pain it caused you. How many times did she leave you? Twice, wasn't it?"

Rafe glared at him with a furrowed brow. "No, it wasn't twice," she said and sighed in frustration because Eden was already getting everyone on her side.

"How many times was it?" asked Cathcart wondering where he counted wrong.

"Five, maybe six," said Rafe flatly.

"What?" Eden blurted in dismay. "I didn't leave you six times. Rafe, I didn't."

Cathcart watched as Rafe scowled at Eden then looked away from her. "Can you tell Eden why you think she left you so many times?"

"Maybe you should ask her to figure it out," said Rafe. "Why do I have to always explain things, and she just gets to sit there and play all innocent?"

"Okay," said Cathcart. "Eden, can you think of five or six times when it could have been viewed by Rafe as you leaving her or abandoning her?"

Eden shook her head at a loss for what to say. "I—" she started and looked shakily at Rafe who would not look at her. "I left after," she paused, "after she cheated on me." She saw Rafe stiffen but stay in control. "I left when I moved out with Jake," she said and swallowed hard. "I haven't left since I moved back in. I don't know." She paused and thought about everything. "Maybe she felt abandoned when I didn't stand up for her when it came to Bronte. I really don't know what else, Rafe."

"Do those things sound right?" Cathcart asked Rafe.

"She's right, it's seven now," said Rafe.

"Seven?" Eden gasped. "No!" She shook her head in denial.

"Help her, Rafe," said Cathcart. "You need to tell her how you're feeling so she can understand why you're hurting."

"Right," scoffed Rafe. "I have to talk to her, but she doesn't have to tell me anything. She doesn't have to think about what she's done to me. As a matter of fact, she doesn't have to think about me at all."

"I think about you all the time," said Eden softly. "I never stop thinking about you."

"Except when you abandon me or leave me," said Rafe scathingly.

Eden put her face in her hands and sobbed, and Cathcart sighed.

"Rafe, you and Eden are here to help each other, not hurt each other more," said Cathcart. "Help her understand what things you feel she did to abandon you. Help yourself by allowing her to understand what you're talking about so she can see things from your point of view."

As Eden cried into her hands, Rafe fought back any sympathy daring to move inside her. "My point of view," Rafe said softly, "like it even matters. Fine," she grumbled. "The three things she already said plus she stopped talking to me, and talked to strangers instead, she had an online affair, before my fuck up too, by the way. Go figure." She gave a bitter laugh. "She left me alone to take care of everything by myself after my father's funeral. She didn't tell me about the insemination or the pregnancy. She started her affair with Jake before she even left my house or me. I guess it was your payback for New York, after all." She paused seeing Eden's wide eyes then Eden looked away guiltily. "She moved in with Jake without telling me she was going. I had to find out when I walked into an empty house. When she decided to come back to me, she didn't tell me she was still talking to Jake, and she lied to me about what was happening." She stopped and scowled at Cathcart. "Maybe there are a lot more things making me feel abandoned than I thought."

"Okay," acknowledged Cathcart. He nodded as he made notes while Eden clasped her hands together anxiously. "A few of those things Eden has addressed, and we can go over them again later, but based on the conversation from last week, let's discuss Eden's affair with Jake and her moving in with him." He addressed Eden. "This will also include the feelings you were having leading you to consider the possibility you should be in a relationship with a man and the anger you were dealing with over the affair Rafe had in New York." Cathcart was surprised by Rafe as she stood from her chair and began pacing the room. "Rafe, is there something on your mind you need to say?"

"No," Rafe said shortly and stood by the window.

Eden watched Rafe as she stood across the room. She tore her eyes away to look at Cathcart who nodded his head indicating she should talk.

Eden cleared her throat. "Last time," she said quietly and stopped to calm herself. "Last session, you said you thought you should have left for Italy after I moved out," she paused to see if Rafe would react, but she stood silently. "I'm glad you stayed, Rafe," said Eden and Rafe looked over at her with liquid eyes full of pain. "I didn't know it at the time, but I was making a huge mistake when it came to Jake. So many things were happening, and I thought I had to leave, I thought you would want me to move out after I, we," she couldn't say after she started having sex with Jake. Cathcart encouraged her to continue, so she took a breath. "After I was having sex with him," she said regretfully and waited for Rafe's reaction.

She watched as Rafe just lowered her head but said nothing, so she went on. "You told me to figure things out, and I thought I was." She waited to see if Rafe would look at her again. "You're right, I should have waited to get into a relationship with him, or anyone until I moved out and you knew exactly what was happening with us. But at the time, I really didn't know our relationship was being systematically infiltrated by Jake and the Stewards. I was convinced it was what I wanted, and I may not have talked to you after I left, but I did think about you."

She wished Rafe would react or look at her again, but she stood silently. "It was one of the reasons Jake couldn't convince me to go with him further than he did. My feelings about you kept me close, and he couldn't convince me to move away from you. The more he pushed me, the more I thought about you. Remember, I told you I kept your letter, and how it helped me. I know you think I was using it for myself, but I know having a piece of you, even in the form of a letter, so close saved Bronte and me."

Eden desperately wanted Cathcart to help or change the subject, but he just nodded for her to continue. She wiped her tears away. "If you had left and had gone to Italy, I don't know where I'd be now, where Bronte would be now. I do realize you staying is what saved us, Rafe, and I'm sorry the things I did hurt you. I think about everything, and I feel sick. I feel sick over the fact Jake and his group were able to convince me to do something I knew deep down was wrong. I feel sick I put my daughter in danger, and yes, I feel sick about not telling you what was happening as soon as I found out. But I can't go back in time and change things," she said and looked from Rafe to Cathcart.

She hesitated, and when they remained silent, she continued. "I was trying to do what I thought was best, what I thought was right at the time. I can see now I did a lot of things wrong, and I hurt you with my mistakes. I just hope you can see I'm trying to tell you I was wrong, and I want to try to fix things with us. I want you to stay with Bronte and me," she declared, hoping Rafe would at least look at her.

She held her hands together tightly to control her anxiety. She just needed Rafe to understand and stay with her. "I want you to see when I told you those things when I said we were a family and we belonged together, it was real. It was the real and true feelings inside me buried for a while by my anxiety and anger, and the confusing feelings I was having about needing to be in a relationship with a man or something different."

Eden did not know why Rafe wasn't responding. Cathcart was watching Rafe closely. Eden swallowed the knot in her throat and continued. "We found our way back to each other because we have a connection, a heart connection that we shouldn't fight. I realize it's a strained connection, but it hasn't been broken. I know it hasn't been broken because I can still feel it, and I don't want to let go of it." She stopped as Cathcart held up his hand signaling her to give Rafe time to respond.

"Rafe, can you tell us what you're thinking?" Cathcart asked firmly.

Fighting the sick feeling inside her at Eden's pathetic attempt to justify herself, Rafe turned to look at her. "You really just don't get it, do you?" she asked shaking her head. "You can divide all our problems up into all the categories you want, but I don't know if talking and making excuses will help anything. It's just all too fucked up, and I don't know if we can get the missing fundamental thing needed back to make us work again."

"This is what we're trying to work on," said Cathcart, "finding a common place to start and rebuilding your relationship. Tell us what you think is missing," he said encouragingly as Eden watched Rafe in misery.

"I've already told you," Rafe said in exasperation, "trust." Trying to control herself, she looked back at Eden. "I trusted you and now look at me," she said and opened her arms revealing what she felt she had become. "I'm so gun shy now, I don't know if I will ever be able to trust anyone again when it comes to love."

She looked away from Eden and thought of everything now lost because of her. "I was so lucky when Greer found me. Who knows if I'll ever find someone like her again? Someone who will take me in even though they know I'm damaged, yet love me anyway, and accept I can never give them all of me. She was someone who was honest and told me she needed more than I could give, but she still accepted what little I could give her and she let me feel her love, even though I probably didn't deserve all she gave me. I may never find someone else who knows being with me will be painful and will love me for just a little while despite the fact we would have to end things someday because I just can't give everything to her."

"Rafe," sobbed Eden, "you don't have to find anyone else. I love you. I'll never stop loving you. You can trust me," she said and broke down in tears.

"You have to stop saying you love me, Eden," said Rafe firmly. "Stop lying to yourself and to me."

"I'm not lying!" Eden cried angrily, "I'm not!"

"Eden," Cathcart said sympathetically, "Rafe told you last week she isn't ready for you to say how you feel to her right now. She knows how you feel." He looked up at Rafe. "Rafe, you may not be ready to hear about how Eden feels, but she shouldn't be punished by you for telling you her feelings. You also can't tell Eden her feelings for you are not true, just like Eden can't tell you how to feel about her. Let's agree neither of you will punish the other for how you feel right now."

"Right," said Rafe, "let's not ever punish Eden for anything. She has no fucking idea what punishment even is," she quipped. "She can take my slap on her wrist. I've been taking her punishment for years."

"I'm not punishing you, Rafe," Eden snapped back and tried to stare her down but couldn't hold against her icy blue-grey gaze and looked away.

"Let's take a step back," Cathcart suggested. "Let's take a moment and calm down."

26

DR. WILLIAM CATHCART waited as Eden sat back on the couch wiping her tears with a tissue, and Rafe paced around the room purposely not looking at Eden. He was glad Rafe had not gotten upset, but he was afraid she was verbally punishing Eden to keep herself from becoming angry. He also thought having Eden speak more this session was helping. It seemed like the less Rafe talked, the more control she was able to keep. The problem was, she had to talk sometime.

"Eden," he began, breaking the long-held silence, "let's go back now to when you left Rafe the first time, meaning after her infidelity. From what Rafe said last week, she feels like you're still punishing her for what happened in New York."

"I'm not," insisted Eden.

"But it feels like you are to Rafe," said Cathcart. "When we talked about it in your sessions, it was the cause of a lot of your anger. Are you sure it's not something still being used against her at times? She said it keeps coming up."

"I'm not punishing her," Eden repeated. "I know I've tried to talk to her about it a few times. I still don't really know what happened or why it happened." She turned to Rafe. "You tell me it wasn't my fault, and there was nothing I could have done, but there has to be a reason why it happened."

Eden looked pleadingly at Rafe. "I know Julia has brought it up and the other girls may have too. I never told Julia to talk to you about it or throw it in your face like she did. She did it on her own. She told me you won't even talk to her about it, and you just get angry. I already told you I was angry about it for a long time, but I'm not anymore. I told you I forgive you, and I have. I have," she repeated seeing Rafe frown at her words. She knew from her talks with Julia Rafe didn't believe the same way she did about forgiveness, but she couldn't help saying the words.

Cathcart watched Rafe cross her arms and turn away from Eden and made a note to go back to the previous subject of abandonment later so they could now move on to a discussion of trust. "Rafe," he said calmly, "Eden has told me several times you avoid talking to her about what was happening with you at the time of your infidelity. This is one of those trust issues you want to work on. Eden can forgive you and still have trust issues. Maybe she needs to know what happened, and what you were going through, so she can trust you and then you can know she's telling the truth when she tells you she forgives you."

"I don't want you talking to Julia!" snapped Rafe angrily spinning toward Eden with her eyes blazing. "I told you I don't like her talking about me with you! What's she been telling you? I know you meet with her all the time! I want her to stay out of my life!"

"She just wants to help you," said Eden softly. "She said she thought there were things I needed to know so we could help you. She keeps telling me I need to grow up, and I'm trying, but I don't always know what she means."

"Fucking Julia!" yelled Rafe angrily. "She's probably saying you did the right thing trying to protect me with the whole Stewards thing, and you did the right thing when you left me, and you did the right thing when you locked me up in Mexico, and you need to leave me again and lock me away!" She yelled out at Eden furiously. "Now you listen to her! Now you just want to be with her all the time! She's suddenly your protector and who you go to for secrets and comfort! Fine! She can have you!" Rafe paced the room angrily.

Eden shook her head in denial. "Stop it, Rafe! You know it's not true!" She stopped herself when she realized she was yelling and softened her voice. "She's your friend," she continued. "She's worried about you. She wants you to get better and for us to be happy. She's trying to help and is just doing everything she can to help you even if it's wrong sometimes."

Cathcart waited for a sign Rafe had calmed. "Okay, it's good we know about this issue, and we'll discuss how to deal with your friends while you're dealing with your relationship issues. Let's go back to our original topic."

"I have a question first," said Rafe softly.

Eden looked away from Rafe's blazing eyes and nodded. "Okay," she said softly.

"It seems to me everything I do or say, or even think at times, causes you problems. Julia and Abby always tell me you walk on eggshells around me. So, my question is this. Where was all your anxiety when you were with Jake?" she asked and her anger grew with each question. "Where was your anger and fear after he tried to take Bronte? Where was it after he beat the shit out of you? Where was it when you almost died?" she asked heatedly. "Where was it!"

"It was there," said Eden shakily.

Cathcart cleared his throat, but Rafe did not move her angry gaze away from Eden. "Rafe, whether or not you could see Eden's anxiety doesn't mean it wasn't there."

"Really?" Rafe scoffed, eyeing Cathcart guardedly. "Was she in here telling you about Jake and all the things he was doing? Are you another person who knew more than I did about what was happening? If you knew, why didn't you call me or the police?"

"No," said Cathcart flatly. "Eden wasn't talking to me about the group Jake was with at the time." Cathcart was sure this was a ploy, so Rafe didn't have to speak about her infidelity. "This is not a place for judgment or blaming. It is a safe place to talk about how things in life are making you feel and to help the two of you understand each other."

"Well," said Rafe evenly, "I don't *understand* where her anxiety was when she was hiding things and lying to me while Jake was fucking with my life!" She turned to Eden and waited for her answer.

"It," Eden stammered, "it was there, but it was better when I was with you. It's always better when I'm with you," she confessed.

Rafe shook her head in disbelief. "No," she said softly. "You're always walking on eggshells around me, remember."

"You're right," said Eden. "I was walking on eggshells, but it was because I was keeping things from you and wanting to protect you. It wasn't because you did anything to me. It was what I was doing to myself."

"Back then maybe," said Rafe unable to hide her suspicion Eden was lying again. "But what about now? I'm still being told those things, so what else are you lying about and protecting me from?"

"Nothing. I'm not lying about anything," said Eden shakily as she saw the disbelief on Rafe's face. "I'm not protecting you," she said softly. "I just don't want anyone to upset you."

"Upset me?" Rafe laughed mockingly. "I think it's a little too late, don't you?" Unable to look at Eden, she turned and walked to the window again. She watched all the cars following the simple rules of the road and wished there were simple rules for her to follow about her life. She thought things were simple once, but now she knew just how wrong she had been.

"Let's move on," said Cathcart from his chair.

"Sure, why not?" snapped Rafe. "Let's let Eden get away with not answering another question and forget about anything she may have ever done wrong!"

"She answered your question," Cathcart reminded her. Rafe scoffed and crossed her arms as she looked out the window. "We were talking about trust and how Eden's trust in you was broken because of your infidelity," he continued and Rafe visibly tensed. "Can you tell us what happened?"

Rafe turned and saw the fear and anxiety in Eden's eyes and knew it was because she still wasn't over what had happened in New York. She would never live it down. It took everything in her to keep her anger from taking over her mind and flowing out into a rage at Eden and at Julia.

She paced for a while then went back over to the window and looked outside. The busy street below was distracting so she closed her eyes. She took a calming breath and tried to decide if she could tell them what had happened. She didn't know if she could or if she even wanted to talk about it. She felt sick thinking about everything that happened in New York then and coupling it with what she knew now. She put her hand to her head and tried to open her eyes, but they wouldn't respond.

Eden watched Rafe as she stood in front of the window and saw her body tense and her hand tremor as she put it to her head. She worried the tremor meant she was feeling too much stress and they should stop or change the subject.

She looked over at Cathcart who was also watching Rafe with interest. "Maybe we should talk about something else," Eden whispered to Cathcart, and he held his hand up to her indicating she should just wait.

Cathcart cleared his throat. "Rafe, why don't you come and sit down so you can relax? You can take all the time you need."

Rafe's eyes snapped open at the sound of Cathcart's voice, and the light streaming in made her eyes water. She wiped her eyes and took another shaky breath then turned and walked back over to her chair and sat down. She saw the pity in Eden's eyes, and she fought the urge to get up and leave again.

Rafe looked down and sighed. "Okay," she said softly and shook her head. "Okay, I see I'm still to blame for everything because of New York, so let's go over again what I did to you. You, and everyone else it seems, can't get through a fucking week without shoving my face in it," she said evenly. "So, do you really want to know what happened?" she asked and looked up at Eden with a frown.

She watched Eden shift uncomfortably on the couch. "Do you need to know what happened to help you with your precious feelings?" she asked as she looked intensely into Eden's eyes while her own eyes burned with the fever of anger. "Okay, no problem," she said and looked away from Eden. "I flew to New York with the woman who was supposed to love me, but she had stopped, though I didn't know it yet."

She looked back at Eden and saw she was about to protest so Rafe continued before Eden could lie. "I was dealing with losing my father, the man who was my lifeline in getting through all the things from when I was young, and who was my business partner, and my only connection to my mother. Suddenly, the one person—" she stopped and shook her head, "the one person left in my life I thought I could depend on." She paused a moment. "Instead of helping me get through it all, she left me there—alone."

She could feel her temper flame and was happy it was there to hide the pain in her heart. "I dealt with all the people there who thought they knew my father, alone. I listened to them talk like they were his best friend to my face. Then they would stop talking when they noticed I was there and caught them while they cursed him and were saying how happy they were he was dead." She put a shaking hand to her head reining back her anger at those people and the situation. "I made sure his body was sent to the crematorium, alone. I sorted through all his things in his office, alone. I had to go through his apartment." She stopped and looked up at Eden with pain blazing in her eyes. "So," she said softly, "do you want to know what was in his bedroom?"

She watched as Eden glanced at Cathcart then back and gave a small nod.

"Okay," said Rafe shakily. "It was my mother's paint and easel box." She gave a manic laugh. "And what did I find sitting on the easel, you might ask? It was the last painting she was working on," she said in almost a whisper. She got up from the chair trying to make the picture in her mind go away. "Guess who the subject was," she demanded feverishly when she was standing in front of Eden.

Eden looked up at her at a loss.

Rafe leaned over and whispered shakily in her ear so Cathcart could not hear her. "It was Maria." She stood up and paced the room, agitated, wishing the room were bigger, and fighting the urge again to walk out the door.

Eden could only watch with worry while Rafe paced and was presenting all the signs she was under stress with her shaking hand, holding her head or putting her hand to her chest, sweating, and the inability to sit still. She wasn't sure if she should say anything or not since she had promised Rafe that she wouldn't talk to anyone about Maria, the girl who was Rafe's first kiss. She could see Cathcart watching Rafe and knew he might ask about it later. She didn't know what to do if he asked her. If she told him, and Rafe got any more upset, she had no doubt things could get worse.

Rafe went back to the chair, sat down, and then leaned forward, looking at Eden intently. "She was making the painting in the last days of her life," she said in misery. "Why did he put the painting there?" she asked as if Eden might know the answer, but knowing she would not. "He had to know I'd find it! He knew," she said, and tears broke free from her eyes. "I know he knew! He wanted to remind me of what I did and make sure I never forgot!" she said in anguish. "He wanted to make sure I was still being punished even after he died!"

Rafe stood up and paced the room again, not paying attention where she was walking. She bumped into the corner of Cathcart's desk and leaned on its top until the pain in her leg stopped. "The woman who was with me to get the apartment listed, Lauren," Rafe started through clenched teeth, "she was the best person for the job. She was smart, aggressive, and beautiful. I knew right away that I should hire her. I remember she came over to the apartment, and she had a kind of copper-colored lipstick." Rafe released a tormented laugh and shook her head from side to side. "I don't know why I remember her lipstick. Maybe it was because it contrasted so well against her smooth black skin and brought out the lighter tones in her dark eyes. She was wearing this," Rafe hesitated and swallowed, "this dark suit over a bright white shirt with ruffles bursting from her throat and wrists. She was striking, now that I think about it. Striking," she said softly.

Rafe limped for a couple of steps then, as the pain eased, and continued to pace and talk. "We had to decide what would stay for staging and what would go to storage. I hadn't been in the apartment for years except for short visits, so I was overwhelmed and glad she was willing to help me. She went somewhere, I think it was the kitchen, and I," she paused, "I went into my father's room."

Rafe sat down again, rubbing her leg, with eyes glazed with memory. "She found me there in his room on my knees," she said heavily then leaned over and put her head in her hands. "She said she tried to call you from my phone, but you never answered." She looked up at Eden. "You never even called me back!"

Eden winced at her words because she knew Rafe was right. She had been going through issues herself and didn't call Rafe back because she didn't want to talk with her or get into an argument about her going home.

Rafe got up, began pacing again as she rubbed her head and put her hand to her chest, trying to relieve the pain developing. "Lauren, she," Rafe hesitated, "she helped me up off the floor and took me into my old room and tried to console me, to help me."

She sat down again and tried to look at Eden but couldn't do it, so she found Cathcart's face instead. She took in his wide dark brown eyes against his tanned skin and sun-lightened hair. She looked down at the notepad in his lap, and the pen in his hand then looked back into his face, noting it finally held the proper impassive clinical expression it was supposed to have. It was comforting. It was much better than seeing pity in his eyes. "I really don't know if I was in control of what happened or not." She shook her head trying to remember while fighting the pain ebbing in her head. "I remember I was crying. I remember her soft, delicate, black hands flowing over me, covering me with warmth, and her beautiful dark face and hair filled my vision and then," she paused and looked up at the ceiling, "and then—just darkness. I don't remember what happened."

She stood quickly and began pacing again with a slight limp. "I don't remember, I don't remember, I don't remember!" she said pouring more anger into each utterance as she made her way across the room and back.

She stood behind her chair fighting to pull memories up from the darkness. "I just remember seeing her dark hands, or maybe they were my hands, I'm not sure. The next thing I knew I was alone again, and I cried then too! You think I was just there fucking her and laughing at you, but it's just not how it was!" she yelled defiantly. "I know, I know it's still no excuse, but it's what happened. Then, when you still didn't call me back, someone came to see me. I think it was her. She came and, she stayed, and she took me out of the house to help me get into a better place. She helped me pretend I was happy as we walked to places I used to go when I was young and talked about people I used to know." Rafe took a shuddering breath trying to remember if she just talked about those people or if she had actually talked to them. Sometimes they seemed so real, but she wasn't sure how it could be true after all these years.

She moved around to the front of the chair and sat down. "I know it was completely my fault because I lost control," she said hoarsely then cleared her throat, "and I've been taking the punishment you obviously think I deserve," she said in distress and wiped away the beads of sweat on her forehead. "I came home, and I told you the truth when you confronted me. I could have lied. Your evidence was circumstantial at best. But I knew what I had done, and I couldn't bring myself to lie to you. I apologized in every way I could think of, but you left me, and I couldn't blame you for it," she said and wiped a tear from Eden's face. "I understand why you had to leave and why you keep punishing me. I betrayed you," she whispered heavily as she looked feverishly at Eden.

Rafe sat back in her chair and looked up at the ceiling again. She couldn't look at Eden knowing there was pain etched across her face—pain Rafe knew she had caused. "After you left, I had to go back to New York and deal with the rest of my father's affairs. Everyone said I went to be with her again. I didn't deny it, because you were gone, and nothing mattered anymore."

She tried once more to look at Eden but couldn't, so she found Cathcart again. "I think maybe the girl woke something up in me I wasn't feeling with Eden. I imagine it felt good at the time to have someone want me again and have someone there to help me through the grief I was feeling about Papa. She probably even talked dirty to me, told me I was great or just talk to me like Eden used to do when she loved me."

Eden looked up to say she loved her but Cathcart signaled her not to interrupt. She fought her tears as Rafe walked across the room, looked out the window, and continued.

"There was really no excuse for what I did except ego, maybe. Jake told me I have a problem with my ego." Rafe laughed as she wiped her hands over her face, regretful that Jake could know anything real about her.

"But maybe it was more like a break from reality. The reality of my papa being gone and Eden not wanting me anymore," said Rafe as she moved around the room. "We both knew it was an affair, and if she would have been there waiting for me, like Abby and the others said, I would have told her I had to stop. I would have told her I had to go home, I needed to get Eden back, and I had to get my life back."

She walked to the mini-refrigerator, got a bottle of water out, and took a sip. "She had almost everything done when I got there, so I was alone again to finish packing the last of Papa's things and take care of all his other business." She stood in front of Cathcart. "I'm not sure I could have gotten through it all without Lauren. Maybe I could have if Eden had stayed, I don't know. I never saw her in person again. I didn't want to see her. I wanted Eden back."

She looked down at her water bottle then over at Eden and saw her looking back at her with tears running down her cheeks. Eden looked just like she did on the day she confessed to the affair. "I just couldn't stop thinking about you, so I came home and tried to apologize again, but you wouldn't even talk to me. I understand. I do," she said as her hand shook. "I hurt you, and you didn't want me in your life anymore. You were completely justified, so after you didn't answer my calls or want to see me, I left you alone, because I knew I had caused my own pain. You deserve to be with someone who won't hurt you."

Rafe looked away and took a breath then walked over and sat her water bottle on the desk. "But now, I don't understand why it mattered, because you stopped loving me long before my father died," she said softly ignoring Eden's attempt to deny the truth. She walked across the room to the door. "I can't do this anymore," she said and put her hand to her head and tried to press away the pain. Finally, with eyes glazed in pain, she found Eden's face again. "I can't live with any more punishment. I understand why you have to do it, but I just can't take it anymore."

"I'm not punishing you, Rafe," said Eden through her tears. "I'm not," she sobbed.

Rafe closed her eyes to the pain in her head. When she opened her eyes again, she could see Eden looking at her with her wide brown eyes, the golden specks magnified by the tears flowing down her face. She blinked her eyes quickly as bruises formed on Eden's face and a dark form solidified beside her. Death put his hand on Eden's shoulder and flashed an arrogant smile.

"*Te vedo,*"[7] she whispered to the dark form. She knew the only way to stop him was to get away from him and from Eden. She had to make Eden understand. She had to let her go.

"Look at me! Look at me!" Rafe cried out and opened her hands to Eden. "What do you see? You see something to be pitied and something to be fixed, and not someone you love! So let me go!" she pleaded. "Just let me go! I have nothing left

---

[7] I see you,

inside me! I have no more room inside me to take anything. I'm gorged to the point of exploding with pain and heartache and loss, and it's all my own doing. I know you just can't understand, and it's okay because it's really not all about you. I know I'm *Caïna,* and I have to pay the price! I'm paying more than you know!"

Rafe's anger flared and her voice shook with pain. "Everyone tells me you're walking on eggshells with me," she said in a menacing growl. "Well, I'm walking on paper thin ice, and it's already cracked beneath my feet. I can feel the cold water around my chest, and it's moving upward. With every thought about what happened, and every ounce of punishment you heap on me, I sink deeper and deeper, until sometimes, I feel like maybe the right thing to do is give up, just let myself sink into the cold water and accept there is nothing left of this relationship before I sink so far that it's too late. Just let it all go and try to start over somewhere far away where I can just stop thinking about you and everything else!"

Before Eden could respond, Rafe continued. "I'm done, and the world I'm looking at has no more light. I see no future, and I see no hope, and mostly, I see no love. I should never have even thought I could have it in the first place." She met Cathcart's eyes with her own filled with desperation. "You have to help her, help her let me go," she said then flung open the door and walked out slamming the door behind her.

"Rafe," Eden yelled frantically as she jumped off the couch to follow her.

Cathcart caught Eden before she could run out. "Eden, let her go. Give her some space. I think you and I need to talk about what just happened and about her other therapist."

"What?" Eden asked in shock. "Why? I can't let her leave!" she said in a panic. "She's upset again! What if she takes off? I need to make sure she stays!"

All the things Julia had been worried about and the things Rafe told her ran through her mind. The asking about money and saying she wanted to go to Italy. She had no idea what Rafe did while she was at home. For all she knew she had already bought tickets and packed her bags. She pulled away from Cathcart.

"I have to find her! There is no way in hell you're going to talk me into letting her go!"

"That's not what I want to talk about," Cathcart reassured her as he blocked the door. "Eden, she just told us she had an emotional blackout, and it happened well before the event at the Conservatory."

He could see Eden didn't understand the significance. "This tells me her PTSD started long before the event at the school and, possibly, the school event added to the stress she already had, and it has sent her spiraling. Her therapist needs to know this, and Rafe needs to be reassessed. For some reason, seeing the painting in her father's room was a stressor event–and we need to know why. She could be having more blackouts we don't know about when she's exposed to stressors."

Eden stared at him as her mind reeled at the thought that Rafe might be driving and having blackouts. She knew Rafe's reaction to the painting had something to do with Rafe's mother and Maria, but she didn't know what, and she was afraid to say anything to Cathcart.

She swore to keep Rafe's secret, and now she was angry with herself and with Rafe. Julia was right. Now someone needed to know what Rafe told her and her hands were tied with the threat of Rafe leaving. And according to Julia, Rafe wouldn't hesitate to do what she had promised. Rafe would leave and never come back if she said anything.

"Please," she said desperately, "I have to go. I have to find her and make sure she's okay." She tried to brush past him, but he held her firmly.

"Eden, I need you to listen," said Cathcart firmly. "If you want to help her, there are some things you need to know."

Eden could feel her heart beating hard in her chest and her anxiety over Rafe building. She just wanted to run after her and find her. "What?" she asked frantically. "What do I need to know? I have to find her!"

Cathcart led her back to the couch and sat down with her. "Breathe," he said to calm her. "I need you to listen and then you can go find her. This is important."

"Okay," Eden said and took a breath to calm herself. "Okay," she repeated wanting him to hurry and tell her so she could go.

"First, when I was transcribing the conversation from last week, I had her Italian outburst translated. Let me read you what she said." He opened the file to read Rafe's words, "She said 'But I try to control my feelings and understand my feelings. I can't have feelings and follow them blindly.'" He looked up, making sure Eden was listening. "But this last thing was most concerning. She said 'Death requires a choice, and I can't hold off much longer,' and then she went to her knees."

"Death?" said Eden and began to tremble.

Cathcart nodded. "I was very concerned, so I contacted her therapist. Did you know she stopped going? She stopped over a month ago."

"She," Eden choked, "she told me she wouldn't quit. She told me she wanted to quit, but I told her she needed to go. I told her I couldn't go to Italy with her if I didn't know she loved me."

"Based on her behavior, she has most likely stopped taking her medications too," said Cathcart gravely. "We have to get her back on them as soon as possible. This may also mean she's having disturbing dreams again."

"Oh, my god," Eden cried and put her face in her hands. "What's happening?" she sobbed. "Rafe had a dream I gave Bronte to death, and now she is saying death needs a choice. What does it mean?"

"It means she needs to be reassessed," said Cathcart firmly. "I don't know if she may become violent and harm herself or you and Bronte, but I don't think we can take the chance. You need to be on alert until we can get her in and reassessed."

"She doesn't want to go back into a hospital," said Eden. "You saw her reaction."

"It doesn't mean she'll have to be in a hospital," Cathcart assured her. "It may just mean she'll be given mandated therapy and we need to get her on some medication. I'll get everything arranged and let you know as soon as I can set up the reassessment. You can tell her it's just another session, and it will be, so you won't be lying. We'll just have different goals."

Please," she said shakily as she got up and went to the door, "I have to go find her! We can't do anything for her if she decides to take off and we can't find her or something happens to her!" She dashed out the door then ran down the hall to find Rafe.

27

EDEN KINGSLEY RUSHED outside to the doctors' office parking lot and found Rafe's car gone. In case Rafe didn't go home, Eden called everyone she could think of to look for her. When she was halfway home, Jude called and told her Rafe's car had pulled into the driveway, but when she tried knocking, Rafe wasn't answering the door. Since Jude no longer had a key, she couldn't get into the house. By the time Eden got home, everyone had gathered on the front steps, waiting for her. Abby rushed over to the car and Eden barely got out before Abby was confronting her.

"What the hell is going on? Why's this happening again?" asked Abby frantically.

"I have to make sure she's okay," said Eden desperately as she pushed past Abby and made her way to the house.

"Eden," Abby called out in frustration as she went after her. "We came as fast as we could. Letty said she'd be here as soon as she can get away. I told her we'd call and tell her what was happening."

"I checked, and all the doors are locked," said Jude as Eden made it to the front door. "I've knocked a bunch of times."

"It's okay," said Eden and hoped it was true. She looked over at Julia, feeling guilty, and then looked away quickly because she had done what she told her not to do—made a promise on her life to Rafe. Now her hands were tied. "She got upset in therapy again," was all Eden could say as she unlocked the door. "You guys should stay out here until I see how she's doing. I don't want her to feel like we're ganging up on her."

"One of us should come with you in case there's a problem," said Julia as she followed Eden inside and stopping in the hallway outside Rafe's bedroom door. "I'll just be here," she said. "If you need me, call out."

"Okay," said Eden as she let out a ragged breath. She went to Rafe's bedroom door, put her hand on the doorknob, and then knocked. "Rafe, I'm coming in." She walked into the room and didn't see Rafe, so she went to the bathroom and opened the door. She found Rafe kneeling and retching over the toilet.

"Rafe," she said and went to help her. "Rafe, I'm so sorry. Are you okay?"

Rafe pushed her away, got up shakily, and went to the sink where she leaned heavily as she got out her toothbrush and got it ready to brush her teeth. "I'm fine," she choked out. "Just leave me alone," she said and began brushing her teeth quickly.

As Eden watched Rafe, it was clear she wasn't okay. She had dark circles around her eyes, her face was pale and drawn, her clothes were sweat-soaked, and she was shaking slightly.

"Babe, I'm so glad you made it home okay. I was so worried."

After taking her toothbrush out of her mouth, Rafe spit into the sink and then rinsed her mouth out. "Please, just leave me alone," she said shakily as she wiped off her mouth. "I need to take a shower." She went to the shower and turned it on. Turning, she saw Eden still looking at her. "I don't need help taking a shower," she said irritably and began to strip down.

"Okay," said Eden softly as she watched Rafe take her clothes off. She saw a bruise had already formed on her leg from walking into the doctors' desk. Rafe got into the shower, and Eden left quietly, closing the bathroom door behind her.

Julia saw Eden come out of Rafe's room looking worried. "Is she okay?"

"No," she said agitated, "no, Julia, she's not okay. She's not, and I don't know what to do," she cried and could not stop the tears.

"Come on," said Julia and led her into the living room where she sat her on the couch, fighting the urge to pull her close. "Let me get the others."

Julia came back in, leading Jude, Abby, and Flynn, and they all sat down around Eden. Julia sat next to Eden and put her arm around her. "It's going to be all right," she said as she rubbed her back to help ease her anxiety. "We're all here, and we'll help however we can."

"What happened?" asked Abby sitting on the other side of Eden.

"We had our second therapy session together today, and it didn't go well again," confessed Eden as she wiped her tears with the tissue Julia gave her. "She walked out, and I panicked. I thought she was going to leave again or she was going to blackout and get hurt."

"Blackout?" Abby asked with concern.

"Well, she's still here," said Jude gently, uncomfortable with Eden crying. "That's a good thing."

"Yeah," said Flynn nodding his agreement.

"She told Dr. Cathcart he should help me let her go," Eden said shakily.

"What!" Abby screeched. "What the fuck? Why would she say that?"

"Obviously, she's not thinking clearly," said Julia. It looked to her like Rafe was pushing Eden away even harder.

"Obviously," Abby said with her typical snark. "Rafe would never say that if she were," she said remembering all of the things Rafe had done for Eden to show her how much she loved her. "She does love you, Eden. You have to hold on to that knowledge. It's just the crazy talking, not Rafe."

"Abby," Flynn chastised while the freckle-faced woman shrugged.

Julia took a breath and sat back, finally resolved in what she needed to say, and how to help both Eden and Rafe. "Eden, she needs to be placed again. I know you don't want to without her agreeing, but you and I both know she'll never agree." She saw the concern on everyone's faces. "You need to call Cathcart, as well as her doctor, and have them do a reassessment to get a recommendation for placement. Then we can either convince Rafe to get more help, or get Katheryn to help you and Letty place her again legally."

Eden was filled with guilt and anxiety. "She," Eden sobbed, "she took away Letty's power of attorney, and she quit her therapist," she revealed, flinching when she saw the shock and anger on Julia's face.

"Goddamn it, Rafe," Julia hissed and resisted the temptation to march into her room and strangle her. "When? When did she stop therapy and make those changes?"

"I don't know exactly," said Eden. "I think she changed her power of attorney as soon as she got home from Mexico. Dr. Cathcart says he found out yesterday that she quit her individual therapy over a month ago."

"Well," said Abby still reeling, "I just want to know what the hell you mean by blackouts. Is she passing out for no reason or is it because of her medication? What's happening to her?"

"No," said Eden as she put her hand on Abby's leg. "She isn't passing out for no reason or because of her medication." Everyone looked to her for an explanation as Eden ran her hands nervously through her hair. "She was talking about what happened in New York after her father's funeral. Based on what she said, Cathcart thinks she had an emotional blackout from the stress she was under." Eden wasn't sure if she could say more without telling Rafe's secret about Maria. "He thinks maybe her PTSD was there before what happened at the school," she confided in Julia. "Maybe it has to do with her mother," she said and stopped not wanting to reveal what Rafe had said about her death.

Julia went pale as she remembered what Rafe told her about her mother and her friend from Italy. She remembered the conversation with her father about some of the men who had PTSD he had dealt with in England. It made her wonder if the Rafe she knew when she was young if she had been suffering from PTSD and if it was the real reason she did some of the things she did back then.

Maybe Rafe wasn't the devil in angel robes and wings. Maybe she was just a scared kid fighting demons in her mind. It certainly explained a lot of Rafe's absences and the wild things she seemed to get herself into all the time.

She knew Rafe skipped school because not only had Julia witnessed her walking out, she sometimes joined Rafe. But there were times when Rafe was gone without explanation, and she always thought Rafe just skipped school a lot on her own or got suspended and chose not to tell her why. Maybe she was sick. Julia just didn't know, and thinking about it was upsetting. She needed to do something, but she wasn't sure what at the moment. She only knew she had to help Eden through this, and she knew it meant making sure Rafe was well taken care of right now. Rafe had been a friend for a long time, and she couldn't abandon their friendship, even if both she and Eden were being pushed away.

"I think we should tell Katheryn what's going on," Julia said firmly. "Maybe she can tell us who Rafe made her power of attorney, and we can contact them to get her help. Maybe she gave it back to you, Eden."

"I don't think she did," said Eden as she shook her head. "I think she would have told me if she had." She wiped her tear. "I'm going to go check on her."

Eden opened the door to Rafe's room and saw her sitting on the floor in her meditation position. She walked over, sat next to her quietly, and just breathed to calm herself. She remembered when they used to do this together, and the times Rafe would tell her meditation was impossible when all she could think about was making love to her. Then they would end up meditating on each other the rest of the night. Eden couldn't help smiling sadly at the memory.

"I'm sorry," said Rafe as she felt Eden sit beside her. She didn't have to open her eyes. She could tell it was Eden from her scent.

"Me too," said Eden quietly.

"You have to let me go," said Rafe softly and hung her head down. "I can't give you what you need any more."

Tears began to flow out of Eden's eyes. "I can't. I can't let go. I love you."

"Why? All I ever do is make you cry and make you unhappy," said Rafe sadly as she saw the tears streaming from Eden's eyes. "Everyone tells me how bad I treat you and how unhappy you are. Don't you want to be happy again?"

"I do want to be happy. You make me happy," she said softly. "You're just having problems right now, and they're hard to work through. But we can get through them together."

"I hope someday, when you think about me," Rafe sighed, "you'll remember some good things about me and not all the bad things I've done."

Eden swallowed hard with the fear Rafe might be thinking about death and dying like Dr. Cathcart warned. "I remember good things about you all the time," said Eden and put her hand on Rafe's leg. "I think about you and dream about you. You're part of me and always will be."

"I can't think of any good things I ever was for you anymore," said Rafe and put her head into her hands. "It's all gone."

"I'll remind you of things," she said softly. "Remember the first time you brought me to your house? You gave me the grand tour, and we ended up here in your room. I don't know if you realized it, but I was a little nervous." She laughed softly. "It was the second time we made love. I was all tied up in knots inside because, the first time we made love, my mind was so clouded over with all the feelings I was having and everything I was experiencing. I had no idea exactly what happened, and I was afraid I would mess things up. I was afraid maybe I couldn't do it again if I was aware of what was going to happen—and I really wanted to do it again." She smiled at the memory. "Do you remember?"

"Yes," said Rafe softly. "Are those times all you remember about me? The times we had sex?" Rafe sighed. "I guess it's better than nothing," she said and lay back on the floor, sad she had been reduced to nothing more than a carnal animal.

"Rafe!" Eden gave a small laugh. "Of course, I remember things about you other than sex. I think I just have sex on the brain right now because I want you so much."

She lay back next to Rafe and closed her eyes. In her mind, she saw visions of Rafe and the things they did together. "I remember going to New York with you for the first time. You showed me all the places you went when you were young. I remember walking along the streets after spending hours in the museums and the warmth of your hand in mine. I remember looking at you across the table when we had dinner with your father and the game you two played about being properly improper and how you tried not to laugh. I remember so many things about you. All our trips and other things we did. I remember just sitting with you as you held me when we stayed home. I remember watching you paint and being amazed at your talent." She stopped and thought about their years together and how happy she and Rafe were before everything happened that led to where they were now. "I hope you start painting again," she said softly.

"Thank you," Rafe whispered to her for helping her remember there were some good times in their past.

Eden lifted herself up and leaned on her elbow so she could look at Rafe. *She has such beautiful eyes*, she thought. She remembered all the times Rafe had said her eyes were beautiful, but couldn't remember if she had ever returned the compliment directly. She leaned toward Rafe and kissed her gently on the lips. "You have beautiful eyes," she whispered and kissed her again. She felt Rafe's body shake and her lips move into a smile. "What's so funny?" Eden asked with a pout.

"That's my line," she said with a grin.

"See, I remember a lot," she said and kissed her again and felt the warmth flow through her as Rafe kissed her back. She felt Rafe's arms wrap around her and pull her closer. "I remember this," she whispered and felt Rafe kissing her face and neck.

She found her lips and kissed her deeply again and felt Rafe's hands go under her shirt and run over her skin, so warm and so sure. She felt Rafe's body begin to shake again and could taste the tears coming from her eyes.

"Oh, Rafe," she sighed and wrapped her arms around her and held her tightly to her as she kissed her gently. It was so rare to see her truly cry, and it made Eden's heart ache for her. "I remember when you used to hold me when I cried," she whispered. "I want to be as good to you as you were to me. Let me hold you and help you," she said softly and kissed her again.

Eden fought the temptation of saying she loved her again because she knew it wasn't what Rafe wanted to hear. She decided her kisses would be those words and hoped that, even though Rafe wouldn't hear the words, maybe she would feel them.

She kissed her again and again with love and wished love could take away all the pain and problems surrounding them. She hoped, for just this moment, Rafe could feel at peace and know she was loved. She kissed her again so she wouldn't say the words in her heart and on her lips. She could feel Rafe hold on to her tighter and knew she was fighting with herself in her mind.

Rafe took a shuddering breath and pushed Eden away gently. "I need you to go," she said in misery. Rafe had to make Eden see that she was better without her. "You have to let me go. I'm sorry for kissing you and touching you. I don't want to break your heart again. I didn't mean to break it," she said and tried to pull away.

Eden tried to pull her back. "No, Rafe," she said fighting tears of her own. "Please, don't say that."

"What? That I broke your heart? I did," she said sadly and pulled away then went to sit on her bed. "Don't you know kissing you and touching you will make it harder for you to let me go? Don't you know it will just give you hope and break your heart again when I can't give you what you want or need? It will! It will, and I'm trying so hard not to hurt you and to help you let go."

Eden sat up on her knees next to Rafe. "I broke your heart too, Rafe. We should help each other because we," she paused realizing she almost broke her rule. She took Rafe's hand and held it to her cheek then kissed it. "You can give me what I need. Maybe not today or tomorrow, but I know you'll be able to someday. It's why I know letting you go again would be another huge mistake."

Rafe snatched her hand away. She didn't know why Eden had to make this so hard. She saw the pity in her eyes again. "Stop looking at me like that," she said shakily. "I know what I am! Why do you keep lying to me? Why do you keep punishing me?"

"I'm not," said Eden as she looked into Rafe's eyes in confusion. "I'm not lying, I'm not punishing you."

"Get out!" Rafe screamed at her and Eden fell back in shock. "Get out and leave me alone! Stop fucking with me and let me go!"

"Rafe," was all Eden could get out.

"You prove it over and over again!" she yelled angrily. "You try to suck me in, but I know what you're doing! You can't make me love you. You can't make me say it! You try to seduce me and tell me lies and try to trip me up, but I won't let you!"

"No," she said not understanding what just happened, "I–I just want to help you."

"Well, you can't! You can't help me! I don't want your help! I want you to get out of my room! I want you to let me go so I can stop the dar—"

"What the hell is going on?" Julia shouted, interrupting Rafe as she charged into the room. Everyone could hear Rafe screaming across the house. "What are you doing?"

Rafe glared at Julia darkly and then turned her glare on Eden. "Your protector is here," she said angrily. "Take her!" yelled Rafe. "You only listen to her and the rest of them who want you to leave me and hurt me! Well, they can all have you! You can be her lover now and be their perfect friend who can do no wrong, and I'll go somewhere where I can be free of all of you!"

Julia helped Eden off the floor as Abby and Jude appeared at the doorway. "You need to calm down! No one wants to hurt you," said Julia firmly. She stopped herself from shouting back how she would definitely be taking Eden since Rafe was hurting her and pushing her way again. Eden had to see how she would be better off free of Rafe. "What happened, Eden?"

Eden shook her head, "I–I don't know," she said shakily. "We were just talking," she said and flashed a look at Rafe.

"Did you upset her?" asked Abby accusingly. "What did you say?"

"Yes, she upset me," said Rafe angrily. "She's a liar!" She looked Julia up and down. "So are you! So fuck off and leave me alone!"

Julia was stunned and wondered if Rafe really did know, somehow, if she got the chance, she would take Eden out of this situation. "I don't know what the hell you're talking about," said Julia heatedly pushing down the guilt of her thoughts, "but I'm not the one who's a liar! That's you, Rafe!

You're the liar! You tell us all you're going to therapy, and now we find out you've lied all this time! You tell us you want time alone with Eden so you can talk and work things out but that's a lie too! Look at what you're doing to her! I was going to let some things slide because you're sick, but I'm not going to let you abuse Eden or the rest of us!"

"Good! Leave then!" seethed Rafe and pointed at Eden. "Take her with you!"

"Please," Eden said trying to stop Julia from going on the attack again and turned to Rafe. "Tell me what you think I'm lying about. If you want, I'll make everyone leave."

"I already told you," said Rafe evenly. "You never listen. You only take and take and take!"

"Is it because I said I wouldn't pressure you about sex?" asked Eden tentatively. "I wasn't pressuring you. I just wanted to comfort you and show you I care about you."

"What the hell, Rafe?" said Abby in dismay. "Since when do you not want to have sex, especially with Eden. I thought you loved her. Julia told us you said you love her but now you're throwing her out. Why would you do that?"

Rafe ignored Abby and frowned at Eden angrily. "Why the *fuck* are you all still in my room?"

"We should go," said Jude. "Come on. Give her some space and the time she needs."

"Thank you," said Rafe and put her face into her hands. *Jude was the only one who understood*, she thought, *the only one who would just leave her alone*. She looked up at Jude pleadingly. "Tell her to let go, Jude. She's done it before. She's done it lots of times, so she can do it again. She needs to let go."

"No," said Eden as she shook her head at Jude and then looked back at Rafe. "I never let go of you, Rafe."

"Liar!" yelled Rafe and clenched her fists in anger. "You just said letting me go again would be a mistake! Again! Again! You said again! So you have let me go! You need to do it again!"

"I didn't mean it like that!" Eden yelled back. "I meant I wouldn't leave you again! I meant, even when I left, I could never let go of you, so leaving again would be a mistake!"

Rafe looked up at Jude. "You see how she lies?" she asked softly. "She spins and twists her words, my words, everything."

Jude sat next to Rafe. "I can see how things can get confusing," she said gently and patted Rafe on the back, consoling her. "Maybe you need some time to relax again," she suggested soothingly. "I can call Susy and see if she can come in again if you want," she said softly.

"No," said Rafe as she rubbed her head. "I don't want to deal with anyone. I just need her to go. I need everyone to go."

28

EDEN KINGSLEY WATCHED all her friends look from Rafe to her and back again in confusion and fear about what was happening. As Rafe lay down on the bed, Jude helped put her feet up and talked softly to her. Eden could feel the telltale feeling of pins and needles starting to surface from deep inside her. The anticipation of the oncoming pain that would soon overtake Eden's body had fused with the fear already flooding inside her mind at the thought of what was happening with Rafe.

She forced herself to breathe, and as everyone left the room, Eden hesitated. She was worried about what Cathcart had revealed earlier in their session about Rafe talking about death. She was afraid to leave Rafe alone right now because of the sudden change in how she was acting.

She followed Julia to the door, and as Julia went out, Eden closed the bedroom door then pressed the lock. She turned to face Rafe. "I'm staying," she said anxiously fighting the pins and needles blooming over her and wondering how Rafe was going to react.

She watched as Rafe looked up and stared at her with blazing angry eyes. She steeled herself for a confrontation with Rafe, something terrifying to her right now. "I've locked the door so no one can get in and bother us. If you want to scream at me and tell me everything I've done wrong, then do it. If you want to talk calmly, that works too. If you want to sit there and stare at me all night, then go ahead."

She was determined not to cower under Rafe's stare. "I'm tired of finding out all of these things you're thinking when you were acting like things are good. I'm tired of hearing all of the things about you I never knew from Julia, and everyone else, that you won't tell me yourself. I'm tired of keeping secrets for you and only knowing half the story. I'm tired of making one-sided deals with you and rolling over and making excuses for you!"

She took a step toward Rafe and calmed herself. "I need to know if you love me," she said softly. "I need to know if you really want to be with me. I'm tired of living in limbo and walking on eggshells as Julia, and the others put it to you. I don't want to watch you spiral out of control and get hurt or have a blackout." She hesitated and felt her anger build at the thought of not knowing anything about what was happening with Rafe. "I want to know why you're talking about death because it scares the shit out of me! I don't want you to die or to hurt yourself or do something stupid like leave the country and disappear from our lives. I need to know you're going to be here for Bronte and for me!"

Rafe looked away from Eden feeling sick because she already had the solutions to all her problems and the answers to her questions. She knew Eden was doing this and saying things to punish her even more. Eden could have left with the others, but instead, she was here demanding things impossible to give and asking questions when she already knew the answers. She just wanted her to give in and give up, but Eden had to be the one to let go. It was the only way death would lose. Eden wasn't the only one living in limbo.

Rafe knew if she gave in and told Eden she loved her, death would take Eden, but as long as she didn't say it, Eden would live. She also knew if she let go of Eden, she would be the one who would disappear into the darkness and she never wanted to go back there.

"Why are you doing this to me?" Rafe asked softly, her voice shaking with exhaustion and pain. "I can't give you anything more. I can't take anymore," she whispered and curled herself up on the bed.

A loud banging came from the other side of the door. "Eden," a muffled voice said through the door. "Eden, open the door!" Julia demanded as she continued to pound on the door.

Eden ignored the pounding. She went to Rafe and sat on the edge of the bed. "Please, babe," she said and brushed Rafe's hair back from her face. "Please, just talk to me and let me help you." She kissed her forehead lovingly. "I'll do anything for you. I love you," she said, knowing it was breaking the rules, but she had to say the words.

Rafe closed her eyes and could not stop the mourning sob from bursting out. "Please, just let me go," she whispered and couldn't stop her hand from going to her chest to ease the pain from the pressure she was feeling. Behind her eyelids, she could see the dark face laughing and could hear him mocking the pain searing through her body. "*Basta!*" she screamed in anger at the dark man. "*Smettila di ridere di me!*"[8]

Thinking Rafe was yelling at her, Eden pulled her hand back. She knew *basta* meant 'stop' or 'enough,' but she didn't know the rest. "I'm sorry," she said softly.

Opening her eyes, Rafe saw Eden's face in front of her. Her light brown eyes were shining with tears, and her bow lips trembled slightly. Rafe sat up quickly. She had to get away from her. She could feel her pressing in and taking the very air

---

[8] Stop laughing at me!

she was breathing. She went to the door leading to the patio and worked to unlock it to get out. She finally got the vertical rod lock to turn, opened the door, and stepped outside. She felt the cold concrete on her bare feet but kept walking.

"Where are you going?" said Eden frantically as she followed Rafe.

"I have to get away," said Rafe. "Leave me alone," she said as she made her way to the main part of the patio.

"Rafe!" Eden called. "Please, I'm sorry. Come back inside, I'll leave you alone," she said as she followed her closely, "just come back."

Making a sudden turn, Rafe faced Eden as she almost walked into her. "Stop following me!" she yelled angrily. She took Eden by the shoulders and pushed her gently back until she had no choice but to sit in the patio chair behind her. "What do you want?" Rafe asked as she leaned over her. "What do you want from me?"

Eden looked up into her liquid gray-blue eyes and haunted face. "I want you to stay with us. I want you to be happy. I–I just want you back, please. I love you. I want us back," she said through her tears.

Rafe knelt down and put her throbbing head on Eden's knee. "We can't go back in time," she said softly, "you said that, and it's true. You have to move on. It's the only way," she said as she looked up at Eden. "I don't know what else to do."

"I can't move on, Rafe," said Eden as she took Rafe's face into her hands. "We just need to take the time to talk and fix things together. We just have to love each other," she said and kissed her lightly on the lips. "I love you."

"I don't understand," said Rafe, confused by Eden's kiss. "What do you want from me? You want me to kiss you, to hold you, to have sex with you? If I do all you ask," she asked her feverishly, "will you let me go? Is that the price I have to pay?"

Eden shook her head at Rafe's words not understanding how she could think she ever had to pay a price for anything. "No, no," she said softly as she shook her head.

"I need to go," said Rafe and started to get up.

Eden leaned forward and caught Rafe, then put her arms around her. "Please," she whispered into her ear and kissed her jaw.

Rafe leaned into Eden and couldn't stop the whimper of pain coming from deep inside her. She knew she would have to pay the price even if Eden denied the truth. She would have to go into the blackness.

She shuddered as her mind let go of her body, and her arms moved around Eden then lifted her head to look at her. *There it is*, she thought as she saw the desire in Eden's eyes demanding her, *the price*.

As Eden moved her face closer, Rafe moved to meet her kiss. As her heart sparked at the feel and touch of Eden, her mind sank down until there was nothing left but inky blackness and deep, gravelly laughter dragging her down further, deeper into the pain, until she disappeared.

Eden couldn't help herself and kissed Rafe when she looked up at her. When Rafe met her kiss, a bolt of love shot through Eden, and it felt so good to feel and taste Rafe's kiss. She felt Rafe's warm hands move up her and over her body. She felt Rafe begin to take control as she kissed her hungrily and pulled at her clothes.

Thrill ran through Eden because it was finally happening and because Rafe loved her and wanted her. She pulled Rafe close and ran her hands over her kissing her back breathlessly. Rafe slid her hands around her again and pulled her out of the chair and onto the cold ground.

The shock of the cold made Eden gasp. "Rafe," she breathed out, wanting to tell her they should go inside, but Rafe put her mouth over hers and kissed her again as she moved against her heavily.

She felt Rafe move her hands up and take hold of her shirt with both hands. She tore it apart so her skin was exposed. Eden took a breath of surprise at what Rafe had done but was sent back into desire when Rafe yanked her bra apart ruining the clasp and took her breast into her mouth.

Eden arched back and felt Rafe move down her body then felt Rafe pulling at her jeans roughly. She sat up and tried to open Rafe's pajama shirt, but Rafe pushed her hands away. Rafe pulled on her jeans like she couldn't see what she was doing.

Eden reached down, unbuttoned and unzipped her jeans, and Rafe pulled her hips up and took the jeans down her. She could hear Rafe's heavy breathing as she threw the jeans aside and crawled toward her. Rafe was suddenly on top of her, kissing her and running her hands over her in desperation.

"Rafe," said Eden as she tried to kiss her back, "Rafe," she said again and gasped as Rafe pushed her back down roughly against the hard concrete. Rafe was holding her down so that it was hard to move and hard to breathe. "Rafe!" said Eden as she began to panic, but Rafe continued to kiss her and suck on her body.

She could feel Rafe put her hand between her legs and pull on her underwear. Eden tried to push Rafe up, but Rafe gripped her hand and held it down as she shoved her legs apart with her leg. "Rafe, you're hurting me!" Eden cried, and Rafe held her down harder. "Rafe! Stop!" she cried in panic, but Rafe kept moving over her and sucking hard on her breasts and her chest and stomach.

She felt Rafe let go of her arm and put her hand back between her legs, pulling at her underwear again. Eden clenched Rafe's hair and tried to push her away from her breast.

"Rafe! Stop! You're hurting me!" she cried out again.

Rafe didn't acknowledge her as she pressed harder into her, sliding her hand inside her underwear, and then she covered her mouth with hers.

Eden turned her head and tried to push her away again.

"Damnit, Rafe!" she screamed. "Stop!" She screamed in a long, loud panic. Before her scream ended, she felt Rafe being ripped away from her.

"What the fuck are you doing, Rafe!" Julia screamed as she pulled Rafe away from Eden. She shoved Rafe away and leaned over Eden. "Are you okay?" Julia felt Rafe grab her shoulder and pull her around then shove her away.

Eden watched as Rafe pushed Julia away, and then bent down and lifted her up and began kissing her again. "Rafe, stop," she said and pushed against her.

Rafe took her arm, twisting it behind her back, then kissed her again as she put her hand between her legs. Eden pulled back and used her other hand to push Rafe away.

"Stop!" she yelled, and Julia pulled Rafe away again.

"She said stop!" Julia yelled at her. "What the hell are you doing?" She watched as Rafe just stared at her. Julia shook her head then turned to Eden to help her.

As Rafe walked toward Eden, she began stripping off her pajamas. Eden looked in confusion at Julia. Rafe grasped Eden, pulling her close to her naked body and began kissing her body and trying to drag her down to the ground. "No! Rafe, Stop!" she said and pulled away.

Eden twisted out of Rafe's arms as Julia pulled her away, then pushed Rafe back hard, so she stumbled but did not fall. Julia hoped she would get the message to back off. There was no question in her mind Eden needed protection from Rafe. She didn't know what Rafe was doing or what she was thinking, but hurting Eden and forcing herself on her was unacceptable.

"Are you okay?" Julia asked, and Eden nodded breathlessly. Julia looked around at the splash coming from the pool and saw Rafe was gone. She shook her head in annoyance at Rafe then tuned back to Eden. "Did she hurt you?"

"I'm okay," said Eden shakily and tried to pull her shirt together.

Jude walked out to the patio after hearing all the commotion as Eden tried to cover herself with her torn clothes and pick up her jeans from the ground.

"What's going on," asked Jude as she took in the scene. Abby and Flynn followed after her. "Where's Rafe?"

29

RAFE SALVAGGIO COULD feel the warmth surrounding her in the inky darkness. It felt good. She also felt a sharp burning pain in her chest and back. The pain was no worse than anything she had felt before. As a matter of fact, it felt good to have a different kind of pain, so she welcomed it and gave over her body to it while her mind left her body behind. The darkness liked it when there was pain, and she could hear its sinister laughter echoing around her.

"Are you ready for me to take you now?" the darkness asked with amusement.

"Yes," said Rafe sadly knowing she had nothing more in her to fight. "Only you can save me. I see it now."

"Who are you?" the darkness demanded.

"*Traditorè*," Rafe whispered and fell further into the dark abyss where there was nothing, and she was nothing.

30

"GET HER OUT!" Eden screamed in terror. "Get her out!" she screamed again as Jude dove into the pool with Julia not far behind. Eden Kingsley's every nerve was on white hot fire, and the agony running through her at the sight of Rafe unmoving at the bottom of the pool was so unbearable, she could feel herself shaking and coming undone. She was living a nightmare, but she was wide awake. "She can't die!" she shrieked as memories of all the times Rafe had talked about death ran through her mind. Her mind let go of her bodily motor functions, and she collapsed to the cold concrete in anguish, not feeling the scrapes on her knees.

Abby held onto Eden as she fell, keeping her from hurting herself, trying to reassure her. "They'll get her," she said shakily. "She'll be fine. She'll be fine." She hoped it was true as she watched Jude and Julia struggle to get Rafe up to the surface of the pool.

They came up out of the water with Rafe who was listless in their arms. Flynn helped Julia hold on to her and Jude pushed herself out of the pool quickly. As Julia pushed Rafe up, Flynn and Jude pulled. They got Rafe out of the pool, and then Julia got out hastily. Rafe lay naked and unmoving on the cold concrete as an eerie white fog lifted off her skin and surrounded her. The warmth of the pool's heated water mixing with the cool air caused the fog. Moving quickly in the wet fog haze, the girls leaned over Rafe to begin CPR. Jude was checking for a pulse, and on the other side Julia was checking to see if Rafe was breathing. Flynn stayed close by in case they needed him.

"I can't feel a pulse," Jude cried frantically.

"Rafe!" Julia yelled with no response. "She's not breathing!" Julia tilted Rafe's head back, pinched her nose, and then blew two breaths into her.

Her hands shaking, Jude placed her hands on Rafe's chest and began pumping and counting to thirty. "Now," she barked out. She kept her hands in place and watched Julia breathe into Rafe once more.

Seeing no response, they began CPR again. After Jude was finished with the compressions, Julia gave two more breaths and turned Rafe's head to the side as water and bile flowed from her mouth. Jude trembled with relief as Rafe began coughing and breathing on her own, and Flynn sat down to recover from the scare.

"We forgot to call the ambulance," Jude said gasping with relief. "Should we go ahead and call?" She pushed Rafe into the recovery position to help her stop coughing.

Julia heaved a breath then looked up at Eden. "I think we should. Once we get her to the hospital, they can keep her there, and we can get her more help."

"No," said Eden as she shook her head, her heart racing in terror. "No! If we do, I don't know what'll happen to her!

"They'll just make sure she's okay," said Jude with concern as she held Rafe up.

"I don't know who has her power of attorney," said Eden through her tears. "What if they won't let me see her? What if she tells them to keep me away? I can't take it."

"We should at least take her to the emergency room and get her checked," suggested Flynn softly.

Eden gazed through tears at Rafe who had drops of water running down her naked body in streams, looking helpless as she leaned into Jude listlessly. "No, no," she cried and shook her head. "We should just take her back to her room and watch over her," she said frantically holding on to Abby.

"Fine," said Julia with a sigh. She could see Eden was about to have a breakdown and figured it would be best to do whatever would calm her. Rafe was breathing, and she didn't have any kind of head injury so it looked like she would be fine. "Come on," she said to Jude and Flynn. They began to get Rafe up to take her back to her room.

Abby held Eden's arm as Julia, Jude, and Flynn took care of Rafe, who was lifeless as they carried her back into the bedroom.

"What the hell happened?" Abby asked as she took in Eden's torn clothes and half-naked state.

"Nothing," said Eden shortly. She tore herself away from Abby and made her way into the house and to her room.

"What the fuck?" said Abby dismayed and picked up Rafe's pajamas then went to check on her.

When she got into Rafe's room, she found Julia getting a fresh pair of Rafe's pajamas out of the drawer and then a towel to dry Rafe's wet body and hair off so she could get her into the pajamas.

"What the hell happened?" she demanded as she tossed the clothes she was holding in a chair. Jude helped get the listless Rafe dried off, Julia got the pajamas ready, and Flynn looked down at the floor nervously.

"I thought she just jumped in the pool," said Julia shakily. "I just thought she dove in to swim," she said trying to control her shaking voice as the adrenaline was wearing off.

"Why is Eden half naked with her clothes torn?" asked Abby. "Why were they even out there? What were you all doing? Why does Rafe have a huge bruise on her leg? How did she end up in the pool?"

Jude helped Julia lay Rafe back in her bed and was worried. "Maybe we should call the ambulance. I don't know what's wrong with her," she said nervously. "I don't think she's conscious."

Julia sat down and leaned over Rafe. "Rafe," she said, "look at me." She shook her gently and watched as her eyes rolled back in her head. "Rafe, come on," she said worriedly. She looked over at Jude and Flynn. "I don't know why she's not responding."

"What's wrong," said Eden as she came into the room from changing her clothes and saw them all gathered around Rafe.

Abby caught her before she could go to Rafe. "She's not responding," said Abby shakily.

"Let me go!" cried Eden and pushed Abby away so she could get to Rafe. She climbed across the bed and bent over

Rafe. She took Rafe's face in her hands. "Rafe, Rafe!" she cried then turned to Julia. "What's wrong with her?"

"I don't know," said Julia shakily and turned back to Rafe. "Come on, Rafe," she said and rubbed her hands as Eden held her face. "Rafe!" she yelled hoping she could shock her awake.

"Rafe!" cried Eden and tried to sit her up.

Rafe could feel herself being pulled up, but she didn't want to go where the pain was, so she fought to stay in the dark. There was no reason to go back, and she didn't understand why she had to go, but the voices kept pulling her from the new comfort she had found in the darkness. She could feel the pain again coursing through her and could feel the tears burn as they fought to escape. She could feel the scream building as the pain increased. Her mind couldn't control her body because it was too busy trying to get back to the dark.

Julia and Eden were thrown back as Rafe lifted her arms and let out a blood-curdling scream. She continued to try to fight them off her.

"Rafe!" yelled Julia as she took hold of Rafe and held her arms down while she flailed and screamed. "Rafe! It's okay, it's okay!"

"Oh, my god," Eden gasped as she could do nothing but watch in terror as Julia held Rafe down, and Jude jumped in to help her.

"It's okay," Julia said to Rafe as she began to calm and looked up at her and Jude with wide-open eyes.

"*Togliti di dosso!*"[9] Rafe cried out. "*Lasciatemi tornare indietro! Non sopporto il dolore!*"[10] she said, and the tears finally ran down her face. "*Salvami*," she said weakly calling to the darkness to save her because the pain was too much. "*Salvami*."

"Rafe, it's okay," said Julia trying to calm her, "You're okay. Focus," she said and took Rafe's face in her hands. "Focus. You're okay," Julia said shakily.

"Get off me!" Rafe cried through the haze of her mind and pushed Julia back. "Leave me alone!" she yelled and tried to crawl away, only to find Eden in her path. She saw the pity in Eden's eyes. "Stop looking at me!" she yelled at her. Rafe lost her balance because her arm weakened and then she fell into Eden. She was too weak to move away.

"I'm sorry," Eden cried and held on to her stroking her wet hair and her back. "I'm sorry."

Rafe found her strength and pushed away from Eden. "Get out," she said weakly, "get out," she said and crawled the other way and found Jude. She reached out to her. "Make her go," she said. "Make her go away," she begged. "I don't know why they're still here. Make them all go," she said shakily and curled up into a ball in the bed to try to lock down the pain again.

Jude looked up at everyone. "Maybe we should do what she says," she said softly. "Give her some time to rest and recover." She looked up at Eden, who was still crying and shaking, and then she looked over at Julia, who still had a look of fright on her face, and up at Abby and Flynn who both

---

[9] Get off me!

[10] Let me go back! I can't stand the pain!

looked lost. "I'll stay with her for a while then let you know how she's doing. I'll see if she wants to let me give her a short massage to relax."

"Right," said Julia recovering slowly. "Come on, Eden," she said and helped her get off the bed. "We'll be in the living room so call out if you need us." She led Eden from the bed, and Flynn opened the door for them.

Eden looked back at Rafe and stopped. The image of Rafe at the bottom of the pool flashed in her mind again. Cathcart's words telling her Rafe was talking about death leaped to the forefront of her mind. Then the image of Greer's angry face telling her Rafe had wanted to die when she provoked the gunman at the school flashed before her eyes. Her knees weakened, and Abby helped Julia hold her up. "I–I need to stay with her," she said then tried to go back to Rafe. She didn't know if Rafe being in the pool was an accident or if Rafe had wanted to die and had done something to try to cause her own death again. All she knew was she couldn't let it happen again.

"No, Eden," said Julia and held her back. "Let Jude stay with her for a while. We need to talk about what to do."

"Yeah," said Abby shaken, "let her rest. See, I told you everything would be okay," she said weakly as they led Eden out of the room, leaving Jude to look over Rafe.

Jude watched the door close. "Okay," she said softly, "they're gone. Can I do anything for you? Do you need a drink or something?"

Rafe whimpered into her pillow as she shook in pain. "I need medicine," she said softly. "I hurt."

Jude nodded her understanding. "Okay, I'll get you something." She went into Rafe's bathroom and found some aspirin. She filled the glass she found by the sink with water then took everything to Rafe. "Here you go," she said as she sat on the bed next to her. "Can you sit up and take this?"

Rafe sat up shakily and took the medicine Jude gave her trustingly. "Thank you," she whispered and lay back down.

"What happened?" Jude asked as she pulled the covers up over her.

"I don't know," Rafe groaned. "I just wanted them to leave me alone. I was hurting, and Julia and Eden were holding me down. I don't know why." She sobbed. "They hate me. I'm trying, I'm trying," she said and covered her face with her hands.

"They don't hate you," said Jude and rubbed Rafe's shoulder and back to keep her calm. "I think you scared them. You scared me a bit." Jude chuckled nervously trying not to show just how much she really was scared of what had happened. "Can you tell me how you fell in the pool?" she asked softly.

Rafe frowned with confusion on her face. "The pool?" she repeated. "No, I don't want to see Susy right now," she said shakily. "I told you, I don't want to deal with anyone."

Jude bit her lip in concern and ran her hand over her face. "Okay," she said softly. "You get some rest. See if you can relax and get some sleep." She tucked the covers around Rafe then turned off the light as she went quietly out of the room.

31

IN THE LIVING room, Julia Hawthorn paced as Eden and Abby sat on the couch, and Flynn sat in the side chair. Julia had changed into some of Eden's dry clothes. Abby had already called Letty to let her know what happened and, after reassuring her she didn't need to come over, Letty agreed to pick up Bronte from Lydia and bring her home tomorrow.

Julia was trying to calm herself, but the memories of what had just happened and the things her father had told her were running through her mind. She knew they needed to place Rafe, and she had to convince Eden to let her help. They needed to figure out who Rafe had made her power of attorney.

Eden was still upset and crying as Abby held her, and it was plain Eden couldn't think clearly tonight. Julia could tell by Eden's state the conversation they needed to have may not happen tonight

"What happened?" Abby asked Eden again for what seemed like the millionth time.

"It—it just all happened so fast," Eden cried. "I was talking to her about staying, and she went out the back door. I followed her," she swallowed and took a breath, "and I thought she was coming around, and she was, we were kissing and," she hesitated, "and then she was holding me down and hurting me, so I screamed at her to stop."

"I heard her screaming," said Julia as she nodded. "I pulled Rafe off her, but Rafe just kept trying to go back to her, so I pushed her away."

"You pushed her into the pool?" Abby asked shocked.

"No, no, I didn't push her in the pool," Julia insisted. "We weren't even close to it. I thought she dove in like she does sometimes. I don't know how she ended up there," she said and shivered at what may have happened if Jude hadn't come outside and asked about Rafe.

Jude walked in after getting a towel from the linen closet and wrapping up in it. They all looked up at her with concern. "She's fine," she told them as she ran her hand through her wet hair. "I gave her some medicine because she said she was in pain and told her to try to relax and go to sleep." She saw their relieved faces and shifted nervously. "I think she's still confused about what happened."

"She's confused!" Julia said angrily. "She was the one attacking Eden! She needs to explain what the hell she was thinking!"

"She wasn't attacking me," said Eden in Rafe's defense, and Julia stared at her like she had lost her mind. "She wasn't hurting me at first, and I started it," she explained anxiously. "I thought—" She put her face in her hands. "I thought we were—" She sobbed.

"You thought you were going to have sex?" asked Abby and took a breath of frustration. "She was doing her wildling thing, wasn't she?" demanded Abby. "I told you! I told you she was reverting back to her old self!" She got up and paced around the room until she was standing in front of Julia. "Now who's reading too much into things?" she asked crossly. "I was right! I was right! I knew it!"

"Calm down, Abby," said Julia angrily. "We don't know if that's what was happening or if it was something else. I don't think Rafe has ever hurt anyone or wouldn't stop when she was asked to stop, even if she was doing her 'wildling' thing like you call it."

"It was like she didn't hear me," said Eden as she thought about what happened. "She just kept going even though I screamed right in her ear."

"I asked her what happened, and she just said you and Julia were holding her down, and you and Julia hate her," Jude revealed as she sat across from Eden.

"I don't hate her," Eden said and burst into a new round of tears.

"Of course, we don't," said Julia angrily. "She's just trying to push us all away! The only time I held her down was when she was flailing around and screaming."

"Well, I'm just glad she's okay," said Jude with a relieved shrug. "I need to go get changed. Let me know if you need me to come back." She got up and folded the towel to leave it behind.

"I'll go too," said Flynn. "I'm just glad you guys knew CPR."

Jude nodded in agreement. "Come on," she said, and they headed home.

When they left, Julia sat down next to Eden. "I know you don't want to talk about this right now, but we have to get her some help."

"I know," said Eden sadly. "I don't know why she lied about seeing her therapist."

"Because she can," scoffed Abby. "She's always gotten her way for everything, and I don't doubt being a good liar is part of the reason why."

"Abby," said Julia in frustration, "you need to stop. We need to focus on what we're going to do to help her, not complain about whatever happened to you in the past."

"I'm not complaining," she insisted angrily. "I'm just saying no one ever knows what she's going to do or how she gets her way!"

"It's okay, Abby," said Eden and held her arm. "I know she's not easy to figure out sometimes."

"Eden," said Julia trying to get her to focus, "we need to call Katheryn and find out who Rafe made her power of attorney so we can get her some help. Look at what's happening. She's lying to all of us and pushing us away, she hurt you and hurt herself, and it could happen again, and who knows what else. She needs therapy in a more secure place for her own safety."

32

IN THE KITCHEN, Eden Kingsley helped clean up after Julia made Sunday lunch for her, Abby, Jude, and Flynn. Julia and Abby stayed late last night to make sure nothing happened with Rafe, but she stayed in her room all night. They finally left to get some sleep, but Julia was back well before noon. After talking Eden into it, Julia had invited everyone over to talk about what happened yesterday and what to do about Rafe.

Eden was still anxious about forcing Rafe into a hospital. Not knowing who Rafe assigned as her power of attorney made the decision even harder. Eden hoped Rafe would talk to them today, but every time she or Julia went into her room, she got angry and demanded they leave.

Jude tried to take Rafe something to eat, but so far, she hadn't eaten anything of substance. Jude finally convinced her to eat some bread and butter in exchange for more aspirin so there would at least be something in her stomach for the medicine.

When everything in the kitchen was put away, Abby made tea, and they took it into the living room. Eden called Letty who had kept Bronte for the night and arranged for her to bring her home after taking her to the park. Then they all sat solemnly thinking about Rafe who was still confining herself to her room.

Eden had told them what she felt she could about the therapy session, but she was afraid of telling them too much because she didn't want to break a trust with Rafe again.

Julia knew if she couldn't convince Eden to place Rafe, she might have to call her father and have him help her with getting Rafe the help she needed.

"I just can't," said Eden as she held onto her warm teacup. "If you saw her and how upset she was about being in the hospital, you would understand," she tried to explain. "She has to agree. Then we won't have to worry about a power of attorney."

"What if it's someone we know, like my father?" Julia reasoned because it seemed the most likely to her. "He wouldn't keep you from her or do anything to exclude you. He would make sure she got the best help available."

"Maybe it's Greer," Abby piped in. "She helped before."

"Abby," said Eden in frustration. "Greer helped put her into the hospital. I don't think Rafe would choose her. Plus," she said nervously, "I'm not sure how kind she would be again."

"I still think we should just call Katheryn," said Julia exasperated as she considered bypassing Eden. "Maybe Rafe chose her. She is her lawyer."

The doorbell rang, and Abby jumped up from her seat. "I'll get it," she said. "It's probably Letty." She walked quickly out of the room to answer the door.

"Eden, we really should talk to Katheryn and see about getting her placed again and finding out what Rafe did with her legal paperwork," said Julia with concern trying again to convince her. "She needs help none of us can give her. She needs to be under care."

"I can't do it to her, Julia," sobbed Eden, "not without her agreeing to it. I told you she'll just see it as more punishment."

"Well, we can't let things go on the way they are," said Julia as she rubbed Eden's back to comfort her hoping Eden would remember she was the one there for her. "She needs us to step up and take control because she can't right now."

Abby walked into the living room nervously. "Guys," she said to get their attention. "Someone's here to see Rafe. I think it's her friend from Italy."

"Gabri?" said Eden in surprise. She wiped her eyes and got up to follow Abby. When she got to the entryway, she saw the dark angelic man she had been introduced to by Rafe. Beside him was a woman she didn't know holding a briefcase. "Hello," said Eden unable to hide the surprise on her face as she shook his hand.

"*Ciao, sono venuto per vedere Rafaella,*"[11] said Gabri with a small smile and looking past her to see if Rafe was coming.

"He has come to see Rafaella," said the woman beside him. "I'm Chiara. I'm Mr. De Angelis' translator," she said and shook Eden and Abby's hands.

Eden stared at Chiara and Gabri nervously. "Rafe isn't feeling well," she said, and Chiara translated. "She's in her room. I'll go see if she'll come out." She turned nervously to go tell Rafe he was here.

---

[11] Hello, I've come to see Rafe,

Gabri gave Chiara a look of concern as she translated and he saw the expressions on everyone's faces as they had come out of the living room. He quickly followed Eden to Rafe's room. When Eden opened the door, Gabri saw Rafe and went to her immediately. *"Eroina, cosa c'è che non va?"*[12] he asked as he sat on her bed. He lifted her up and took her into his arms. *"Now I am here,"* he said consolingly in Italian.

Rafe wrapped her arms around him and began to shake and cry into his shoulder. *"Gabri,"* she whispered and continued in Italian, *"Gabri, how are you here? I'm sick again, I don't know if I can get better."*

"No, Eroina," he said compassionately. *"You will get better and I will help you. I promised you I will always help you."* He held her while she cried and kissed her head and cheek.

Eden watched as Gabri held and kissed Rafe gently and Rafe cried in his arms. A surge of jealousy went through her. He was doing something she had been denied. He was holding and consoling Rafe. She looked over at Chiara questioningly.

"He calls her Heroine," she translated. "He told me it was from their childhood. He has been talking about her non-stop. He loves her passionately." She nodded toward them. "He tells her he will always take care of her."

"Why is he here?" asked Eden shakily. "Did she call him?" She looked over at them as they spoke to each other much too softly to hear.

---

[12] Eroina, what's wrong?

"Oh, no," said Chiara. "He has not heard from her, and she didn't answer his emails or calls since maybe a few months or more. Her last email was curious, so since he came here for work, he wanted to see her in person. Has she been sick long?"

"Yes," said Eden nervously, "things have been getting worse. We were just talking about what to do for her because she had a big setback yesterday." Rafe and Gabri were speaking louder, and Eden hoped Chiara would translate. "Can you tell me what they're saying?"

"You don't speak *Italiano*?" she asked surprised. "Gabri said you two have been together for six years."

Eden wrung her hands nervously not telling her they were apart for almost two years. "I don't," she admitted. "Rafe speaks Italian to Bronte all the time, but I never learned very much."

"Yes, Bronte. Is the baby here?" she asked and looked around.

"No, she is with her Zia Letty. She should be here soon." Eden looked back over at Rafe.

"I will tell you what they are saying," Chiara said in her accented English and patted Eden's arm. "Mr. De Angelis said to translate all his words as well as others so nothing is mistaken unless otherwise instructed."

Chiara listened to the conversation and then translated for Eden. "She says she is *Caïna*. The *Traditorè*. Meaning traitor or betrayer. It is from Dante, he is very famous in Italy." She smiled, proud to discuss a famous *Italiano*. "We all learn about him in school at some point. Gabri tells her she is not the betrayer. He says she is only a child of Cyprian[13] the Fair and they will travel together back to the mother of love. He says he will lift her from the icy water again, and she will see the truth."

"I don't understand," said Eden confused. "What does it mean?"

"It is Dante, from his poem Divine Comedy." Chiara shrugged like Eden should know all about the poem. "She is speaking of the first part, Inferno. The first son, *Caïna*, or Cain you call him. He murdered his brother, so he is the betrayer of his family and is encased in ice to his chin down in the ninth circle of hell, as all are who betray their family."

Eden shook her head and looked in the room, watching as Gabri talked gently to Rafe in Italian.

Chiara continued her translation. "She calls herself the *Traditorè*, the betrayer, so she aligns herself with *Caïna*. She says she feels the coldness enclosing on her."

Chiara paused to think how to explain the rest of what was said. "Mr. De Angelis, he tells her it is not the truth. He refers to the third part of the poem *Paradiso*, Paradise. He is telling her she is one of the rays sent down by Cyprian the Fair, and she has surrounded so many with her light of love she is sure to ascend to Paradise. He says the world still holds her here because the love she has inside her is much needed." Chiara smiled at Eden. "They have interpreted it very romantically. I don't know if it is what Dante had in mind, but childhood passion is in play."

---

[13] chē-prian

She saw Eden's confusion. "The more common thought is the Third Sphere of Heaven is meant for those who, unlike those who have temperance, are unrestrained in their love. They are needed to fill the world with happiness and pleasure, sometimes to bless not to just one person, but many, with their affection and passion. My explanation may be too simple also. Dante is complex and is used for many purposes from politics to religion and everything else you can think of." She smiled and nodded toward the two. "But theirs, it seems, is passion."

Eden observed the two again and watched Gabri wipe Rafe's tears from her face. She felt another sharper stab of jealousy. This time it was for the love they had for each other, the love she felt very separated from. "What are they saying?" she asked trying to hide the sick feeling running through her as she leaned against the wall.

"He is telling her he will take her away," said Chiara with a nod. "He will take her to Milano, and they will watch the beautiful people together while they drink caffè and they will walk the streets and buy beautiful garments then make sure they spin on the, uh," she hesitated, "the balls of the bull," she said with a short laugh. "It is a tradition there," she said then listened for a moment. "He says they will go to Firenze and sun in the garden under the Palazzo Pitti then they will go and be overwhelmed by beauty at the Uffizi and walk the paths of Da Vinci and the de Medici's. They will go to Roma and talk with Michelangelo then discuss again just how large all the stone penises are the Pope keeps in baskets in the cellars." She put her hand over her mouth to stifle her laugh. "They are very irreverent." She paused to listen again. "He is telling her she will stay with him, and he will take care of her. Everything is good."

Eden watched Gabri as he got up from Rafe's bed and walked toward her. She didn't feel like everything was good at all. It was like some kind of bad dream she couldn't wake up from, and this angel walking toward her was here to take Rafe away from her. She couldn't speak as Gabri showed his concern for Rafe and spoke in a language she didn't understand.

"Mr. De Angelis says you should sit and speak about Rafe. He wants to know if you have a private place," said Chiara.

"Yes, yes, of course," Eden stammered. "We can go to the living room, and I'll ask everyone to leave for a while." She led them back to the living room, and everyone stood up, overflowing with curiosity when they walked in the room. "Everyone, this is Rafe's friend Gabri. You may remember when Rafe introduced some of you to him. He is the friend who was our donor for Bronte." Everyone said hello and looked expectantly at Eden. "Uhm, we need to talk privately, so I hope you understand. We need you to go for a while. I'll call you so you can come back," she promised them.

"Sure," said Jude and started to lead Abby out by her elbow as she started to protest. "Come on," she said. Flynn followed them out.

Julia could tell something was wrong with Eden by looking at her. "Eden, I'd like to stay," she said covertly watching Gabri and his translator who was telling him the conversation. Julia knew exactly who Gabri was, and though they never hung out, she had always been jealous of him because Rafe spent all of her time with him after her move back to Italy. There were many times when Rafe had chosen Gabri over her, even when she knew Julia's schedule allowed her limited time in Europe sometimes. She looked directly at the man she had considered competition for Rafe's attention for so many years. "I've been Rafe's friend since she moved to America when she was fourteen and I'd like to help if I can."

"Mr. De Angelis asks if you are Julia," said Chiara and Julia nodded. "It is good," she said, and they sat down with each other.

Gabri turned his gaze on Eden. It was rare to see Rafe in tears. It infuriated him, and he wanted answers. "What are you doing to my Rafaella?" asked Gabri in halting English. "How have you made her this way again?" he demanded.

Eden's heart crashed inside her chest as he called her 'my Rafaella' so possessively. She looked over at Julia anxiously. *Rafe is not his*, she raged inside herself. *She is mine.*

"Gabri," Eden started when she gained control of herself, "she's had a lot of things happen to her in the last year, including being held at gunpoint. She's suffering from PTSD, and the doctor thinks it started before being held at gunpoint. But none of us know anything except she saw her mother die and saw her friend who died taken away and got his blood on her. She's apparently been having emotional blackouts, times when she can't remember what happened."

She held back the information about Maria because Rafe told her only the two of them knew about her. She wondered if she had to keep her promise if Rafe was leaving her with him and not coming back.

"We also know she blamed herself for her mother's death and her father exploited her guilt and used her mothers' death to punish her," added Julia to let him know she knew the most about Rafe.

Chiara translated their words, and Gabri spoke to her animatedly and angrily in Italian. Finally, she turned to speak with them. "He says, who are these doctors? He asks why you did not let her go to Italy when she was asking to go? Why did you not let her go where she knows she needs to be? You and the doctor obviously know nothing of her father and mother or of their friend or how to help her. She should be where she got help before."

Eden shook her head in confusion. "Before? Gabri, she never told us she had help with this before. We didn't know."

Gabri looked up at the painting Rafe did of Eden and frowned. He then spoke to the translator. When he was finished, she nodded and turned to Eden and Julia. "She would not say anything to you, Julia," said Chiara. "But he says he is surprised she did not tell Eden since you are her family. She should have told you if anything happened, she needed to go to Italy. But maybe since her father died, she thought she would not have to go. Her father is like all the old families and keeps things like this very private."

"Things like what?" asked Julia when she saw Eden was at a loss for words.

"He is not sure he should talk to you," said Chiara. "He wants to go talk to Rafaella again. He thinks something is very wrong because of the last email he received and you don't know things a family would know. He is afraid the email came because you are holding her without consent again."

"What?" Eden asked in dismay. "What are you talking about?" she asked getting upset.

Gabri said something to Chiara and left to go talk with Rafe. "He says I have to stay because it is a private matter," said Chiara.

"Do you know what he's talking about?" asked Julia. "Do you know what was in the email she sent him?"

"No," said Chiara with a shrug. "I am only Mr. De Angelis translator since a few weeks ago. I know only they are childhood friends, and he has been very worried about her. He calls her Eroina, which means heroine, and describes her as his Wild Angel, and I think he is in love with her." She smiled and blushed because she may have revealed too much about her employer. "He showed me a photo he carries of her baby and calls the baby his gift to her. He mentioned a golden mother too, which I am thinking must be you," she said to Eden and blushed again.

Eden had no idea what Gabri was talking to Rafe about or what Rafe was telling him. She only knew Rafe wanted to leave and go to Italy, and he was prepared to take her. She leaned close to Julia. "Maybe we should call Katheryn," she said shakily.

Julia was about to reply as Gabri walked back into the room looking very unhappy.

Gabri spoke quietly to Chiara for a few minutes then Chiara nodded and turned to the two waiting women. "Mr. De Angelis requests Julia excuses us so he may speak with Eden alone," she said and waited for their reply.

"It's okay," said Eden before Julia could protest. "Call," she mouthed so only Julia could see and hoped she would call Katheryn and let her know what was going on.

Julia sighed and nodded to Eden. "I'll just be next door with Jude and the others," she said and hugged Eden. She stole a look at Gabri for a moment before walking out of the living room then out of the house.

33

WHEN THEY WERE alone in the house, dread ran through Eden Kingsley as she faced Gabri De Angeles. Eden sat down in the chair slowly and could feel the subtle threat filling the room. The anxiety building made it feel like her heart was being squeezed inside her chest. Eden clasped her hands together to keep from shaking as Gabri took his seat again next to Chiara. This man knew Rafe and all about Bronte, and now he was here telling Rafe he would take her away. On top of everything, her head was spinning because he had alluded something like this had happened before.

"Gabri," she began nervously, "please, tell me what you're talking about. What happened to Rafe?"

Gabri began to speak, and Chiara translated. "Mr. De Angelis wants you to know Rafe told him that Julia, though she is a longtime friend, is not helpful and it is the reason he asked she not be present when he speaks to you. Rafaella is very upset with her and the others, as well as you. Now Rafaella is saying she is betrayer to you. What happened? Why is Rafaella saying this?"

Eden nervously ran her hand through her hair. She thought Rafe had told him what happened, and now, with his sudden appearance, she was feeling unsure and anxious.

"She had an affair," she said flatly. Gabri looked on expectantly after Chiara translated. "It was before we knew I was pregnant. I found out when the woman she had the affair with, the realtor who was selling her father's apartment, sent flowers to Rafe here, and I read the card." she cleared her throat remembering the pain she felt at reading the note. The words in the note were burned into her mind. "It said, 'I had a wonderful evening, my darling. Lauren.'"

She stopped and looked sadly at Gabri. "When Rafe got home, I confronted her, and she admitted to the affair. I was hurt and angry, and I left her," she said shakily. "Talking about the affair was one of the things she was so upset about in therapy. She talked about what happened, and it was then we found out she had an emotional blackout while going through her father's things. She said Lauren took her to the bedroom, and then she doesn't remember anything more about the initial affair except waking up next to... to her."

Eden looked from Chiara to Gabri and bit her lip. "I love Rafe," she said softly. "But the affair hurt me and caused a lot of anger in me, and I left her for a while. I've worked so hard to get back to her. And now—" She shook her head unable to continue.

"She says you are still punishing her," Chiara translated for Gabri who was frowning.

"I'm not punishing her," said Eden trying not to be defensive. "I'm not. The subject seems to come up a lot, and it upsets her."

Gabri sat silently for a moment, thinking about what Eden had told him. "Are you sure she had an affair?" Chiara translated.

"She admitted she did," said Eden wondering why he would ask such a question.

"Yes," relayed Chiara, "but you say she does not remember. Did she admit it right away?"

"No, she admitted it after I showed her the card from the flowers," said Eden uncomfortable with the interrogation.

"So, she denied it first, yes?" Chiara translated. "Mr. De Angelis is saying he does not think she had an affair. He wants to know if you confirmed it with the realtor woman."

"I. . ." Eden hesitated under Gabri's stare, "no, why would I?"

"He says, you tell him Rafe is explaining things she does not remember," said Chiara. "Maybe, since you accuse her, she thinks it is true and creates a scenario in her mind to make it real to her."

"Why would she? If she didn't have an affair, she could have told me the truth and proven it to me if it didn't happen," said Eden wondering if he was trying to let Rafe get away with bad behavior.

"Could she?" Gabri asked through Chiara. "You just said she was sick and had an emotional blackout. How do you know when she was talking to you she was not still sick?"

"She told me when she went back to New York she saw her again but didn't continue the affair," said Eden frustrated by his questioning.

"And you confirmed this too?" Chiara asked Gabri's question.

"Of course not," said Eden, affronted. "I took her word for it."

"It seems like it is very easy for you to think Rafe did this with so little proof," translated Chiara. "He says, it was only a few months before he was here, and she was so excited about having a family. He asks, why do you punish her? Even if she did do this, she was sick. She has no blame at all. She is still innocent. Her mind was not there, so her heart was not either."

"I—" Eden stammered at his logic, "I didn't know she was sick at the time."

Gabri frowned and shook his head slowly. He spoke to Chiara for a moment then let her translate. "He says you should have certainly known she would be sick with grief for her father."

Eden flushed red with a mix of anger and guilt at his berating. There was so much more, but she was afraid to tell him about her own online indiscretion. She already felt defensive and knew he would not accept her defense for her own behavior. From what Rafe said in therapy, she did not accept it either. "I know she's sick now, and she was getting help. She told me she was going to Italy at the beginning of the year, and I just found out today she quit her therapy," she said wanting to change the subject. Right now, she just wanted to make sure Rafe did not leave like she planned. "We're trying to get her more help."

Chiara translated her words to Gabri then listened to his reply. "Mr. De Angelis says Rafe is right to go to Italy. It is where she will get better."

Looking from Gabri to Chiara, the anxiety inside Eden threatened to overwhelm her. She looked up at a sound of the doorbell and was relieved someone else would be here. "That might be Letty with Bronte," she said softly and got up to answer the door.

As she opened the door, Eden was shaking, and she was happy it was Letty and Julia. Bronte reached for her, and she took her in her arms, then hugged and kissed her. "Hello, baby," she said softly.

"Is everything all right?" asked Julia as she saw how pale Eden was and how anxious she was acting. "I left a message for Katheryn. Hopefully, she'll call me back soon."

"What's wrong?" asked Letty. "Whose car is out there?"

"It's Rafe's friend, Gabri," she said trying to hide her anxiety. "He's in the living room."

"Where's Rafe?" asked Letty with concern.

"She's still in her room. She's still not feeling well," Eden answered and turned to lead them into the living room where Gabri was waiting.

"Does she know he's here?" asked Letty.

"Yes," said Eden and shifted Bronte on her hip. When they entered the living room, Gabri was standing to greet them. "Gabri, this is Bronte," she said and stood in front of him. "I think you may know Letty, Rafe's cousin, and you met Julia a little while ago."

Gabri smiled at Bronte. "*Ciao, bambina,*" he said gently. "*Sei bellissima.*" Bronte nuzzled shyly into Eden's neck as he spoke to her. Gabri spoke again then nodded to Eden.

"Rafe was right, the baby is wonderful," Chiara translated.

Gabri looked up and smiled. "*Rafaella,*" he said and went immediately to her. He took her arm, helped her to the couch, and sat closely to her. "*I'm glad you feel better. I'm meeting the baby girl,*" he said gently, glad he did not have to use a translator with her. "*She is even more beautiful than the pictures you've sent.*"

Rafe held on to Gabri's arm as she sat next to him and leaned close speaking in her childhood language. *"I'm glad you got to meet her. I think she looks like you."*

Bronte struggled out of Eden's arms and walked to Rafe holding out her arms and calling on her Mama to hold her. Rafe picked her up and put her in her lap.

"Look at her beautiful eyes," she said as she looked into Bronte's eyes and showed Gabri. *"They are so similar Eden's. Can you see the golden color in them?"* she asked as Bronte put her arms around her neck and told Rafe she loved her in her attempt to imitate Rafe's Italian. Rafe kissed her and whispered in her ear making her giggle.

"She loves you very much," said Gabri. *"Now you have the love of two angels and one is really called wild!"* He laughed and Rafe laughed softly too. *"I know,"* he said with excitement, *"let's sing a little song."* He reached into his jacket, pulled out a small tin whistle, and began to play. Bronte was immediately mesmerized, and they laughed at her amazement.

Eden watched the scene unfold nervously. They looked so much alike, all three with dark hair and skin, and Bronte's facial features were so much like Gabri's there was no doubt he was her father. The music had broken through Bronte's shyness, and she had climbed into Gabri's lap reaching for the small instrument and saying 'mine' to him. Gabri let Bronte hold the tin whistle and was showing her how to blow into it to make music. Eden looked over at Julia with wide, anxious eyes.

Julia took Eden's arm annoyed at Rafe for shutting them out by speaking Italian. "Are you all right," she said softly. Eden nodded, but Julia could tell she was upset. "Let's go to the kitchen," she said softly then gave a concerned look to Letty. "We're going to make drinks for everyone," she announced to the room. "We'll be right back." She dragged Eden out of the living room and into the kitchen.

When they got to the kitchen, Julia began getting out glasses, and Eden sat at the counter. "What did he say to you? Why is he here?"

"The translator, Chiara, said Gabri hadn't heard from Rafe and was worried. He's here for work so he decided to see her in person." Eden looked up at Julia with fear in her eyes. "When he was talking to Rafe, the translator said Gabri was telling her he would take her with him. You heard him. He said he's worried she's being held against her will again."

"We had to place her, Eden," said Julia defensively. "She needed help. She may need it again now because she isn't getting better."

"He said she could get better in Italy," she said softly. "Julia, we can't let her go if he really is here to take her with him. If she goes to Italy, she may never come home," she said and began to cry at the thought of never seeing Rafe again.

"Katheryn will help us," said Julia hopefully. "We just have to let him visit. Let him see that we can take care of her. Then he'll be satisfied and leave. I'll try Katheryn again," she said and pulled out her phone and dialed. The call went to voicemail so she left another message. When she hung up, she turned to Eden. "Come on, stop crying, and wipe your tears. Let's get these drinks in there."

They walked back into the living room with the drinks tray and found Gabri and Rafe singing a song to Bronte. Gabri was playing his tin whistle, Rafe was singing and would tickle Bronte making her giggle at certain parts of the Italian song.

Eden's heart pounded in her chest again and knew her anxiety was from all the things she remembered Jake saying to her, but she couldn't help being fearful they might want to take Bronte, and she would lose both of them. She knew it was irrational. She knew Rafe could not legally take Bronte because they had joint custody, but the fear shot through her anyway.

"Here we are," said Julia as she sat the drinks tray on the coffee table.

Letty looked up at Eden with a smile. "Eden, you should have seen it. Bronte was trying to sing the song with them, and Gabri taught her how to blow the whistle. It was so cute!"

"I'm sure it was," said Eden with a weak smile. "Maybe they can sing another song."

Rafe looked up at her and gave a small smile. "Gabri says she's not too young to get involved with music lessons. We should find her a teacher," she said softly then turned to Gabri. "*Gabri, I must show you something. Wait here,*" she said in Italian. She put Bronte into his lap and went out of the room.

"Gabri," said Eden softly, "would you like to stay for dinner? I'm just making chicken and some side dishes."

Chiara immediately translated. "He says thank you, but no. He does not think he will be staying much longer."

"Oh, okay," said Eden, hoping Julia was right about him just visiting.

Rafe came back into the living room carrying a framed painting and her camera. She sat back down next to Gabri ignoring the others. She knew it was rude speaking in Italian but she did not care. Gabri was beside her now and they had the right to speak their own language. *"This painting was made by Bronte. I was going to send it to you for Christmas, but I'd like you to have it now."*

"È incredibile," he said and began talking to Bronte. *"You are very talented and lucky to have such wonderful mothers to teach you so much."*

Bronte laughed as he tickled her. As she played with him, her large brown eyes shined happily, and Rafe took several pictures of them together.

"I didn't get a chance to find her a new art teacher, but I will as soon as I feel better," said Rafe and stroked Bronte's dark hair.

"Rafaella," said Gabri quietly, *"I think you should come home with me to Italy. You are not doing well here with these people. They don't know how to help you as I do. I do not want them to lock you in a room again. It's inhumane,"* he said firmly.

"I'm trying to get home," said Rafe and a tear found its way out of her eye. *"I made a promise that I would stay here until after Christmas for Bronte."*

"*You can't make that promise, Rafaella,*" Gabri reasoned. "*You're sick, so they cannot force you to keep it. If they do, they are not good people to take care of you. I spoke with Eden. She doesn't know anything about how to help you. She says herself that she doesn't know what to do for you. I can see you've kept everything from her,*" said Gabri with worry. "*What is the reason? Do you not trust her? Or maybe you thought you wouldn't get sick ever again?*"

"*I never wanted her to look at me with pity,*" said Rafe with a frustrated frown.

"*Oh, Rafaella,*" he said and sighed. "*We both know that you must be in Italy. Come with me,*" he said gently.

"*I know,*" said Rafe softly. "*It's so hard for me. I tried.*"

Eden turned to the translator when she heard her name. "What are they saying?"

"I cannot translate for you. They said if anything needs translated Rafe will do it, or they will let me know. I'm sorry," she said and looked away.

Eden took a breath of shock. "Rafe, what were you saying? Are you okay?"

"I'm fine," she said with a frown then turned her attention back to Gabri. "*I know that things are not going well here, but how can I leave and still be a mother to her?*"

"*You're sick, Rafaella. She needs you to get better more than she needs you to be here right now. How can you take care of her if you get sicker?*"

"*I need to think, Gabri. I need to think*" she said and put her hand to her head. "*I need to go lay down.*" She got up and walked out of the room and into her bedroom, leaving them alone with Gabri again.

"I'm going to check on her," said Eden and followed Rafe.

34

ENTERING RAFE'S BEDROOM, Eden Kingsley found her lying in bed. It was clear by looking at her that Rafe was sick. Her face was pale and drawn with dark circles around her eyes, and she was still so thin from not eating when she was on the other medication. Eden sat down on the bed next to Rafe and ran her hand over her gently. "Rafe, I'm so worried about you," she said as she leaned over and kissed her head gently. "I love you. What can I do to help you?" she asked and brushed Rafe's dark hair from her face.

Rafe looked searchingly at her face and took a shaking breath. "You have to let me go," she said softly. "I can't do this," she said and turned away from her. "I need you to leave now. I need to think, and I can't with you here."

"Please," Eden said trying not to cry, "I can't let you go. I can't." She wiped the tears from her eyes. "I never want to let you go, Rafe. I love you too much. I'm sorry for everything," she sobbed. "Tell me what Gabri was saying to you. I don't want you to leave with him. We need you to stay with us, please," she said desperately.

Rafe closed her eyes and sighed heavily. *She never listens*, she thought sadly. "I just need you to leave me alone right now. I told you, I need to think."

"I wish you could forgive me," Eden said softly. "We need forgiveness for each other. I know you don't believe it, but I forgive you, Rafe, I do."

Rafe turned with a look of disbelief. "You don't," she said sadly and shook her head, "I know you don't. You prove me right all the time."

"No," said Eden shaking her head in denial of Rafe's words, "I do forgive you."

"Stop saying that!" said Rafe as she sat up and crawled to the other side of the bed to get away from Eden. "You're lying to me!" she yelled as she got out of bed and turned to face her angrily. "Get out!"

"I'm not lying," Eden insisted anxiously. "I'm not, and you know it!"

"Do you even know what forgiveness is? Do you even really understand the concept? I don't think you do!" Rafe shouted angrily. "It's impossible to give actual forgiveness. Whoever told you it was possible to give it or even receive it was lying to you and tricking you!"

"No, it's not true," said Eden, "I know what forgiveness is! It's—it's if you do something wrong, or you hurt someone, you ask for forgiveness to show you know you did something wrong and you're truly sorry. If they forgive you, they understand you're sorry and you know you were wrong. This way you can both heal and learn from the mistake."

Rafe shook her head. "That is not forgiveness! That's what you think forgiveness does! You've just relegated it to a fucking apology!"

"Well then, what is it?" Eden demanded angrily.

"It's absolution, release without recourse, giving up the claim of vengeance, punishment, and resentment, and no one is capable of it because we're human! We don't forget! We always remember! The best we can do is to try to obtain some justice, either internally or externally somehow, depending on the transgression. This way we can feel the debt owed for the wrongdoing is paid in part or in full!"

Eden was stunned, not sure what to say. This was just as confusing, if not more so than what Julia had told her. "I don't understand what all you said means," she said softly trying not to cry.

"It means you keep punishing me, so you don't forgive me!" Rafe yelled at her. "You all keep punishing me, and I can't take anymore! When will my debt to you be paid? It feels like it never will be!" she screamed and put a shaking hand on her chest. "I can't take it," she said softly and sat on the bed in pain.

"*Rafaella*," Gabri called out as he flung open the bedroom door. He saw her and went immediately to her knelt down and put his arms around her. "*What's going on? Why are you in this situation? You should be calm.*"

"*She continues to punish me. I can't take anymore,*" she sobbed into his shoulder. "*I'm disappearing again. The darkness promises no more pain and that it can save me. I thought I might trick it and not disappear again, but I was wrong,"* she told him sadly.

Gabri closed his eyes in sorrow for her and kissed her head. He took her face in his hands and looked intently into her eyes. *"Ti vedo,"*[14] he said softly. *"I will help you and keep you here,"* he said and tapped her forehead gently and smiled warmly at her. *"Maybe we can cure it here too,"* he said and tapped her chest over her heart. *"I'm sorry that she punishes. I don't think you are Traditoré. I will prove it to you, if you come with me. Would you like to come?"*

"Sì, I think I have to go." Rafe looked at Gabri unable to hide her despair from him. *"I'm sorry, Gabri. I thought I wouldn't have to go back this way."*

"Oh, Eroina," he said with a sad smile. *"I wish it were different too. We will get over this again. We are strong."*

Rafe laid down weakly, relieved Gabri would be there for her again. *"Take me home now,"* she whispered. *"I'm tired of fighting."* Gabri stood and Rafe reached out and held his arm. *"I need to get my father. I promised to take his ashes back,"* she said softly. *"I also have to get my mother's things."*

Gabri held her hand then bent and stroked her face. *"Naturalmente, mio Rafaella, naturalmente,"*[15] he said sadly.

Eden had watched as Gabri knelt in front Rafe looking her in the eyes and touching her head and then her chest so familiarly. Her anxiety throbbed through her body as she watched Rafe lay down and Gabri stroke Rafe's head and

---

[14] I see you,

[15] Of course, my Rafaella, of course

speak gently to her. The only words she knew were *ti vedo,* I see you because Rafe said it to Bronte when they played.

Gabri turned to Eden and then noticed Chiara who had followed them. Gabri spoke to Chiara, and she nodded then he walked out of the room. "He says you should follow," she said to Eden.

"What did they say?" Eden asked nervously.

"Follow," said Chiara and left the room.

As they walked out, Eden saw Julia hovering near the door. As Gabri and Chiara passed her, Julia took Eden's arm. "What's going on?" she asked softly.

"I have no idea," said Eden, panic clear in her voice. "They were speaking in Italian so fast. I have no idea what they were saying. Gabri wants me to follow him." They went into the living room where Letty was holding Bronte, and Gabri was standing in front of the fireplace speaking with Chiara who was at his side.

Chiara cleared her throat and motioned for them to sit down. She waited for them and took her cue from Gabri who nodded his head. "Mr. De Angelis requests I tell you he has had a serious conversation with Eden, and he can see she has great concern for Rafaella. He has also had a troubling conversation with Rafaella, and he hopes you will understand he is unhappy with her situation."

"We know she's sick," said Julia suspicious of where the conversation was going. "We've been discussing what's best for her and hope to convince her to be placed in a hospital with doctors who can help her."

"We've been going to therapy," said Eden nervously. "She was going on her own, and we just started going together to work on some of our relationship issues." She watched as Chiara translated then nodded as she listened to Gabri.

"Mr. De Angelis says he understands you have been doing what you think is your best, and is appreciative," said Chiara and paused. "However, he has decided Rafaella must come home now."

"Come home?" Letty asked in confusion. "She is home, this is her home."

Julia looked over at Eden and saw her begin to tremble, so she put her hand on her back to let her know she was there to support her. "We think, given the fact she is trying to rekindle her relationship with Eden, and she has a daughter here, she should get help here where she can be with family and friends." She had wanted Eden to realize she was better off without Rafe, but she never wanted anything like this to happen.

Chiara relayed Julia's words and nodded as Gabri spoke softly but intensely to her. "Mr. De Angelis says you have a good point, and he will now go and talk with Rafaella," Chiara said then took a seat nervously as Gabri left the room.

Julia stood up, watched him walk out, and then turned to Eden and Letty. "I'm calling Katheryn again," she said, taking out her phone and dialing. She looked suspiciously at Chiara and knew she might relay her conversation to Gabri. "I'm just going to take this in the kitchen," she said and left the room.

"Eden, what's happening?" Letty asked looking from Eden to Chiara.

It seemed like Gabri had been gone a long time when there was a sharp knock on the front door. Chiara stood up with her briefcase and the painting Rafe had given to Gabri. "That will be our driver checking on us," she said and left to meet him.

As Eden watched Chiara walk out, dread ran through her, and she jumped up from her seat. As she made it to the hallway, Gabri came down the hall from Rafe's room, carrying Rafe in his arms wrapped in the blanket from her bed.

"Rafe!" Eden cried out in a panic as Gabri passed by her, "Rafe!" she called again, her cries drawing the attention of Letty and bringing Julia from the kitchen.

Gabri ignored Eden's calls as Chiara opened the front door. He gave a passing nod to Chiara as he carried Rafe outside to the waiting car.

Chiara forced a folded piece of paper into Eden's hand. The message delivered, Chiara turned quickly, leaving the group of women to watch as the front door closed with a firm click.

To be continued in Book Nine — Cyprian the Fair ...

NOTES

Translations: For translations of Italian, French and Spanish use: www.Babblefish.com

The chapters in this book were arranged with the intent of saving paper. This chapter style saved 21 pages. Original Total Book Pages 316 — Final Pages 295.

Music mentioned in this book.

No financial incentive was given for the mention of the following artists in this work. The author is a fan and felt mentioning them worked in the story. For the use of their name, credit is given, and links to their work are below.

Enjoy!

Ginger Doss

Website: https://www.gingerdoss.com
Facebook: https://www.facebook.com/GINGODOSS
Twitter: www.twitter.com/gingerdoss
Instagram: http://instagram.com/gingerdoss
YouTube: https://www.youtube.com/user/Ginger0440

ABOUT THE AUTHOR

C.L. CATTANO LIVES in the Midwestern U.S. with her partner and their dog somewhere between the city and the forest. With a joy for traveling, she and her partner have visited many countries and have a love for meeting people and learning about the places they visit. When possible, she likes to include references in her work about the things she has learned, the places she has been and people she has met while on her travels and in her everyday life.

Cattano has a variety of creative interests including, but not limited to, creating fine art, writing, photography, and supporting women in the arts. She considers herself a 'Jack of All Trades' dabbling in what she terms the 'whimsies of her soul' that pull her toward happiness and fulfillment.

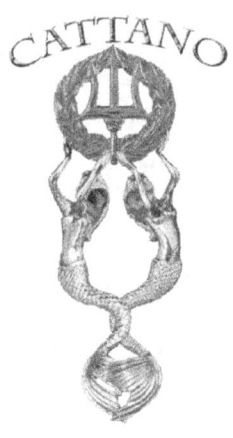

OTHER BOOKS

By C. L. Cattano

Cursed Hearts is a love story transcending time and gender. Two souls, separated by a gift from a bored demon on All Hallows Eve, have been searching through time for each other and have been incarnated as both men and women.

Over time, the gift became a curse and a game for the demons. Connected by the power of love, the two souls have finally met again, and now they must fight for a life together.

Will love prevail? Will they finally be able to live together again for a lifetime? They have one night to figure out the riddle and get it right to break the curse.

NOTE: 18+ Lesbian Romance. Some light erotic moments.

Available on Amazon Cursed Hearts

Salvaggio's Light Series

It takes true love to survive secrets, lies, and betrayals from within and without.

Get ready to settle into this epic contemporary drama-filled romance entwined comedy, lust, danger, thrills, regret, tragedy, suspense, and love.

Available on Amazon

Check out the Salvaggio's Light Facebook page to join in the discussions and fun! www.facebook.com/pg/SalvaggiosLight

Join the CL Cattano Mailing List www.clcattano.com

I love getting fan mail, and you can contact me at clc@clcattano.com

REQUEST FOR REVIEW

Thank you for reading **Salvaggio's Light** — *An Epic Contemporary Romance Serial.*

I hope you enjoyed book eight, **Traditoré**, and will consider leaving an honest review. It only takes a few minutes, so I encourage you to go now and leave a review!

Need help writing a review?
Try the Random Review Generator by A. E. Radley!
It's Free!

http://aeradley.com/review-generator/

www.ingramcontent.com/pod-product-compliance
Lightning Source LLC
Chambersburg PA
CBHW070636260626
47161CB00007B/2720